The Japanese Wife

Kunal Basu was born in Calcutta and has travelled widely. He teaches at Oxford University and is married with one daughter. Author of three acclaimed novels – *The Opium Clerk, The Miniaturist,* and *Racists* – he has acted in films and on stage, written poetry and screenplays. *The Japanese Wife* has been made into a film by India's celebrated director Aparna Sen.

From the reviews of *The Japanese Wife*

'It's absolutely exquisite.' – *DNA*

'Kunal Basu deserves to be thanked for bringing short stories back into reckoning.' – *The Telegraph*

'[*A*] delicately rendered telling of ordinary people reacting to extraordinary situations.' – *Business Standard*

'[*The Japanese Wife*] makes one think of dreams, memories, discoveries, unexpected love and fortuitous gifts.' – *Society*

'Love, longing, grief. The non-layered stories are well crafted, attention paid to small details and the reader's interest sustained all through.' – *The Hindu*

'…poignantly rendered, it's often portrayed in strikingly visual terms.' – *TimeOut*

'…these stories are a tribute to imagination.' – *Mint*

'Kunal Basu uses both the zoom and the wide angle to bring his short story to life.' – *Mail Today*

'It's hard to pick a favourite from this collection – each is a story worth treasuring.' – *Sunday Mid - Day*

Also by Kunal Basu

- *Racists*
- *The Miniaturist*
- *The Opium Clerk*

The Japanese Wife

Kunal Basu

Tirtha
Much love!
Kunal
6th April 2013
Kalkata

HarperCollins *Publishers* India
a joint venture with

New Delhi

First published in India in 2008 by
HarperCollins *Publishers* India
a joint venture with
The India Today Group
©Kunal Basu 2008

ISBN 13: 978-81-7223-903-9

Kunal Basu asserts the moral right to be identified
as the author of this book.

First published in paperback in 2009

4 6 8 10 9 7 5 3

HarperCollins *Publishers*
A-53, Sector 57, NOIDA, Uttar Pradesh - 201301, India
77-85 Fulham Palace Road, London W6 8JB, United Kingdom
Hazelton Lanes, 55 Avenue Road, Suite 2900, Toronto, Ontario M5R 3L2
and 1995 Markham Road, Scarborough, Ontario M1B 5M8, Canada
25 Ryde Road, Pymble, Sydney, NSW 2073, Australia
31 View Road, Glenfield, Auckland 10, New Zealand
10 East 53rd Street, New York NY 10022, USA

Typeset in 10/12.6 Galliard BT
Jojy Philip New Delhi - 15

Printed and bound at
Thomson Press (India) Ltd.

for R

Contents

The Japanese Wife

S he sent him kites. They came in a trim balsa wood box – light as paper, but large. At Canning's harbour, postmen admired the alien markings on its wrapper. 'From where?' asked a new recruit. The experienced ones smiled. Like a giant street sign, it rode on a cycle rickshaw, the hooting puller struggling to clear its delicate edges from the snarl of the dock. Then, it sat on the ferry, all tidy and proper, held by a proud mailman. It crossed the Matla without spilling a drop on its canvas-brown cover neatly tied with black cord. Chattering kids formed a circle around it; peasants gawked over their drooping shoulders; even the bearded sadhu abandoned contemplation of waves for a quick glance. It was a safe passage, barring a few jabs from little grimy fingers checking the box for what was inside. At Shonai, the landing was tricky – the swollen river had drowned the island's meagre jetty. Men formed a human chain on the slippery bank and the box passed from one pair of outstretched arms to another, pausing briefly at each transfer. When it reached the dry shore, an eager crowd cleared its way to yet another rickshaw. From there it moved smoothly through village paths lined with the swaying tamarind and neem, ignored by sleeping dogs, trailed by more children, creaking slightly at uneven bends.

His aunt received the box like a returning bride. Waiting with neighbours in front of their yellow-and-white home, the only one in cement and brick, she let the younger women welcome it indoors – to his room. There, it sat all afternoon in the cone of a shadow, listening to the purr of mating cats, in the company of an unmade bed and a dresser full of knick-knacks, facing a painting of a rising sun over a flaming volcano.

Entering the room, Snehamoy closed the door behind him, feeling faint from the heat and the day's excitement. Fellow teachers arriving late had informed him of a certain box that bore his name – in English, along with markings in an alien alphabet – making its way over the Matla. Finishing his lecture, he had announced a snap test in arithmetic, giving him time to think. Exactly at four, after the bell had rung announcing the end of the school day, he had mounted his cycle and made his way back through the rustling trees. Once inside, he stood facing the box propped up by his bed like a timid visitor, then started unwrapping the canvas-brown cover just as impatiently as he had opened his wife's first letter from Japan, twenty years ago, similarly marked with two alphabets.

They called him by many names – Snehamoy Chakrabarti, a teacher at Shonai's secondary school. The first two syllables, Sne…ha, standing for 'affection' in Bangla were reserved for his aunt, the young widow who had raised him after both his parents had drowned in the Matla. 'Sneha…!' she called him from her kitchen, just as she would when he was young, going around the village looking for the truant boy. Just as before, he came to her running, urged by a growling stomach. To others, he was known more formally by his profession – Mastermoshai – teacher, a master in solving the unsolvable, a BSc in mathematics from a college in faraway Calcutta. Behind his back they called him Japani – the Japanese; scrawled the letters with chalk on the blackboard, or called out from dark groves as he went pedalling through the village. Even the visiting school inspector on reaching their island would ask to be shown the house of a certain Mastermoshai – the one with the Japanese wife. That he had married secretly, was well known ever since his return from Calcutta at the end of his studies – the only one among the lot of villagers to have a foreign wife. A secret marriage that was now open; as normal as letters; as ordinary as his aunt's daily stories about her beloved Bou – the daughter-in-law. Ordinary, except for the arrival of kites.

For twenty years he had opened a great variety of mail – book boxes smelling of sweet glue, cartons marked 'fragile' holding Hokusai prints, a silk sack filled with mountain cherries, scarves rolled tight like children's pillows in thick parchment wraps, cards and letters exuding perfume, and rustling sheaves of washi. And they came over the Matla in dusty mailbags, jostling with peasants. Except the one at the very beginning.

The first, as he often recalled, was simple, almost bare. Yet, in many ways it was the most charming, the unexpected, his first brush with the other kind, native or foreign. ....*Dear Snehamoy*, it read, *I was waiting for your letter. Yes, I shall be your penfriend. The meaning of my name is 'gift.'* It was signed *Miyage*. He found it brief, but revealing. For the next few months he wrote brief letters to his penfriend, spending more time revising his English than the calculus that came naturally. Having made the first move, discovering her address in a magazine, he felt shy unlike his city friends all too willing to show off. He wrote about his college, his aunt, and the river. When she wrote about her own river, Nakanokuchi, the words flowed. He told her of his anger towards Matla – for flooding their village and devouring his parents; of its treacherous churns; the stink of floating carcasses. He wrote of its months of contentment following the monsoon – all swollen and calm – reflecting the bamboo groves like ageing spears; of his passion for gazing at idle boats dotting the mudflats and the yearly pageantry of fishermen celebrating the gift of the river. He confided his strange excitement, lying on the banks and listening to the lapping waves, as if they were the endearments of his long lost mother.

She sent him a print of a marooned village, asked, *how do you pronounce Snehamoy?* He wrote her the trick of rounding the tongue to whistle, then combining the 's' and the 'n' in a soft hiss. Preparing to graduate, he wrote less frequently for a few months. When he sat down next, it was to inform her of both his decision to take up a teaching post at their village school, and his aunt's keen interest in arranging a match for him with a friend's daughter.

For three years in the city, he had wormed inside his cocoon – the comfort of mathematical problems and their solutions, the bimonthly trips to see his aunt, regular visits to the post office to have his letters weighed, and waiting for the postman to deliver Miyage's replies at the college hostel.

Fellow students pulled his leg, called him the bumpkin. Someone spied on him, stole his letters and announced the village boy's adventure. ...*Dear Miyage, I am lonely here...* he read aloud from Snehamoy's unfinished letter. *My aunt brought this girl over last time I went. She was shy...* His friends demanded an explanation. What business did he have hiding Miyage from them? What did Miyage mean anyway? One of them threw him the unsolvable problem – would he marry the village belle or the Japani?

In her next letter, she was strikingly different, almost a stranger. After the usual beginning, she changed the colour of her ink and wrote in piquant blue… *now, Snehamoy, I must tell you something important. I would like to offer myself to you as your bride. Please tell your aunt I will make a good wife. If you accept, we'll be married.*

More than anything, he sensed a relief – from the anxiety of having to take the next step, departing from his routine. In his single-most courageous act, he lifted his pen and accepted Miyage's proposal, spending the next month agonizing over the likely encounter with his aunt. She had taken it lightly at first – the penfriendship, the pen-marriage – chiding Snehamoy for neglecting his health, till she saw in his eyes the resolve of the Matla.

'Miyage…what does it mean?' She had asked, breaking her vow of silence. Recently married, Snehamoy told his aunt about the shy beginning, the courtship, the proposal – told her everything.

'When will the two of you meet?'

It hadn't occurred to either, he had confessed, to discuss the prospect of a meeting.

Sitting on his bed, he heard his aunt's footsteps. She saw him lost in his thoughts before the recently arrived box.

'What did she send you this time?' she asked with the assurance of a confidant.

'Kites.'

As in old sayings, arrivals came in pairs. Waking to unfamiliar sounds, Snehamoy found a boy skipping rope in their courtyard. He heard more than the usual bustle from their kitchen – straining from his bed, he caught sight of a younger form huddled beside his aunt, shrouded by the oven's smoke. *Who is she?* he thought, turning over in his mind the few visitors who came to their island braving the infamous Matla. More than casual visitors, there seemed a certain permanence about them, the child ducking in and out of the rooms with ease, as if he had been born there. He heard the boy call out to him…. 'Kaku!' *Uncle…?* Sitting up on his bed, Snehamoy fumbled with his glasses and caught a pair of eyes inspecting him from the kitchen. In a flash he knew who she was – the shy girl her aunt had chosen for him twenty years ago.

In a hushed tone, his aunt gave him the full story over lunch. The girl had been married off soon after Snehamoy's refusal and lived in a nearby village till tragedy struck not long ago. Suddenly widowed, she had left with her son, unable to put up with her unfriendly in-laws. Snehamoy listened silently as his aunt described their misfortune. 'She'll be safe here,' he heard her say. 'Plus, you could raise the boy as your own, just as I raised you.' Seeing him frown, she scolded him, 'You can't shirk your duties, Sneha... life means more than simply writing letters.'

As he cycled to school, Snehamoy began composing his letter. How would he break the news to Miyage? It was one thing to inform her of the sudden arrival of distant relatives, quite another to announce the return of his once would-be bride. It was she, Snehamoy was certain, the prospect of their marriage, that had prompted Miyage's proposal to him. What would his wife do now? He felt confused. Distracted by his thoughts in the classroom, he made a rare mistake before his students and left hurriedly. Back on his cycle, he started pedalling north towards the river's bend, leaving behind the village pond buzzing with bathers. He passed peasant women returning from fields with huge stacks of hay, and rung his bell in greeting. Bullock-carts piled high with rice sacks made him stop briefly, but soon he rode past the familiar mudflats towards the river.

As always, he brought his woes to the river, and as always, it cleared the slate for him. Certainly, it was no stranger to her letters or his. Over the past twenty years he had consulted it at every critical bend. During her depression after her mother's death, he had read aloud Miyage's dark and brooding letters tinged with self-pity. And the river had spoken, lending him words to console her. He had written to her in agony when their village had suddenly erupted, flames of hatred scorching the peasants' huts. Gazing at burnt logs from funeral pyres, he had scribbled...*wait for me...in the end I'll come to you floating down this river*... Here, he had discovered his true love for his wife; the urge of a lonely letter writer had given way to a lasting bond. Like a married man, he had grown used to coming home to her, to her things – the gifts she sent him regularly; he waited for her letters as if he was waiting for her to return from her daily visit to the market. In his personal portrait gallery – one that lay in a weathered file at his bedside – she smiled in a series of gently ageing faces. He greyed with her, advised her on her health. She prompted him to mind his savings and the loans he was eligible for but never took out. During monsoons, she'd remind him to wear socks over his slippers to avoid the bloodsucking leech. With the assured status of a Bou, she scolded him for neglecting his aunt – not taking her to see a doctor for her recurring malaria. He wrote about the bazaar women with gaudy made-up faces, who loitered around at night and gestured lewdly at passers by. He could hear his wife giggle, teasing him... *go to them Snehamoy, I know you would like to! Don't come back to me, I can live without the...* They fought over periods of silence, blaming each other, then blaming the lot of postmen. He could swear he saw her waiting for him one evening by Matla's shores, as he came pedalling blindly down the muddy road after a rare evening with mohua – the local brew.

In twenty married years they hadn't met even once. Yet to Snehamoy it had mattered little. Even others, including his aunt, had ceased to notice Miyage's absence over time. Every now and then, it'd come up – a visit to Japan. They had toyed with the idea, then postponed it like a vacation. *Too expensive*, he wrote; *let's see*, she wrote back; *we really mustn't, who'd care for my aunt? Maybe you could come to Shonai for just a short while; how short? Let's see...*

'When will she come?' His aunt would ask in the beginning. 'You must see your wife....she must live in her husband's home. Letters won't make babies you know!' Their meeting, hovering on the horizon, had always seemed as an extra, nice to have but not essential. Having weathered the storm of gossip and snigger, he felt confident of their marriage. He knew he had Miyage as securely as any man did his wilfully wedded wife, even if she didn't sit by his side on the banks of the Matla.

His mind returned to the widow and her child, and he saw the solution instantly – to wait a few days before writing to Miyage. After all, mother and son could still be just visiting. Despite his aunt's designs, the two might in the end return to her in-laws to live out their troubles. Then, he'd write and tell his wife, make her jealous. Like an ageing couple they could chuckle over the threat of indiscretion just passed.

As he returned home from the river, he felt light, almost lightheaded. Stopping briefly at the market, he bought an exercise book for the boy and a ripe melon for his aunt. A cool wind blew through the latticed boughs of the tamarind, and he cleared his throat anticipating the yearly touch of cold. Entering his room, he closed the door behind him. Both windows were shut, and it seemed warm and cheerful inside. Something almost imperceptible had changed. Snehamoy looked carefully from one corner of the room to the other, till he was assured of everything being in its place. Except, someone had tidied it all up – emptied the spilling ashtray, straightened his desk, drawn curtains over the windows, swept the floor, removed the kite-box, and hung a picture – Miyage's portrait in black and white – on the wall facing the bed. He gaped at his orderly surroundings, then grabbed the picture and wrenched it off its hook. ...*Only the dead must hang on the walls not the living*...his heart froze for his dear wife.

The boy found the kites hidden in a dark passage of the house. Unable to lift the box, he pushed it along its narrow edge till it landed on the floor with a thud. Snehamoy helped him take out the kites, lifting each delicately by its staff, and spread them out on the courtyard. The women came out of the kitchen and exclaimed.

'When will you fly them, Kaku?'

'Fly?' The idea hadn't occurred to him, but seemed to appeal to everyone.

'Your Kaku doesn't know how to string a kite let alone fly it! You'll have to call your friends over,' his aunt got the ball rolling. The widow smiled in approval. They fixed the day of celebration for Biswakarma – the god of machines – to be their kite-flying day. But first, they'd have to be ready with rolls of line to fly the kites, lines sharpened with a coating of finely ground glass to cut those of their rivals. A suitable field must be found, one with a good view of the horizon and free of trees to prevent the lines getting tangled up in the branches. Their hearts pounded at the thought of a kite-fight. Like a sensible teacher, Snehamoy sat the boy down with his exercise book. 'If each kite takes five hundred feet of line to fly, how many feet would twenty kites take?' The boy frowned. 'Only five hundred feet for each kite! What if they get tangled with others during a fight and keep circling away needing more and more?' The two spent a whole afternoon asking neighbours for empty glass bottles. Snehamoy's aunt smashed them in her kitchen, then ground the shards in a pestle, pricking her thumb in the process. Glue was added to the glass granules, and a touch of vermilion dye to have the lines stand out against the blue sky and the clouds. After returning from school, Snehamoy joined the boy in stringing lines from one end of their courtyard to another. Then, like seasoned workers, they wrapped their palms in soft cotton cloth, took lavish dips in the pail of abrasive and went from one end of a line to the other, carefully applying a uniform layer over it. In the end, they sat back in the kitchen and admired the brilliant maze turning their courtyard into a field of red pepper.

For days, pedalling to and from school, Snehamoy heard the village buzzing with the impending kite-fight. Rival groups of boys formed teams and were spurred on by a shopkeeper who was offering his Indian kites free to anyone willing to brave the foreign invasion. Yet, on the day of the grand contest, as the first of the Japanese kites came out of the box and heaved by its fliers went up over the school building, there was a pall of silence. It was a giant Baromon, devil-faced, crushing the helmet of a samurai warrior between its awesome teeth. Scarlet and ochre, it hung still, face up, refused to be cowed by the stiff breeze. *Brahmin!* The spectators renamed it after the mythical Brahmin of Mahabharata, the one who had devoured his own share of warriors. Standing in a circle with the boys, Snehamoy strung the kites, gaze fixed on the sky. Like characters in a play, they made their appearance one by one. The jaunty Tsugaru whirred like an airplane through a clever loop fixed on its back. The crowd went into a roar over the kabuki faces – bald men with comical sideburns; and delicate ladies – their hair tied up in fancy buns. They floated in the sky, like stained glass windows lit by the afternoon sun. A sudden calm drew giggles as the bows dropped and the faces turned circles. 'There goes Mastermoshai's wife…!' Someone sniggered. By then the lines were crossing and tangling up the kites, with a steady stream of taunts spurring on the flyers. Just when Snehamoy thought they had emptied the kite-box, the boy reached inside and scooped out more. Instantly, the field buzzed with humming and whistling kites shaped as cicadas, gnats, dragonflies, dancing carps, even a few ugly clams. It felt like a carnival and drew the crowd's applause.

Snehamoy saw his aunt and the widow watching the show, both enthralled. He felt proud of Miyage's kites and handed out the last – a Nagasaki fighter – simple in appearance but agile. Then the local fighter came out from behind the clouds, one with a long shimmering tail. For a brief moment, the Indian and the Japanese eyed each other from respective corners of the horizon. As the sparring started, they zipped in towards each other like low-flying combat planes. The blue Nagasaki, with the sky as its cover, had a natural advantage; the homegrown red had the crowd behind it. By then the light was falling, and all other kites had been pulled down, their lines rolled back, leaving the sky wide open for the final show. In a clear field, intentions were plain. The Nagasaki tried a deceptive loop – coming in from above and dipping over the other to set a trap. Reading the plan just in time, its rival wriggled out managing to avoid contact. The crowd, exhausted by the day's excitement, cheered and groaned in turn. Snehamoy sat down on the grass, the boy holding on to his arm nervously. Like a seasoned warrior, the red climbed down from the clouds, almost touching the roofs of the village huts. Then in a majestic move, it reversed its course and rose, cutting through the line of its enemy in one clean sweep, ending up, once again, as a speck in the sky. *Bhookata....!* Gone! The Nagasaki took a dip, its line sagging, and floated away. A group of boys chased after it, carrying long sticks like fishing rods. It flew past the school and over the paddy fields in gently rolling waves, then crossed the mudflats and floated over the Matla. For a brief moment it stood paralysed in mid-river, before taking the final plunge.

Returning home, Snehamoy felt elated. He sensed a special bond with the boy – his kite-flying partner. The whole episode seemed preordained – beginning with the arrival of the box, the hectic pace in their courtyard, and the afternoon's finale – as if his wife had planned it all from far away. Sitting on his bed, he watched the acrobatics of fireflies through the window, reminding him of the kites. He smiled. Before falling asleep, he glanced at a largish envelope on his table. Holding it up against the lamp he could see folds of a smaller envelope within it bearing his name, from Miyage.

The aftermath filled him with guilt. He had planned to take the boy to school with him the next day, but the letter upset his plan. Munching on his breakfast of tea and ricepuffs, he opened the envelope and read along casually, until the ink suddenly changed colour to a soot black....*now Snehamoy, I must tell you something important. My doctor says I am sick, very sick. He has asked me to leave my job and go to live with my brother's family in Shirone. I think I will be fine soon. You mustn't worry. I am sending you my will in a closed envelope. You may read it when I am no more...*

His first reaction was to sit down to reply. Then, sensing the occasion, he paced his room. Dressing quickly, he left for the school, alone on his cycle. As he passed under the tamarind drooping with yellow blossom, he made up his mind. The time had come, he thought, to take leave from his school, the leave he had postponed for years, just to be able to spend it all at once when he visited Japan. Now he must devote as much time as possible to his sick wife. He felt a responsibility that went beyond regular letter-writing or exchanging gifts, rather a need to be in constant communion with Miyage. And, he'd have to spend hours with his friend – the village homeopath – describing his wife's symptoms to receive a proper diagnosis, advise Miyage every step of the way till she was fully cured. In her adversity, *their* adversity, he found a strength that surprised him as he sprinted on his cycle through the narrow lanes.

At the end of the day, as news of his wife's sickness and his leave spread from the school to their neighborhood, he found his aunt and the boy's mother waiting for him outside their yellow-and-white home. They received him silently, then his aunt asked, 'Will you be going away now...?'

He shook his head.

'Will she come to live here then?'

He shook his head again.

'Then why...?' She sighed, unable to decipher her nephew's motive, and turned to enter the kitchen, 'At least you'll have more time for the boy now.'

Increasingly, Snehamoy spent his days at his desk, writing to Miyage and simply thinking of her. His next great occupation was indeed the boy – his arithmetic and his questions. 'Where is Japan?' the boy asked one day. Answering that was simple. Then, 'Why did you marry her?' he asked, pointing to the geisha doll on his desk. 'Is she a fairy? Will she send me gifts too? I want to marry her,' he declared, shutting his book after homework. On another occasion, he alarmed Snehamoy... 'My mother wants us to go away from here.' The widow, though, had started to take charge of their household. Every morning she waited outside his door till he left for a walk around the village. Then she'd set about with pail and broom, rearranging everything in his room – capping his pen, recovering his lost slippers from under the bed. In deference to Snehamoy's wishes, she had left Miyage's portrait alone, the rusty nail sticking out of the whitewashed wall as a reminder. In his quiet way he had started adjusting to her presence as well – he didn't mind her curry that tasted saltier than his aunt's, or the bowl of warm water she had the boy deliver to his room for his morning shave; even took to her quaint chants for Lakshmi – the household goddess – at dusk before their shrine. 'Are widows allowed to worship Lakshmi?' He asked his aunt. 'Well, this *is* her home, isn't it?' his aunt retorted. 'Nothing wrong with her prayers then…' The boy started calling his aunt Dida – Granny. Yet, try as he may, he couldn't see the widow as a little sister in distress, seeking her brother's shelter like Miyage. He noticed a growing distance between himself and his aunt – his confidant. She seemed less interested in his reports on Miyage's health. 'Are you sure she takes your advice seriously? What makes you think she cares for your homeopathy? They must have better medicines than us in Japan…much better…' At times she even refused to discuss the matter with Snehamoy. 'You shouldn't worry, her brother is taking care of her now.' Only the boy shared his worries, running to his room with Miyage's letters delivered by the postman and waiting patiently by the door as he finished reading. 'She is better now,' he'd lie, smiling kindly at his anxious face.

A month into the monsoon, his aunt came to his room and sat down on the bed after he had finished helping the boy with homework. She told him about the widow's plan to pawn her gold to pay for her son's thread ceremony. It would be an expensive affair, his aunt told Snehamoy, with offerings to the priests and a lavish feast for the neighbours. He listened with interest. Busy with his pupil's arithmetic, he had overlooked other rites of passage. 'You must go with her to Canning, Sneha…it's risky for a woman to go all alone to these places…' Not out of resentment but inertia, he tried to extricate himself: 'But the river is now in spate. Wouldn't it be better to wait a few months?'

'The priests want it to be now.'

'Couldn't *we* offer her the money….?'

'Would you?' His aunt gave him a strange look.

His fears were unfounded. Riding the ferry on their way to Canning, he felt he was returning to his college in Calcutta after a trip home. Nostalgia for those brief years held sway as they passed villages at the edge of flooding. He ignored the disappearing mangroves on the banks, the submerged jetties, and flood warnings posted on the ferry terminals on their way in. Hunched over the railings, he scarcely noticed a huddled form beside him, clutching a suitcase, eyes fixed on the heaving floors of the boat. At the harbour, he helped her off with her suitcase. Unfurling their umbrellas, they stepped carefully over puddles along the slippery bank. As they passed by the market, the smell of dried fish and rotting vegetables made them screw up their noses. He eyed the melons, piled high like cannonballs, stopped briefly to stock up on cigarettes, ignoring the urgent calls of a sickly woman sitting by a heap of scarlet eggplant.... 'Buy cheap before it goes to rot!' Threat of the river had seeped into wet bones bunched inside a shed with a corrugated roof that passed for the harbour's main market. He waited for her to catch up, then let her lead the way as they entered lanes with shops full of dull metal and flamboyantly coloured items for household shrines. She stopped to check the price of a copper lamp, the kind with five lotus-shaped heads. He waited as she bargained for a box of sandalwood incense. Following a definite plan, she took him past rows of dazzling finery and confectioners selling rock-sugar candies he remembered stealing from his aunt's cupboard when he was young. Instinctively, he reached to pay as she chose a black stone Shiva. Then, she made him wait outside a beaten doorway, and went in with her suitcase.

Snehamoy felt hungry. And yet, he sensed a comfort that he hadn't quite expected from the journey or his companion. He found her shy, but confident with a knack for the practical. *She has suffered,* he thought, and felt guilty at not having offered to pay for the boy's ceremony. Holding her Shiva and a basket of lotus, he sensed the vast gap between their lives, as well as the bond that had sprung from sleeping under the same roof. As he sat before the pawnshop, he resolved to break the ice, ask her why she wished to leave their home with the boy.

She seemed relieved as she came out, smiled at him and asked if he was hungry. Then they walked through the drizzle and returned to the banks – to the hovels serving rice and the day's catch. Sitting across a narrow wooden table, they ate silently. He watched her bent on her meal – wondered what she had looked like twenty years ago. All he remembered was her shyness and the same averted look, except when she glanced at his empty plate and deftly flicked over a piece of fried eggplant, as if she knew that Snehamoy was still hungry. He held her arm over slippery tracks at the dock, and sat with the crowd at the back of the ferry. The Matla seemed strangely calm.

He recognized the postman on the ferry, without his mailbag. He smiled at Snehamoy. For the most part he sat gazing at the widening horizon as they approached the Bay of Bengal. This time he was aware of her by his side, swaying with the ferry. *What did she think of his choice?* He wondered. *How had she felt being rejected? What did she think of him now…?* He went over their similarities – both separated from their loved ones – she from a dead husband, and he from…then stopped himself quickly. His was still a letter away. He thought about her gesture over lunch. Ready for conversation, several times he cleared his throat, searching for words. He felt he didn't need to know anything about her, that nothing about him was unknown to this shy woman. The boy came to meet them at Sagar, yelling against the breeze…. 'No letter for you today, Kaku!'

Snehamoy woke that night to a different sound – sobs coming from the far end of the courtyard. Fumbling with his glasses, he lit a cigarette. Passing the sleeping boy on his mat, he crossed the kitchen, stopping to check his aunt's deep snoring behind the closed door. He found the widow huddled on her bed – just as on the ferry – looking out at the dark night and the fireflies, dancing like kites. In his single-most impulsive act, he reached out and touched her face streaming with tears, then held her sobbing form firmly against his own.

*I must tell you, Miyage, of what happened last night….*he started to write, each time unable to continue. Waking at a ghastly dawn, foggy and damp, he sat motionless at his desk. He felt bound to write and tell Miyage, as he had always, about everything. Even in her illness, she must be informed; as his wife, she had a right to know. He knew she would be distraught. Worse, she could see this as the end, as his way of dealing with her sickness, his escape. *You can take up with the widow now, Snehamoy…she must be as lonely as you are…* He could imagine her reply; hear the self-pity seeping between the lines. But he feared that there wouldn't be a reply to his confession, that his wife could end their marriage just as easily as she had started it – silence replacing the strokes of her pen. His aunt's words haunted him....*how would you know if something happened to her? Who'd inform you if she....* He'd know of her death only when her letters stopped. And he feared that her letters would stop once he wrote to her about himself and the widow, that he'd never know any more how Miyage was, if indeed she was alive. Yet, his compulsion was stronger than his fear. Without the truth, his letter would be worthless he thought, just as without the letters their twenty years as a couple would amount to nothing. Deep within himself he reasoned for her...*what good is a man who isn't loyal? Why shouldn't she fly away from him like the kites?*

After he had dispatched the boy to the post office with his letter for Miyage, Snehamoy paced his room with the small envelope that had come on the day of the kite-fight. Holding Miyage's will, he was convinced this was her last unread letter to him, that no more would come riding over the Matla, delivered by the smiling postman. Dead or alive, here were her final words. With trembling fingers, he peeled its edges and taking out the sheets, spread them over the table. Then, he started to read...*my dear Snehamoy,* she had written in crimson.....*when you set your eyes on this, I will be no more...*

The storm struck Shonai with a venom, erasing the boundary of tamarind and neem. As usual, it blew off the hay from peasants' huts and damaged the school building. Fortunately, the ferry had stopped plying and docked at a safe harbour. It returned in autumn when the river was full but calm. In the lull of winter, the only passage of significance was the untimely death of Snehamoy Chakrabarti, the mathematics teacher at the secondary school, from the killer mosquitoes that spread a wider havoc than the river. Besides friends and neighbours who knew him well, the whole village mourned his loss – the orphaned boy who had studied in the city but returned. The teacher who seldom erred before his students. Words weren't enough to console his poor aunt. At her request, the headmaster had written to Snehamoy's wife who lived far away informing her of the terrible loss.

Then she came – head shaven, wearing the white of a Hindu widow. At Canning, she boarded the ferry. Sitting upright, looking out towards the horizon, her alien features drew attention. Reaching Shonai, she crossed the muddy path over the banks, called for a rickshaw, and asked to be taken to the house of the teacher, the one with the Japanese wife.

Grateful Ganga

They met on Flight 59 to Delhi. Within minutes they were entwined, his head nestled in her tank top. Eyes closed, his right arm went around her seat. Cheek touching cheek, her perm blanked his ear from the engine's groan. He heard her sigh; she felt a vein throbbing by his ear. Their breath quickened and after a while she shut her eyes too, holding tight this man she had met just minutes before. Knees touched, then she raised hers to hook him in place; the plane was rocking.

Leaving the Khyber Pass thirty thousand feet below, they entered the tranquility of green hills, free at last of the sudden panic caused by the turbulence. Seat belt signs off, a stewardess reached for empty cups squiggling on the floor like marbles; a child in a bassinet screamed; there was a rush for the toilet, to expunge ugly scars of tea and coffee spilled by the venomous storm. The scream woke them, but the embrace lasted a touch longer. Then, he said, 'Sorry,' and excused himself. She went back to combing her hair, felt a dampness on her arms, breathed the aircraft's cologne on her chest. Something tore at her thigh, and she swore, *what the fuck*.... discovering a Marlboro lighter dislodged by the turbulence. In a quick motion, she rose and checked the overhead locker, then settled down all tidy and cool. When he returned, she smelled more of the plane's cologne; also, he seemed taller than she had imagined. Clearly embarrassed at his panic-stricken behaviour, he offered his card in a burst of formality and waited patiently while she finished reading....*Yoginder Singh*; *Ajanta Exporting Company; 37 Karol Bag; New Delhi 110001, India; Phone: 2647 7321; Fax: 2647 7111*. Then he asked, 'You, madam?'

'Evelyn.'

Soon after, they were served. Heads bobbing up and down over steak or bean curry, they felt reassured by the tinkle of steel on china and fizzing plastic cups. The tea, as usual, loosened his tongue.

'First time in India, madam?'

'*Evelyn*,' she corrected him. 'Yep.'

He fidgeted with his Marlboro lighter, 'Your husband living in Delhi?'

She told him, her husband was dead. By the time they had bisected Punjab, flown past the bird sanctuary and released the landing gear over Qutab Minar, she had told him the details – the untimely death of Andy Hofner from drugs, and his last wish that his ashes be strewn over the Ganges. Fascinated and perplexed, Yoginder asked for more details. Why the Ganga? Had her husband ever lived in India? Maybe he was a businessman engaged in export-import...? Surprised at his ignorance, Evelyn told him the legend of Andy Hofner – the king of rock and psychedelics – a touring genius who had chosen the Ganges, although he had never visited India, because he believed it was the world's expressway to the stars. She was carrying his ashes in a cask, she said, and pointed upwards at the locker. Yoginder folded his palms and fell silent.

From the queue for taxis, he saw her pushing her cart, arm around an oversized wooden box. Like other western faces, hers was plainly sleepy and dazed. He saw her change money, and chase after a flying bill; mime unsuccessfully at the counter marked 'Hotel.' She was floating, he thought, like a butterfly without a perch. At his turn, he stepped out of the line and dragged his suitcase along to join her in a conversation with the solitary policeman. She was seeking directions to a payphone, and Yoginder asked her if she knew anyone in Delhi. 'No,' she replied. Did she know which hotel to go to? 'No.' Would she stay long in India? 'No,' again. In a flash of courtesy he offered to host her at his ancestral home in Karol Bagh. 'Great!' said Evelyn. Hopping into a cab together she passed out from jetlag.

Waking at strange hours, she saw the house as it was – a series of afterthoughts. Doors opened onto doors, steps led up to a blank wall, a winding corridor spread like a maze around the rooms with no window in sight. At midday it felt cool inside. A captive breeze ferried the dampness of drying laundry throughout, scattering birdseeds over the dark stone floors. She thought she heard music – the kind that comes and goes like a passing train – reminding her of her apartment in Santa Monica with Andy strumming his guitar.

Waking late on her first morning, she had stepped gingerly out of her room and tried to find if anyone was around. She passed unlocked doors, worried about startling someone. The music seemed to follow her, and the twittering of invisible birds. On the first floor balcony she met an elderly man in white, bent over a thick volume. Betraying no surprise, he folded his palms at her, introducing himself as Yoginder's father. 'They call me Papaji.' Yoginder was out for work, he said; Bahuji – his daughter-in-law – had just left to go shopping; his younger son was visiting the hospital, and the children were at school. Only he was at home reading his dictionary, he said, not without a touch of pride.

'And you must be Evlyn.'

In her haste, she had appeared unduly curt. He had led her gently back through the winding corridor and an open courtyard with a birdcage, to her room where a giant poster of a woman in black hid the loo's door.

'Thanks, Papaji!' She had escaped, breathless.

That evening she met everyone. At dinner, they introduced themselves following a rehearsed script. Papaji, of course, was excused, and sat with an approving smile as Vijay and Viswajeet recited a poem each for 'Evlyn' auntie, ignoring her feeble attempts to insert the missing 'e.' She felt like a guest of honour and asked what their names meant. 'To win,' said the youngest, feigning a mighty stroke of a cricket bat. The elder, resembling more the father, bit his lip... 'The winner.' 'Conqueror of the universe,' corrected Papaji. 'The Victory Brothers!' He beamed proudly at Evelyn. Yoginder's younger brother had just returned from the hospital. 'He is a paediatrician.' Papaji took advantage of his stuffed mouth to tease him. 'But he has no children of his own, not even a wife!' There was laughter all around and in the din Yoginder introduced Ajanta, busy serving dinner. She smiled serenely, and asked if Evelyn's room was okay. She said she had made custard for her and asked, 'You all must be having custard everyday in America?' Towards the end, Yoginder made a short speech, welcoming Evelyn into their modest home. For the benefit of the rest, he recited her mission, describing her husband as 'a great singer, like our own Kishore Kumar.' Everybody, Evelyn sensed, had already been briefed, and there were nods of approval. Then, turning towards Papaji, Yoginder broke the news – the Ganga was in spate, flowing well over the danger mark. District authorities had issued flood warnings and the highway to Hardwar was closed. He said he had called Mr. Malhotra, the district collector's brother-in-law, from his shop, and even he had advised caution. 'It happens every year… there's really nothing to worry about,' the paediatrician tried to lighten the danger. But Papaji was firm, arguing against risky behaviour. 'Going now is out of the question. It would be called tomfoolery in English, wouldn't it?' He looked at Evelyn for approval. Then father and elder son suggested Evelyn spend a few days in Delhi waiting for the Ganga to recede. 'Bahuji can take you shopping,' Papaji said. Ajanta acquiesced with a smile.

Evelyn felt comforted, among strange people in a strange city. Unlike other situations, she sensed no urgency, none at all. Failing to evoke a past, it held a wondrous sway – a fine mix of disbelief and rest. She felt she wasn't responsible to herself or to her hosts; neither the actor nor the audience. The journey that had started with Andy's nervous breakdown at the Silver Bowl in Las Vegas – the body slamming, the howls, the speed and the sudden collapse – had somehow departed from a known script and come to rest before an unlikely birdcage. Try as hard as she might, she found it difficult to remember what it was like before she had boarded the flight for India that left JFK an hour late. It was true that until then she hadn't given much thought to her destination, embalmed her senses for a quick in-and-out that'd free her from Andy's dying wish and bring her back to her Poppy. Embracing her daughter – her only child – at the airport, she had a hug ready for her return. She knew, as most recent widows do, that she needed to cross into the aftermath; that she must now learn to live alone without Andy, after decades living alone with him. And Poppy, once again, was likely to be the missing link between one stage of her life and the next. Taking a drag on her last remaining cigarette in the open courtyard, she resolved to make the most of the river's caprice – catch up with herself, release her soul held hostage to a band, as groupie and godmother.

She sat on her bed and cast her eye around the room that belonged to the recently evicted Victory Brothers. Michael Jordan shared a wall with flashy cricketers; a Batman mask sat on the dresser; Metallica stickers struck out from the headboard (*Metallica!* She was amused), and the pin-up of a long-legged woman in black, zippers flashing, graced the loo's door. She winked at her …*All right babe!* She noticed a rack full of tapes, a sad looking guitar, and a bike. Then she let out a scream. Someone had moved Andy's box from her bedside table. Frantic, she searched under the bed and inside the deep loft; unzipped her suitcase in a frenzy, rushing out finally from her room, drawing attention by her wails. Papaji called instinctively for the boys, but they were fast asleep. The doctor emerged wide-eyed through one of the unlocked doors with a frown. A bare chested Yoginder seemed perplexed. In a white cotton nightgown, Ajanta alone appeared serene. Leading Evelyn by the hand, she crossed the courtyard, passed through the winding corridor and entered the household shrine. There, engulfed in sweet incense and glowing under brass lamps, the mortal remains of Andy Hofner kept company with the gods – a dancing Shiva, the benign Lakshmi, a jocular Ganesh, and the photo of an old priest sporting a bandanna.

Lying awake from jetlag, she listened to them snore. The house seemed perfect as a recording studio, picking up notes and amplifying them, leaving nothing to the imagination. She wondered how she'd sound through these paper-thin walls, and if she snored at all. On the verge of falling asleep, she remembered a minor detail, smiling to herself – over dinner, Yoginder had described their chance meeting at Dubai airport, feet planted safely on earth, when in fact they had met on the plane. Dozing off, she could still smell his cologne on her chest.

The damage, as she later recalled, happened mostly at night in the open courtyard waiting for the first drop of rain. And there was music, inevitably. Early evenings, they'd gather together, Ajanta and Evelyn, to display their booty to Papaji, who sat on a large wicker chair and pronounced on their shopping like a boxing jury after each round. Yoginder returned later and changed into a large flapping kurta, looking like the Maharishi without the beard. As the evening wore on, the children congealed on homework, Ajanta migrated towards the kitchen, and Papaji returned to his dictionary, leaving Yoginder and Evelyn alone in the courtyard. Early on, the talk had turned to music and she had summarized her preference for him.

'I like first-person music.'

'What's that?'

'Music about yourself, not somebody else.'

'I like them too.'

He asked her about Andy's music, and she launched into a memoir, covering three decades, numerous beginnings and ends, laced with the sort of intimacy that would've left many an avid fan drooling for more.

'He liked rock and roll, nothing else. Mind you, there was nothing phony about him. I've seen a lot of them go around making money from rock, but not Andy. He could really make you howl and move! He used to say our heart beat is four by four, baby – just like rock and roll... wop bop a loo bop...'

Yoginder listened silently. But from his eyes, Evelyn knew he understood. On one of those evenings, he invited her to his room and sitting next to her on the bed unveiled his collection of tapes, walking her through his favourites – the magical Mukesh, a charming Rafi, an impish Asha, the majestic Lata, and of course, the dead but undying Kishore. In his quiet way, he asked Evelyn if her rock and roll was fit for dancing.

'Sure, you can boogie to rock!'

He thought for a moment, then carefully fished out a tape and played.... *Piya tu ab to aja, shola sa man daheke aake bujhaja...*

Who's she! Evelyn sat fascinated. The voice, spliced from a coy Ella and a devilish Diana, churned with lush Flamenco and gave her goosebumps.

> *tanki jwala thandi hoja*
> *ayse gale laga ja*
> *a-hha a-hha a-hha a-hha*

She could imagine a woman in red, slithering down a greased pole, shaking, letting her body do the talking – drawing out every inch of spunk from the band, giving it a run for its money.

'Farout... !'

Yoginder laughed, moving in rhythm with the *a-hha a-hha a-hha a-hha*.

'What's she saying?' She asked, looking him straight in the eye. Rock it wasn't for sure, but a scream, a tease, a howl, a burning sensation.

Bent over his tapes, Yoginder seemed to be searching for words. Also, he had turned red and got up to raise the curtains for a whiff of the night's breeze.

'Well, it says....
>   come here my love
>   fill your gushing desire
>   cool that burn, baby...'

He fumbled for words, turning more red, beads of sweat glistening on his temples, facing the window with his back to Evelyn. Then, Papaji's voice, booming and clear, filled in the missing line through the paper-thin wall... 'Come into my arms, love!'

Clearing his throat, Yoginder had left the room.

They listened to more music – without translation; raw, on the rocks. Occasionally, Ajanta would join them, singing along in a schoolgirlish voice. Her taste was plain. And she chose to prefix each song with an apt label – a patriotic song, a wedding song, a love song, a song of sorrow. For the most part, Yoginder listened silently, yet his eyes spoke, caressing the music in a way that reminded Evelyn of Andy. *He's really on a high*, she thought. She heard the whole neighbourhood tuned into their music. There were competing notes, and arrogant blasts threatened to drown all from time to time. Yet they seemed to cast a spell on her. 'There is nothing he likes more than his music,' Ajanta had confided in Evelyn during one of their shopping trips. 'He goes to sleep and wakes up to his Kishore.' She had exaggerated – 'The player is on for twenty four hours... even when he isn't home...!' – then proudly displayed Yoginder's player full of fancy features like programmable memory. 'He bought it from Frankfurt only on his last foreign trip,' she said.

With interest, Evelyn examined Yoginder's things. While Ajanta reigned over much of their bedroom, her husband's concession was at the edges. Away from the bed, the mighty dresser and the full-length mirror, he had chosen the meagre windowsill for his player and his tapes, basking under a pin-up of the Konica Girl – a full-figured Japanese beauty cavorting on Hawaiian beaches in a flowery bikini. A red light bulb glowed above the cassette-rack, turning the leaves of a creeper the colour of Fall.

Over the next few days, she learned more about her hosts. She understood, for example, that the binding glue to this house of numerous afterthoughts was a death that had occurred twenty years ago when Yoginder was still in college. When his mother failed to return home after a visit to their ancestral Punjab, encephalitis was an unknown word in Papaji's dictionary. The shock had affected everyone. Retiring early from his government job, Papaji had sought the absent matriarch in her beloved house and spent hours before the birdcage. The dictionary he had found to be suitably distracting – a prompt for meaning to the thoughts that sprinted through his mind. The younger son, still in school, missed the caring touch; the house had become a camp for lonely men. It was then that Yoginder had bloomed – as provider and patron. Like his father, he too had quit – exchanging his passion for books for a partnership in exports. At work and at home, he had fast become the Yoginder everyone trusted. Within a decade, he had freed Papaji from balancing his accounts every day, made a doctor out of his brother, and added more rooms to their home in Karol Bagh. Even when the worst was undoubtedly behind them, they turned to him – the one who succumbed only to a fear of airplanes.

A good man wasted… Evelyn thought, eyeing Yoginder's bulging midriff. As she sat beside Ajanta on the solemn occasion – the arranged courtship between the younger brother and his prospective bride – she felt curious. Despite the elaborate cover, the scheme was transparent to Evelyn even without the benefit of words. After the mandatory greetings, the children were dispatched to their rooms. Papaji too had withdrawn… 'It is a matter for young people,' he had explained to Evelyn. With Ajanta hustling to-and-from the kitchen, it was left to Yoginder to loosen up the tongue-tied prospects. And, predictably, he relied on his music. Soon, they were chattering among themselves, checking out the tapes. After a steaming round of tea, Evelyn was introduced – as a tourist and a friend – leaving Andy out of the picture. Ajanta asked the young woman to sing, and the doctor pricked up his ears. She sang in an even, rehearsed voice. *A safe audition*, thought Evelyn. Ajanta translated the lyrics for her, and provided the appropriate label – a song about monsoon. More tea had the young couple talking to each other, and Evelyn caught Yoginder looking out of the window. He had withdrawn just enough, following his music drowned by conversation. Then everyone ganged up on Evelyn and asked her to sing, rattling off requests straight out of the Hall of Fame. Politely she explained her inability to sing Elvis songs, or those of the Beatles and Abba for that matter. While she admired Michael Jackson, his style was quite unique, and Madonna simply unacceptable. So, borrowing the children's guitar, she played her chords...

> 'If you see me now ... baby...
> holding flowers
> turning over in misery
> if you come too close ... baby
> beyond shame and ...memory
> if you lay your hands
> on me ... baby ...'

There was a round of applause, and soon the prospect got up to leave. Ajanta, Yoginder, his brother, and Papaji went into a huddle, and from their tone Evelyn gathered all had gone well. Helping Yoginder pick up the tapes, she asked why his brother too hadn't auditioned like the young lady. He broke into a laugh, saying that it was so much the better that he hadn't. Would he, Yoginder, have sung for his bride to be? she persisted. He nodded. And what would he have sung? She cocked her ear and smiled impishly. He raised a finger, asking for a sec, then turned on his player.

> *gulabi ankhe jo teri dekhi*
> *sharabi ye dil ho gaya*
> *sambhalo mujhko o mere yaro*
> *sambhalna mushkil ho gaya*

Entering the room abruptly, Ajanta had caught Yoginder looking straight into Evelyn's eyes – just as the song went ... *your eyes, the colour of wine, have me drunk; save me, o my friends, save me fast.*

That night, sitting on the terrace, she lit her cigarettes from glowing butts and tried with all her might to recall a single instance from her past that woud provide the necessary jolt. She tried anger – as in Andy's first betrayal; fear – of giving birth; power – of a thousand megawatts blasting through the night. Even forced herself to remember the death of her first child, who had he lived would be as old as Yoginder's eldest. But like a bad trip her images flitted by unwilling to lend company. She wondered if Andy was playing his last trick on her by getting her stuck thousands of miles away from her Poppy. Yet, she didn't feel trapped, or powerless – simply loath to use her power. Her eyes wandered towards Yoginder's room, basking under the red light. The curtains were parted, and she thought she heard low voices and a sigh; a thread of smoke seeped through the opening. The music had stopped, and for once the birds were quiet as well. Now and then a breeze blew in from the north rattling the panes and Evelyn imagined a woman in red slithering inside the room, shaking, moving it wild to that incredible *a-hha a-hha a-hha a-hha*.

Shit! she swore, flooded by a known sensation.

The warning, or so she thought, was sounded by the brother. A few days later, he inquired casually at dinner about the state of the river. Ajanta looked up from her plate and stared at Evelyn. She shrugged, promising to find out more from the American Embassy. Yoginder mentioned calling Mr. Malhotra again. Yet, she knew it from the tone, knew it from Ajanta's almost complete absence from the terrace in the evenings, and her ploy – using the Victory Brothers to trap their father with homework. Their shopping, once a daily celebration, had petered out into occasional trips to Janpath. Now, Ajanta brought along her Indian friends as well, avoiding one-to-one contact. Outwardly, her serenity was intact, and she managed a series of casual exchanges… 'You must come again for the wedding, and bring your daughter.' She had even tried to pry into Evelyn's 'real' identity – if indeed she had met Yoginder at Dubai, not at some business meeting in Europe. Only Papaji remained unmoved, still busy with his dictionary, still confirming the problematic, like 'psalmody,' or 'papillary.' The music, of course, was her high. Sitting in the open courtyard or on Papaji's balcony, less frequently in his bedroom, Yoginder would hum while she played along on the guitar usurped from the boys. It reminded her, obliquely, of the band's early road-shows, reminded her of Andy crooning in their trailer. She remembered his obsession – with freedom, stripping himself bare of anything that moved. *Minimize contact*, he'd goad everyone on, until all that mattered was a million-faced animal gyrating before the stage to his beat. Gradually, he had infected them – Evelyn and the band – with this disease called freedom, till they slept alone, wept alone, joined only by the ritual of orgy. Sitting on an ink-dark terrace, Evelyn heard Andy laugh as she played chords for this man tied to a million posts and humming his favourite Kishore.

That week she received the final notice. Returning in the evening after her chores, she found the door to her room shut with a sign, 'Doctor is in, please be seated.' She could hear children wailing inside. Looking for Ajanta, Papaji, or the boys, she couldn't find anyone except the indecipherable maid. She wondered what had happened to her meagre belongings – her suitcase and Poppy's photograph by her bed. Used to hospitality, her stomach growled. She wished she had Yoginder's office number, and panicked briefly before settling down at a teashop facing the house. Sooner or later, she reasoned, the family would return, or the doctor finish with his patients. Finding her on his way back from work, Yoginder ordered another round of tea and listened to her silently then excused himself to investigate the matter – returning an hour later to escort her back to her room through the winding corridor, still empty. The maid brought her dinner over, for the first time, and she lay on her bed smoking, not venturing into their evening's courtyard.

Next morning she visited Andy at the shrine. Relieved to find the box, she sat with her eyes closed, drawing in the incense, listening to the pigeons gurgle under the window. Instinctively, she knew her journey would soon resume and once again Andy would accompany her only part of the way. Opening her eyes, she found Ajanta praying. Her face was puffy, and her lips murmured silently. Just as Evelyn was about to rise, a voice, barely audible, stopped her in her tracks…
'When will you leave, Evlyn?'

'Soon, Bahuji,' she had dropped the familiar for the formal.

The tomfoolery occurred over breakfast. Once again, Papaji had drawn Evelyn's attention to etymology. Did she know that the word 'loot' came from Hindi, or Sanskrit rather? She exclaimed, reminded of the lootbags she had stuffed for Poppy's friends on her last birthday. She had let slip about her own birthday, her very first outside the U.S. 'You mean *today!*' Papaji was surprised. Finishing his breakfast quietly, Yoginder gave her a wink.

At midday, he knocked on her door. Stepping into her room, he sat on the bed and invited her to a party with just a few of his friends to celebrate her birthday. The family, busy with the wedding, couldn't come, he said, lying boyishly. He offered to pick her up after work from Janpath near the Tibetan shops, and passed his hand over his hair, 'It's a secret, okay...?'

Afterwards, she closed her ears and screamed, tumbling on her bed. *I have no clothes!* She pondered her choices – Kurta? Tights? A flashy ghagra? Plain-old-vanilla jeans? – settling finally on a red body-hugging shoulder-less zipper down the front dress. *What the heck*, she thought, *we are getting thrown out, aren't we?* Catching the eye of the woman on the poster, she winked. The rest of the afternoon was sheer frenzy. A short nap at four soothed her nerves and she left the house through the back, hailing a cab amidst general admiration.

At Janpath, she paced nervously, glancing at passing traffic and fingered the Tibetan beads. Hawkers called after her... *Memsahib, change money? Real peacock feather, pure gold chain, leather bag, madam...* Someone tried to sell her roses. Her watch had stopped and her pounding heart made her forget the details. Where did he say they'd be going? All she remembered was his truant smile. He surprised her, arriving not in the family sedan but on a black motorbike. Slowing down by the curb, he flicked his head and in a flash she was gone scattering the crowd. With a clever dodge, Yoginder broke free of the traffic, and they emerged under a flaming sunset on the highway north. He rode like a real biker, she thought, pushing lanes, banking steeply to pass, never resting on his laurels. And she smelled his cologne once again.

Passing dusty avenues he pointed out a Nehru-this and a Nehru-that to her. The only place she recognized was the old fort with its overgrown lily pond. Approaching the suburbs they were greeted by truckstops and temples. A thunderstorm seemed to follow their trail, raindrops smelling of open fields. After a while, Evelyn stopped paying attention. His words flew past her blowing hair, and the old comfort of her first night at Karol Bagh returned – she felt neither the actor nor the audience. After a quick stop for cigarettes, they arrived at a dhaba – an open-air diner for truckers – where Yoginder's friends had gathered to celebrate her birthday.

She fell for the men at first sight – perched on their motorbikes under a tree, sensed a frivolity that belied their office-going potbellied grooming. She met the bikers, wearing their mandatory Indian moustache and drinking beer from tall brown bottles. There was Ramesh – the bank guy; Saxena – the customs agent. All had eyes that spoke of music. First things first, they wished her with a bunch of roses she recognized from Janpath. Then Devinder took a group photo – Evelyn perched on a bike, the others surrounding her. He said he owned a photo shop, reminding Evelyn of the Konica Girl. Yoginder sat at the foot of the tree and made the real introductions. There was one among them who could recite all five thousand recorded songs of Rafi; another had a voice that could pass for the legendary Mukesh; Saxena, the customs agent, was a specialist on dance numbers; Nitin a whistling expert. When it came to Yoginder, they yelled in a chorus... '*He* is the real Kishore, the dead one was just a fake!' Drinking beer from her bottle, Evelyn gave a knowing smile.

Over dinner she learned that the gang met every Sunday, without the wives, to spend an evening with music and beer. Yoginder was their uncrowned leader, but they respected each other as in a healthy band. With growing ease, they asked her about her dead husband and his music, asked her about drugs ... speed, crack, LSD.

'Load of shit darling,' she said, feeling a little drunk. She told them her entire drug history beginning with the innocent ganja. 'In the beginning there was this thing about changing your consciousness, then it became a survival thing. And, Andy – the greatest bastard – knew all along that it'd kill him someday. He became like a bad payphone, you know.... in the end drugs went in but nothing came out, absolutely nothing.'

It had started to rain in large, warm drops. Ramesh took off after his favourite Mukesh, the others chipping in and turning on the high beams of their bikes. Their spirits rose with thunder, and suddenly they were all singing, waving their handkerchiefs, clapping and winking at each other. Evelyn added her own la-la-la. As the storm grew severe, the clearing turned into a puddle and the dhaba owner hastened to down his shutters. Perched on Yoginder's bike, she saw him sitting under the tree, waist deep in golden slurry. She felt a shudder. Then, revving their engines, the gang left, shouting, 'Next time Yogi!' and waving to Evelyn.

Speeding back on the highway, she felt she was passing a dark tunnel. The gale bothered her less than the strange evening bringing back flashes of the band. I've been through it all, she thought, and nothing works better than to have somebody you love hold you. She felt the fear of midair turbulence, and kicked off her heels. Then, hooking her legs around Yoginder, she held him tight and screamed against the wind ... 'Sing me your song, Yogi...' Careening past a traffic island, he stopped before a hunched monument and parked in the middle of a glistening road looking like an empty runway. They were both wet – she on the bike; he on the middle of the road. He had smiled like a truant.

'*Hume tumse pyar kitna, ye hum nehi jante....*'

Evelyn understood every word. ...*Don't ask, for I know not how much I love you*...

'*Magar ji nehi sakte tumhare bina.*' ...*Know this much that I can't, can't live without you*...

In full view of a deserted road, she drew him close by his drenched shirt and kissed him. Then whispered into his ear, 'This is your lootbag, big guy!'

Within a week, all arrangements were complete. The Embassy confirmed the river's ebb. Mr. Malhotra called with bus-timings to Hardwar, and Papaji told Evelyn the story of Ganga – the daughter of the mountain. In a sudden spurt she went shopping by herself and bought a full Rajasthani outfit for Poppy to wear on Halloween. She bought herself peacock feathers, and a plane ticket back to the U.S. for the night of their return to Delhi. In the good old days there was talk of a family pilgrimage. Ajanta had planned sightseeing, including a visit to the famous temple of Shiva; the children could skip school for a day, it was suggested. Even the doctor had agreed to come along... may be Bahuji could find a bride for him in the mountains! Evelyn was tickled by Papaji's idea – building a small shrine for Andy by the river – of recurring visits to India that would have her transit via Karol Bagh. Yoginder, as usual, had offered to help with lodgings at Hardwar, checking out the ashrams known for their delightful vegetarian fare. Now she didn't know what remained of that plan. After the night at the dhaba, she had seen Yoginder just once, reading his newspaper on the balcony. He was growing a beard, she noticed, and had the same smile as on that night. He had motioned her to sit, but she was on her way out to buy her gift for Papaji – an American dictionary. On her way back, she bumped into Ajanta, literally, on the doorsteps. She was painting a design on the floor with a thick rice paste. Smiling serene, she described some ceremony or the other, and

Evelyn almost blurted out ... *you mean to celebrate my exit!* Instead, she told Ajanta not to bother with breakfast as her bus would leave early. Then she remembered to visit the shrine and retrieve Andy decked in flowers. On her bed she found a card from the Victory Brothers, 'Goodbye Auntie Evlyn.'

Breaking the ice, Papaji revealed the plan over dinner. Given his health, he excused himself first from the trip. Bahuji too would be busy, from the wedding that was just round the corner. The doctor was submerged under a sudden onslaught of streptococcus, while the children had maths tests that week. So, Yoginder, he said clearing his throat, would accompany Evelyn to Hardwar for the last rites of Mr. Hofner. A modest guesthouse had been reserved for her, and Yoginder would spend the night with Mr. Malhotra, the district collector's brother-in-law. In an efficient use of time, they'd return to Delhi the following day and go straight to the airport for her flight home. He had chosen the right words, but his eyes seemed to hold a deeper story. Ajanta stared at her plate and Evelyn knew this was her final concession, the last act of hospitality. Trying her independent-western-woman bit, she suggested mildly that a chaperon was unnecessary, but Papaji cut in sternly – the river was unknown to her; for a proper ceremony, a shradh, she'd need a priest as well, 'and those scoundrels were out to fleece even a beggar!' He apologized for his expression.

That evening, she sat on the terrace all by herself. The maid brought her tea and she took in the city in slow drags of her cigarette. She heard the usual bustle – flower-sellers, a wailing child from the doctor's chamber, an airplane coming in low with its landing gear. Out of habit she glanced at Yoginder's room and saw the Konika Girl peeping behind the curtain. The red light was on, but no music.

For the most part they rode in silence – Evelyn on her seat by the window, and Yoginder with his feet up on the dashboard and chatting with the driver. The two of them seemed to be on a roll, laughing their heads off. From time to time she'd catch his eye, and he seemed neither distant nor close. *All part of the great Indian hospitality,* she fumed – *hugs, hellos and a very big farewell....* She stared at dozing heads and like a bored shrink tried imagining their dreams. Who were they romancing – a secret lover, or a poster girl? Stealing glances at Yoginder, she saw the same instinct in him as in her dead husband – a freedom that glowed like a cosmic sex appeal. As he brought her tea at a stop, she knew they were one – Andy and Yoginder – her husband had died scorching his guts for his music, while her lover wore it like a garland around his neck.

He met her at dawn, bare chested, with his week-old beard and a string of marigold. Carrying her cask under her arm, she held his hand and walked past countless temples, chanting devotees and shops ferrying steaming tea. Entering the river, she turned for a moment to face the sun, then slipped into glacial waters. From a distance she saw him rising above the flow like a rock, arm raised, motioning her to follow. She saw his boyish grin.

'... Love me, Yogi?'

From his throne of rocks he saw her floating – like a lotus leaf half-submerged, her eyes the colour of wine from the morning's chill.

'... Yes, baby.'

Lenin's Café

I met my father eleven years after his death, in Zürich at the Limmatquai where swans come to feed. After the first wave of disbelief, he said, 'Let's go to Lenin's café.'

Surprisingly, he looked twenty years younger than the sprightly seventy three, when I saw him last. I remembered him as still a handsome face: a shock of well-groomed silver hair, mellow wrinkles under a pair of brilliant eyes, and a firm nose that rose sharply for a man of the valley. Instead, he seemed to be in his fifties, sporting his majestic forehead, eyes alert under dark-tan bifocals, and a pencil moustache courting strong but pleasing jowls.

And he walked with a familiar assurance, always knowing his way, waiting patiently at the light, acknowledging courtesy with a simple gesture. Dressed smartly for an early European summer he resembled every bit the energetic publisher, a Marxist known to friend and foe as a true gentleman, the scion of aristocracy, a connoisseur... the man I knew and called Baba.

As in the numerous black and white photographs of him that lay wrapped in old newspapers, he was instantly recognizable: Baba at forty, clipping buds in his terrace garden; posing in his study with Soviet visitors; cradling my sister proudly at the Konarak temple; and at fifty, smiling at his desk under the gaze of Vladimir Ilyich.

Lenin, of course, was always around him. At our house in Calcutta, he graced the walls, filled bookshelves, dotted end-tables and study desks, and sat – a grey stone between rows of scarlet geranium in the garden, weathered, but without the moss of neglect. (I remember a caustic visitor – 'You have put him out to pasture!' to which Baba had gallantly replied, 'He belongs to the Reds!'). His portraits were evenly divided between us, the siblings, but Baba kept the best for himself. The Chinese scroll with accompanying verses in calligraphy came down from the ceiling to the marble dinner table; the more prosaic ones of the Stalin era changed walls with every makeover; stylish woodcuts from America lay trapped in the attic of my college-going sister. Baba's favourites – those that hung prominently in his crowded study – were of Czech and Bengal variety. The first because the smudged charcoal sketch had taken liberties, giving him the look of a passionate composer; while the second was clearly off the mark: a middle-aged middle class Bengali, *Leninbabu*, up and exalted by virtue of his soul.

Yet, neither the artefacts nor rows of books steeped in insecticide reflected the true bond between Baba and Lenin. Inexplicable to his comrades, it was both subtle and full, without a hint of flattery – a natural intersection that was deeply familial. Indeed, to us, the children, the bald Russian was the sort uncles are made of; an uncle who was dead, yet teeming with stories.

Crossing the footbridge at Rudolfstrasse, passing neat stalls of beer and bratwurst, I felt for the missing wallet.

'I have enough,' Baba said, and we strolled along.

Screaming gulls had magically transformed the city of icicles. A week after Sechseläuten the streets were swept clean of popsicle ends, burnt charcoal from barbecues, and streamers that had lined Banhofstrasse all the way from the railway station to Bürkliplatz. After a brief flirtation the city had regained composure: dark suits went about their normal business, mothers shepherded children along sidewalks, and giant sale signs greeted shoppers on both sides of the Limmat.

Within the span of a few weeks visitors had filled up the city, waiting patiently before Grossmünster for a glimpse of Charlemagne on his horse. The studious took notes in hushed silence at the church of Reformation, where the anguished soul of Zwingli – his body torn to pieces – raged from the dark and austere pulpit. The elderly and the suave, heads tilted, stood enraptured before Giacometti and Munch at the Kunsthaus, while the more adventurous had sought out the *Dancing Shiva* upstairs at Rietberg.

Out in the open, tourists gathered at the piers of Zurchersee waiting for boats that would take them to the Alps. Scared swans turned circles at the centre of the green lake. At cafés one heard the chatter of self-assured Europeans descended from ski slopes, their gear piled nearby, rubbing shoulders with weekenders from Geneva and Berne. Large maps changed hands as Americans at the threshold of their European adventure pondered their options. Venerable Japanese elders stared balefully at sprouting terraces before rows of gingerbread homes. At the schaffi, tour groups were being entertained with cider and gemutlichkeit.

Arriving at the big circle, we turned left, choosing the guildhalls over prim and officious homes. Not far away lay Joyce in his tomb; and the brooding strains of Wagner's *Tristan* filled the cobblestone streets. Here at last one could catch up on the last eleven years.

Like an unprepared actor thrust on centre stage, I felt the urge to offer the opening line. Yet, it was hard as we had come to a halt before the city's walls, where each word and its echo risked sounding a false note upsetting our pleasant walk. So far, it had been quite simple – a matter of engaging with a voice, a smile, a known gesture – without the urge to reveal or extract. Disbelief, like an unexpected gift, had diverted attention from the real; the walk had loosened my tongue but choked the senses.

The problem was the hereafter. It was difficult to judge how much he knew and how well. There was much to say, and I knew Baba to be a good listener. Yet, the unreality of the European summer stood in the way of the stories that clawed at my throat – the misadventures of his errant son that were a world apart from this single-minded serenity.

He listened patiently, looking straight ahead at a coy bird. At the telling of each episode, there was either a nod or a flick of the eyes. He seemed to know, and yet be curious about recent trajectories – births and deaths in the family; failed marriages; scandal and disease. And, during what must've seemed like an unusually circuitous journey, I managed to tell him all: from the time he had suddenly complained of chest pains to this day in Zürich when summer had arrived early. Only then did it occur to me to mention Lenin.

In many ways it was more difficult than the rest. To a communist who had faced prison in India for harbouring Lenin's books, I couldn't bring myself to describe the unthinkable: a Lenin in chains – his bronze torso shackled to gigantic cranes and suspended in mid air – awaiting banishment following his disgrace. Nor did I have the heart to report on the wrangling over burying his corpse, let alone the quiet defacement of his name from the Baltic to the Urals and beyond. I wished to tell him as little as possible about Lenin, and move on.

'I was in Moscow last year, and met your friend.'

Baba asked a few questions about Ranjit, his childhood friend from Calcutta who had escaped British prisons in India during the late thirties. With help from frontier guards, he had crossed the treacherous Hindu Kush and made his way over to Tashkent. Much later, when friends had given him up for dead, his voice boomed in Bengali from the *Soviet International Radio*.

I told him about Ranjit's daughter now living in New York, and of his alcoholic wife from Latvia. 'What happened to his little project?' Baba asked, with a gleam in his eyes. I had no choice then but to talk about the sad and charming flat on Ulitsa Vavilova.

He lived in one of Moscow's towering blocks from where one saw nothing else but other blocks. On a misty November morning when I arrived at Ranjit's eleventh floor flat, few residents were home, and all one heard through the open window were sing-song phrases in Spanish from a neighbour's parakeet. Inside, it resembled our house in Calcutta: brimming bookshelves, busy tables, an old gramophone, and Lenin.

For his seventy-odd years, Ranjit had eyes that probed and darted as he spoke. A quick examination of features confirmed my genealogy: most definitely, I resembled my father; and he had shared my laugh over encounters with dour Russians and lovely ninochkas. Wearing a typical Bengali robe, ends flapping, he looked like an ascetic without the least trace of asceticism.

And I had asked him about his pet project – linking Lenin with Bengal, although the bald Russian had never set foot on the eastern valleys of the Ganga – the land of anarchists and poets, where he had become a household name among the home-grown revolutionaries. There his writings had raised storms in teacups, set friend against friend. The children named after him grew up to become the petits bourgeois or the proletariat that they were destined to be and it wasn't unusual to find public appeals to the disappeared in the papers – *Lenin, return at once....*

On that November morning at Ulitsa Vavilova, Ranjit and I had flitted between two studies – my father's in Calcutta and his in Moscow – till I broached him again on his project. Fixing his alert eyes on me, he had sighed, 'What's the use now…?'

Throwing a crust to the swans, Baba turned and looked at me, reading the same question on my face. Then we started walking again.

A gentle turn of the road took us past Bellevueplatz, and at the corner of Torgasse we strode into the Odeon.

On hindsight, it would've been wiser to order a Rösti, even Berner sausages with noodles. Both of us were slow to gauge our appetites lurking under the rush of memories. After a quick look at the menu, we settled down with dark Viennese coffee beneath the wooden ceiling at a corner that resembled a medieval crypt. Unlike the pavement cafés, the windows were shut, but the afternoon light spilled through the panes. Seeking the edges of crystal – the neat rows of casseroles and the chandelier – it rebounded endlessly like a captive in a prism. As in a luminous theatre, it drew a curtain around the translucent haze of spring.

Baba seemed relaxed. It was his turn to talk. Taking off his glasses and wiping them slowly, he returned to his old banter, recalling the wayward ways of his son – the 'Lord' – of our charming but chaotic Calcutta house.

'So, does the Lord still rise at noon?' Before I could protest the exaggeration, he had delved into minute details, citing for a millionth time the slips and the misses, amidst uncontrollable fits of laughter. He asked me if I'd ever hold down a proper job, and chided me for my 'habit' of falling far too frequently in love.

With unbridled relish, we told ourselves stories we both knew. Then, almost as magically as he had appeared by the river, Baba pointed towards the table by the window. Lenin was sitting there in the corner, looking out at the swans.

It is pointless describing him: he looked exactly as his portraiture, perhaps a little younger – in his forties – when he lived as an émigré in Europe still out of reach of his Russian followers. He resembled, in every sense, the lodger at Monsieur Kammerer's – the cobbler's second floor home at Spiegelgasse. From the guildsmen's quarters halfway up the Zürich hill, he must've trooped down the narrow street weaving his way past rows of handcarts to reach the café, carrying his daily quota of newspapers under his arm. Between sips of tea, he turned pages noiselessly, and from time to time checked his watch.

We exchanged glances, Baba and I. So *this* was nineteen sixteen: Europe was at war, the Bolsheviks were barely a year away from seizing power, and Lenin's days in exile were about to end. Baba, of course, had just been born in the grand mansion of the lawyer whose name struck awe and envy in Calcutta. We fixed the required chronology in silence, and eyed him over our coffee.

He was talking to a short and burly man sitting across from him. As he rubbed his Socratic brows, Lenin seemed a touch irritated, and kept looking towards the heavy mahogany door. The air had suddenly turned cold, and it felt more like late February.

'They are waiting for a meeting of the Iskra.' With Baba's whisper, it came back to me in a flash – *Iskra…the spark…*the clandestine journal of the Bolsheviks, the voice of the revolution; the real power centre and the stage for power struggles among the revolutionaries.. *Iskra, the spark that ignited a flame!*

Within minutes, they were all there – the editorial board – sharing Lenin's table. To his right sat Vera – Vera Ivanova Zasulich, the classic Russian bohemian with flaming red hair and slightly flushed cheeks, rolling a cigarette, her blouse peppered with ash. Unmindful of the delay, she was talking rapidly in a high-pitched voice with an older man in a frock coat, looking like a preacher. He, of course, was Plekhanov, the dean of Russian Marxism and Lenin's teacher. The elegance of the two was hardly matched by the rest: Martov, hiding behind his foggy pince-nez, his face in a perpetual twitch; Axelrod sporting a rabbi's beard, and the burly Potresov.

They were talking, all at once, and delving into rolls filled with sour cucumber and Swiss-style fried potatoes. Edging closer on our seats we tried to catch the words, Baba translating for me relying on his fluent Russian. At that very moment, Plekhanov was emphatic, championing the *Niederwerfungsstrategie* – overthrowing the enemy, over *Ermattungsstrategie* or wearing down the enemy. Serene, frosty and mocking, he looked every bit the perfect professor with the civility and indifference of an educated man. It drew a smile to Lenin's Mongol eyes and a fretful lull among the others. But Axelrod, the milkman, was the most agitated. Stroking his dishevelled beard, the fugitive from Siberia tried to put on the brakes.

'But George, you make the revolution seem like a game of chess!'

Over condescension and some more arguments, somehow the rabbi and the professor agreed to a plan to contain the Tsar before attention shifted to Martov.

It seemed strange that they should be meeting here in Zürich. Somehow, Paris with its sizable number of Russian exiles seemed like a more fitting venue. There at *Café d'Orléans*, not far from *Lion de Belfort*, the cast would've been infinitely more attractive: the journal's editors among poets and ballerinas; at Lenin's flat even on King's Cross, around the kitchen table, engulfed by the fumes of a burning supper.

Martov was speaking, and Lenin listened intently, with the powerful half-turn of his neck. It appeared to be a discourse on fundamentals, and Martov – shirt open at the neck and cuffs shooting through his sleeves – shook with emotion. It had to do with the duma – the Russian parliament – and whether or not it merited the support of the revolutionaries. His pince-nez slipping down with each thrust of his shoulders, Martov was pleading for unity among the revolutionaries, among those who chose to remain in the parliament and others who thronged the barricades outside. 'They are just the same, comrades! We must have the freedom to fight wherever we want...choose our own playground.' There was a pathetic quality in his pleas, a kind of softness that tinged even the most strident argument. Eyes wavering, he was searching for support.

It was the first time I heard Lenin speak. His guttural speech made him out at first to be a poor speaker. But he seemed to grow with each phrase, bringing a stillness around the table.

'We are talking about a revolution, not a tea party.'

Arm extended, he appeared to weigh each word before pronouncing. 'And we are talking about a revolution in deeds not in words. The dictatorship of the proletariat will decide who fights where.' Relentless in attack, his jabs set Martov's face into violent tremor. The grandfatherly Plekhanov had fallen silent with an aloof air, and Axelrod fidgeted with his knife.

The café seemed to have filled with newcomers, dressed in winter's long coats and a cornucopia of hats: berets, astrakhans, and fur-trimmed bearskins. A thin crust of snow covered the cobblestones outside. Voices – Russian, German, and French – drowned the clash of cups and saucers. My eyes were drawn to a lean man with a snarling moustache and a sensuous mouth, perched on the window sill like a great bird of prey. 'Trotsky,' Baba whispered, and added, 'He's not on the editorial board. Plekhanov wouldn't have it!' A man with close-cropped hair sat smiling on a nearby table – Gorky, his arm around Andreyeva, star of the Petrograd stage. They had just returned from Capri, and Lenin raised an arm at them in salute.

But it was the voice of a woman, calm and commanding, that restored order – a little woman, frail and sickly, but with a noble face. Bringing the house down with a thunder, it was none other than Rosa Luxemburg.

'You fighting cocks must realize that workers all over Europe have pinned their hopes on you. You Russians should stop fighting among each other and think of Paris, Berlin....'

'I've seen Paris. Odessa is better!' An impertinent Trotsky brought peals of laughter. In the din, Vera Ivanova leaned across the table and whispered in Plekhanov's ear, 'You, George, are a hound. You will shake a thing for a while then drop it...but Lenin is a bulldog, he goes for the death grip!'

It was time for a second cup. Motioning over one of the hard-eyed, pinch-lipped fräuleins, looking eternally suspicious, we settled down once again and like eager schoolboys resumed our eavesdropping.

By then, time and place had ceased to matter. How else would one find our visitors, spread out as they were all over Europe, sharing a cup under these carved ceilings? Yet, to a dead Bengal Marxist and his errant son, the thrill was unabated by any such doubts.

Equally amazing, the table exuded a bonhomie despite the ferocious arguments. It was the vivacity that made me forget the tragic ends – deaths, bouts of insanity, and exile that awaited the visitors to Lenin's café. On that summer afternoon in Zürich, I did not see a disillusioned Plekhanov, repudiated and ill, dying in Petrograd as his disciples ran amok devastating his home like the Tsar's winter palace. Try as I might, I couldn't imagine a bludgeoned Trotsky in Coyoacan or the hanging torso of a frail Rosa and their assassins that preyed beyond the walls of the Odeon.

In what must've been a momentary lapse, Lenin was chiding Trotsky for his rotten sense of direction. In the midst of laughter and Plekhanov's caustic glare, he was narrating the arrival of 'Pero,' the pen, to his flat in London. Nadezhda Konstantinova had guessed a countryman from the loud knocks on the door at dawn and worried lest her English neighbours should become suspicious. Lenin had taken the country bumpkin for long walks visiting the city's landmarks, 'But every time I left him to return on his own, he was late!' He would worry for Trotsky's safety, when in fact it wasn't the snooping agents of the Tsar who had managed to trap him, but his own Ukranian nose that made him march in the wrong direction.

'And you've led Rosa astray too with your nonsense about a Permanent Revolution. It's because she doesn't speak Russian too well.'

'But she speaks excellent Marxism!'

They addressed each other by a familiar 'ty.' From time to time, Gorky would embark on a series of invitations to his comrades to visit the boatmen of Capri – 'The narcissi are in bloom now... When you come, Giovanni Spadaro will teach you to catch fish with your fingers!' He looked imploringly at Lenin. The actress held him steady during his coughing fits. 'Yes, Alyosha dear, they will come.'

Next, Martov with his shy and nervous laugh, described the incident of the ill-fitting shoes. After a meeting with Russian students in Paris, he had accompanied Trotsky and Lenin to *Opéra Comique* where the wily Lenin had passed off his new shoes to Trotsky. Overjoyed at the unexpected gift, Pero had pledged his lifelong loyalty to his leader, then winced his way back cursing the ill-begotten heels.

After levity, it was time for real sparring. The short and burly Potresov was talking to a grim-faced Axelrod, and unexpectedly threw the first punch.

'The party belongs to the workers, Vladimir Ilyich. They will decide the future of Russia, not a handful of intellectuals drinking coffee by themselves.'

Finding the perfect opening, Martov buttressed the argument, 'All strikers have the right to be party members, not simply those who can argue better than others.' And then, the third of the trio, Axelrod spoke up, 'There are so many voices – you can't price in kopeks or count in hours. The dictatorship of the proletariat will stifle them all.'

Grim and forbidding, his arms folded on his chest, Plekhanov, demanded an explanation, 'And whose precisely will this dictatorship be?'

'Of the editorial board, dear...' There was a definite flutter in Ivanova's eyes.

Even Trotsky had edged closer to the table, and started a nasal monologue on preserving the natural flow of the revolution. It was time for Lenin.

⚘ ⚘ ⚘

The flurry had settled into a constant drizzle. The blue hills of Rapperswil had turned hazy, and the streets were empty. The banks of the Limmat glowed under rows of gas-lamps, and their arches cast crisscrossing shadows on the snow – like a fence of barbed wire. Silent boats floated by. Baba too was looking out, and seemed neither sad nor wistful. A crackling fire drew us forward on our seats, bringing us closer to the table by the window. But for once I was drawn not to our visitors, but to the ferries on an icy river. The wind had died, and shiny icicles hung low from the branches. In many ways it reminded me of memory itself – spouting like an endless reservoir, broken only by a silent passing. In its cold preserve it left nothing to chance, blending the flows, and I saw not one but many rivers. In that twilight, I saw Baba standing on the bridge over our very own Ganga, framed by a tropical sunset with the badge of Lenin on his buttonhole. I saw him waiting patiently in line before the onion domes of Moscow, and share heartfelt laughter with his friend Ranjit in his sad but charming little study marked by the sing-song of a parakeet. Brooding shadows carved out our luminous café from the darkening Alps. Inside sat Lenin. At those borders, I glimpsed the perfect chasm between a dream and its consummation.

Like Pasternak's 'lunge of a rapier,' the leader of the Bolsheviks had scattered his detractors, denouncing 'garden liberals' and amateurs stuffed full with grandiloquence. Eyes darting, he had challenged Martov, 'Not a party *of* workers, but a party *for* them!' branded Potresov's vision as the 'utopia of an electrician,' and cheered Rosa's proposal for a grand international of the proletariat... 'That's splendid, smells terribly of revolution!'

Then they left in a trail of hats almost as suddenly as they had arrived. Beret in hand, Lenin had pointed to the door, and his stern eyes were smiling once again. A sheepish Martov left with Vera Ivanova trying to clear the air with the *Song of the Volga Boatmen*. The novelist and the actress joined in the refrain. Stroking his mane, Axelrod was still arguing. With Potresov in tow, Plekhanov waited for a streetcar. The lean Trotsky and Rosa looking even frailer than before had decided to brave the drizzle. By the time Baba had finished paying, Lenin was already halfway up the Zürich hill.

And then, yet again magically, the Odeon returned to the gay summer afternoon. Once again, the blue hills rose above the mirror green lake and the cackling of swans could be heard over the rush of clearing tables. A troupe of elderly nuns from the Fraumünster cathedral came in for their afternoon tea and scones, and sat at the table by the window. Groups of tourists in baseball hats peered in, then decided to move on towards the lively parasols laid out beside the square. Nearby, émigré Yugoslavs had whipped up a frenzy on their accordions, and a small crowd stood in a circle clapping to their beat. Baba and I got up to leave.

It was just then, after a whole morning of shuttling between tables, serving wine and Kirsch, Raclette and Rösti, coffee and cakes, and braving the pangs of two opposing seasons, that a pinch-mouthed, hard-eyed fräulein finally tripped and fell over her heels. The crash that was likely heard as far as Oberdorfstrasse, sent pitchers and plates flying, emptied milk over the wooden floor, and brought gasps of unspeakable horror to the picture-perfect cove of serenity.

Framed by the mahogany door, Baba let out his hallmark laugh, rolling on his heels, neck arched in triumph.

I knew he had found his story, for Lenin.

Lotus-Dragon

❋🜚🜚❋

'When Goddess Nugua undertook to repair the Dome Of Heaven at the Great Mythical Mountain, she fashioned 36,501 pieces of stone, each 120 feet high and 240 feet across. Of these she used only 36,500 and left the single stone that remained in the shadow of the Green Meadows Peak. However, the divine hands of Nugua had touched off a spark of life in the stone and endowed it with magical powers. It was able to come and go as it pleased and change its size and form at will. But it wasn't happy having been rejected by the Goddess, and was given to sighing over its ill fortune.

As it was thus bemoaning its fate one day...' She interrupted his reading in her small but firm voice, 'I'd be happy if I were her...left alone to be free.'

'But you'd like it to be a she-stone, wouldn't you?'

'It had to be a she to have been left behind.'

'What would you do then? Seduce a foolish monk and turn him mad...is that what you'd do?' He kissed her lightly.

'I'd change form, become the Goddess.'

'And size too?' He pinched her. She ran her nails through his greying hair. Besides his heart, she heard the rustle of casuarinas.

Normally the bed would creak. Everything creaked. The fridge would hum; hot water gyrate in the '50s' plumbing. They'd hear someone's doorbell...*Yankee doodle went to town*....

Turning over on his stomach, he read on from the *Dreams of the Red Chamber*, chuckling every now and then at the adventures of the delinquent stone. 'And thereupon its friend, the monk, exercised his infinite powers and turned it into pure translucent jade.'

'I hate jade,' she said, 'Feels like slippery soap.' He raised an eyebrow. Both were reminded of their shopping in a Hong Kong alley, going over neat rows of jade. She broke the silence.

'I wouldn't have bought anything....just checking if you'd....'

'I knew you wouldn't. I know what goes on inside your stone head!' Then he turned on his side and drew her into his arms, nudging the last piece of cheese from her hand onto the carpet. She picked it up in her toes, tried an awkward flip. He laughed. Resting an ear on his tummy she heard the Great Mythical Ocean.

The year had started with a surprise announcement. None among his economist friends at Delhi University suspected Dr Rudra Narayan's quick-fire affair with Suppie, Dr Supriya Sircar, a specialist in Shakespearean tragedy, would descend into marriage without the customary drama of a long and drawn out romance. The two had considered eloping, but a busy teaching term got in the way. In the end, the honeymoon drew bigger gasps than the marriage – a second for both. Her Bengali friends expected a mountain visit given that her first was spent by the sea: to Darjeeling perhaps, even farther, to Sikkim. The Keralite groom – one could predict with eyes shut – would head south to the beaches, sparking the couple's first 'healthy argument' before the unhealthy ones inevitably followed.

China! Rudra had mumbled something about a teaching stint in Beijing, but the excuse faded in the face of the destination. *A honeymoon with a billion observers!* It was an opportunity hard to miss – making fun out of obvious envy. *Whatever you do don't violate the ceasefire!*

'I'll expect a full report when you return' – Pritish, their Maoist friend, gave Rudra a conspiratorial look at the going away party. 'He means a full report of your bed side manners....if it was better than last time!' – his not-so-Maoist wife, Maya, giggled over her drink.

March was auspicious. Their dream flat fell right out of the blue onto the very spot they had hoped, and once they had moved in, the business of planning took them out of circulation. The impossible arithmetic of fitting everything they ever wanted to do in China into four weeks led inevitably to arguments – a cruise on the Yangtze threatening to bury Xian's terracotta warriors and with it a trip east to Shanghai. Suppie called her friend Rita who worked at the Chinese Embassy for tips and received an earful about smelly toilets. Frequent dining at the *Blue Dragon* brought chopsticks under control, and they managed to wrangle out of friends a pirated copy of *The Last*

Emperor. Spread eagled on the floor of their sparsely decked flat they read aloud *The Dreams of a Red Chamber* – the novel they had gifted each other to mark a momentous 1989.

'Will you teach the Chinese to speak English?' Maya asked Suppie as she drove them to the airport. She shook her head, 'I'll be a lazy memsahib.'

'A brown memsahib in China!'

'Mmmm….straw-hats, jodhpurs, servants…penning my diary over afternoon tea….'

As she settled into her 'villa' – the one-bedroom suite at the university's residence for foreigners – she was struck by how similar Beijing was to Delhi. Neighbours announced themselves across paper-thin walls. The smell of frying food followed them through the corridors. Just like back home, there were queues everywhere; throngs waiting for buses and busy street life in badly lit streets. It felt as if they hadn't left India after all, but travelled to a place where no one spoke their tongue.

Despite a mild dose of culture shock, the honeymoon was as it should be. They'd spend a whole afternoon picnicking at the Summer Palace, empty but for gardeners cleaning the ponds of dead lotus leaves. On busy and dusty avenues they learned to go with the flow, ignore the traffic lights like the other cyclists. Falling back, he'd call after her. Glancing over her shoulder, she'd catch him – a smiling face in a sea of strangers. In the evenings, lying naked on the carpet together after a hot shower, they'd read to each other from the *Red Chamber*. Sometimes that'd be the pretext, at others the result.

In April, they missed friends – quietly at first, then urgently. She felt the absence of familiar voices interrupting her in the middle of her favourite show, the haggling washer woman, and the gossip at her college canteen. Daydreaming, she'd see herself waiting anxiously all by herself in a small chamber, and go over everything that she dearly wished to forget. On her early postcards she didn't write but drew faces: smiling faces; lips sealed. By her own judgment, Rudra suffered less than her. He was friendlier to the other 'Foreign Experts' than she was to their wives. From their suite they saw Swedes and Germans, the Japanese, and Americans sounding like Americans.

That was till they met Wang. On a day when Suppie was out shopping and Rudra was back from his classes, she returned to find him gushing over his student interpreter. 'He speaks English like the

Beijing Man but is willing to learn!' He had thrown her a questioning look, inviting a resolute defence.

'Mine isn't a working holiday like yours.'

'But it won't be much work anyway...'

'I am here to absorb, not work.'

'Fine, absorb him then. He seems like a nice boy.' She was certain they had spent the afternoon discussing politics. Two empty cups stood on the TV.

'He loves coffee,' Rudra winked. 'It's expensive here.'

Next morning Wang was at their door promptly at nine. Outwardly, he looked like other Wangs – shirt tucked in neatly, the double-knot showing on his shoelace. Unlike her Indian students back home, he had no trouble slipping into first names. 'You can call me Byron,' he said. 'Byron? As in...*tis strange but true; for truth is always strange; stranger than fiction?* He laughed boyishly, and Suppie felt an instant bond. After a bit of coaxing, he wetted his lips and recited properly....

> *The mountains look on Marathon*
> *And Marathon looks on the sea;*
> *And musing there an hour alone,*
> *I dream'd that Greece might still be free'*

Then they walked arm in arm into Don Juan: '*Marriage from love, like vinegar from wine – a sad, sour, sober beverage – by time.*' And, '*all tragedies are finished by a death, all comedies are ended by a marriage....*'

'Who said that?' Rudra asked coming out of the shower.

'Byron.'

'And the English call him a Lord....pssst!'

Out for sightseeing they spoke all at once. Flushed with poetry, Suppie kept on: 'Who gave you that name?' 'Me,' Wang shot back over the driver's shoulder. Rudra was quick to follow suit. Passing the Bell Temple, he enquired if Byron was a Buddhist; jammed by Sunday shoppers at Muxidi he asked for a report on the free market. Suppie marvelled at the women in pantyhose. Did he like them? – she nudged Byron, pointing at a flashy poster with women in stockings on it. He nodded. Did his girlfriend like them too? He shook his head; he didn't have a girlfriend. Their driver, speaking no English but keen to join in, pointed at the red star over the National Library.

Arriving at the Forbidden City, they blended easily among Chinese and foreigners. Byron stopped at a stone turtle and they posed for photos. 'This one's good for longevity.' The two egged Suppie on, but she was reluctant. 'Who cares for longevity; shouldn't life be short and sweet like a honeymoon?' Rudra insisted and she climbed gingerly onto the turtle's back, then watched the two slip away, dissolving quickly in the crowd. She screamed at Rudra... 'Now you know why that stone was a she!' Sucking on sugared plums, Byron reached to pay. Rudra stopped him. Halfway into the park that flanked the palaces, Suppie said, 'I'm hungry.'

At the restaurant they saw his sober side. Fidgeting with knife and fork, a full life-sketch was available within a few minutes. He was from Inner Mongolia, Byron said, north of the Great Wall. But in Beijing it didn't matter where he was from. Here everybody was the same – eating the same rice, riding on the same dusty avenues. He wrote poems when he wasn't studying economics or interpreting for foreign guests, and hoped to return home after completing his degree.

Our little Mongol! Suppie feigned alarm. Playing the tour-guide, Byron asked if they'd been to see the Beijing Opera, tasted Beijing Duck and gone shopping. Playing the visitor, Rudra enquired of the length of the Great Wall. Suppie was keen to buy lanterns, the kind she had seen at *Blue Dragon* in South Delhi.

'Tídeng?'

'Yes, yes...with painted glass panels.'

Returning on Changan Avenue, they slowed down in front of the giant square. There were few lights on Tiananmen, alive with a holiday crowd. Babies squealed, couples sucked on popsicles, old men squatted around in circles; columns of smoke rose steadily over Mao Tse Tung's mausoleum in the middle. At the monument to the martyrs they saw a wreath of paper flowers and a red banner that read *Not Afraid To Die*.

They took him under their wings. Before long, he became their friend, their child – like newlyweds they planned around their newly born. It began to feel more like a visit than a honeymoon. Returning early on one of his teaching days, Rudra raised his fist and shouted slogans – 'Inqilab Zindabad! Zindabad! Zindabad!' – distracting Suppie from her reading.

'What now, dear?' She looked up from her book.

'Strike! Strike! Strike! Strike!' By the time he had briefed her on the situation – the campus troubles sparked by a hunger strike at Tiananmen Square – Byron arrived.

'Students are boycotting classes not books,' he announced grimly, holding up a list of demands. A hunger strike! Wasn't that too much? 'Will the government listen?' Suppie didn't recall reading anything in the papers. 'Who's behind them?' Rudra wanted facts, hard facts.

Leaving their flat, they were ensnared: marching students jammed the streets, and the crowd swelled at busy crossings; a stream of bicyclists waving brilliantly coloured flags flashed them 'V's. They held on to each other as in a flood. Suppie took out her camera, catching a glimpse of the giants – the university's basketball team – bowing to deafening applause as they arrived to join the marchers. All around her, the crowd cheered, sang or simply beamed at the slogan-shouting students. Ducking under Rudra's arm, she snapped a doll-face holding up a sign in English...*Don't Ask My Name*. And another...*The People Won't Forgive You*. Loud hissing greeted caricatures of government leaders painted on banners, and a shrill volley of whistles. A hassled policeman gave up his charge and left, as trucks rolled in swaying with young bodies. Once they knew the destination of the march, Suppie wanted to go. 'Well, maybe go as far as we can...' shrinking in the face of the distance – a good twenty four kilometres from their university to Tiananmen. As they listened to Byron, the day's events fell into place: the bustling campus, empty classrooms, and the marching students. Intrigued by the sudden outpouring, Suppie wished she had paid more attention to Carolyn – the visiting American professor of Chinese politics holding daily court at their cafeteria. Running between lines of marchers, she shouted at Byron... 'Why aren't you with them?' For a moment, they lost each other in the crowd, but there was no panic. It felt like a natural part of their travels, fitting well with readings about emperors and revolutions – forbidden and thrilling.

Opting out of the march after an hour, they rested in the shade of a pagoda. The heat reminded them of the changing season. Suppie was still active with her camera, disappearing from sight to climb up the stairs and peer through the turret-like windows for aerial shots of the city. The bottled water came in handy. Perspiring just as much as he would in the heat of Kerala, Rudra quizzed Byron over the student protests.

'Who do you think will win in the end, the students or….' He stopped in mid-sentence seeing the tense look on Byron's face. Maybe he doesn't want to know….or didn't care one way or the other…. With the Chinese it was always a matter of force, he thought, remembering Pritish and his lusty treatise on the revolution. In his mind he started to compose his 'full report' for his friend, beginning, as always, with a snigger or two – the mark of a disbeliever.

'The students will fight till they win,' Byron spoke clumsily, eye on the ground, sounding obstinate.

'You mean they'd fast till death?' Rudra showed disbelief. 'Let me tell you about a man called Gandhi and his fasting unto….'

'Why students? Why should they alone suffer?' Suppie had come down the pagoda's stairs and stood eavesdropping on the two.

'Because they have nothing to lose but their degrees, dear!' Rudra snorted.

'When you are naked, you have no fear,' Byron sounded gloomy. She frowned at both.

A bullhorn woke them at midnight. *The International* blared in through the curtains. Rudra hummed along… '*then comrades come rally, the last fight let us face, on our flesh has fed the raven, we've been the vulture's prey*…' Suppie gave him a surprised look and he chuckled about his radical college days. 'Back then everyone was a Maoist, weren't they?'

'I can't imagine you fasting…not even for a single day!'

'No!' he laughed, 'Pain never equalled profit by my calculations.'

Unlike their neighbours, they ignored the temptation of getting up from bed and peering through the windows to catch the action. Marching feet closed in on their residence, surrounded their private pavilion as she smothered his humming with her weight once and for all.

Officials had been sent to Tiananmen, they were told a few days later, to scold the students and force them to leave. There were rumours of a millions marchers set to gather at the square on May 4th – the anniversary of an uprising that had taken place decades ago.

'Where are the police?' Rudra asked as they toured the Lama Palace in the heart of Beijing. It felt a bit tame by Delhi standards. Student protests without a single bomb! Scooting around on their bicycles they were yet to spot burning tyres or gutted cars. Or have eyes turned red from teargas. No strangers to strikes, they expected every day to bring the pot to boiling point.

'If it was Delhi, by now there'd be a dozen dead,' Rudra smacked his lips as they waited for Byron to return with joss-sticks from the temple's stall.

'There'll be more than a dozen dead if the fasting goes on much longer.' Suppie sounded blue, trying hard to cheer herself up as she eyed a basket of luscious red peach – the Chinese symbol for longevity. 'Maybe the leaders will go to Tiananmen with peaches for the hunger strikers!'

'Peaches fired through the barrel of a gun!' Rudra scoffed at the idea. She sensed a relapse of her old anxiety. 'Who do *you* think will win in the end?'

'Me!' He shrugged. 'How would I....'

'You *are* the professor, aren't you? Shouldn't you know about these things?'

He laughed and took a bow. 'And you? You're a professor too...a Shakespearean, no less! Would you predict a comedy or a tragedy?'

'A tragedy, methinks....' She said with a glum face.

'And is that because you love them?'

'They're simply better. Just think of Shakespeare's tragedies.'

He crooked a brow. 'Why? What makes you so sure?'

'Because life is about suffering.'

'Who said that?'

'Buddha.'

Rudra kept silent for a moment then burst out laughing, 'You mean Shakespeare too was a Buddhist!'

She was first among the three lighting joss sticks and whispering silently as she prayed at the shrine. 'Whom did you pray for?' Rudra asked her as they left the temple.

'For the students.'

Arriving back at their flat, Suppie offered to make a round of coffee for everyone but Byron was in a hurry to leave. 'They want you to stop going to class for a short while,' he mumbled to Rudra before Suppie could insist that he stay back. He mentioned a meeting of university heads that had taken place a few days ago. 'They don't want foreigners to mix with the students now. You can return to class when everything is normal again.'

'But the classes are half empty anyway!' Rudra scoffed at the idea. 'There's no point trying to hide your dirty laundry from us!'

'What are you supposed to do here then?' Suppie cast a quick look at Rudra.

'You'll go sightseeing every day with me as your guide,' Byron smiled through his gummy mouth.

'You mean visit the Forbidden City again and buy more lanterns?' Rudra sounded bitter.

'No, no…there's more to see…the Fragrant Hills, Badachu temple….and don't forget the Great Wall!'

A delegation of deans visited them next morning to apologize for the empty classrooms, and suggested their esteemed guests enjoy the rare sights of Beijing and surroundings till business returned to normal.

For the first time in her life, Suppie felt like a memsahib.

It didn't take their learned noses long to figure out how the movement was going. Besides the BBC, the mood on the streets provided a fairly accurate reading: more flags, louder slogans, and screaming ambulances ferrying the fasting students to hospitals didn't promise a quick and happy ending. Loud doorbells woke them up most mornings with news of yet another twist in the plot. The universities were about to adjourn sine die – a frazzled Swedish economist went about in panic one day, only to be calmed down over lunch by other foreign experts. The *real* news broke faster than rumours – Suppie's screams bringing Rudra out of the shower, dripping all over the carpet, as they both watched the Premier declare martial law, ban foreign broadcasts, and order the army to drive the 'hooligans' out of Tiananmen.

Wherever they went touring, their faces stayed turned towards the square, as if keeping watch on an erupting volcano. Crowds were thin at every site they visited, and despite the luxury of having a whole palace or a temple to themselves, they fretted over their Great China Plan that now lay in tatters. On the morning of their planned weekend trip, Rudra fumed when told that they were to stay put in Beijing. 'Why can't we go to Xian?' 'Because there might be no planes to fly you there!' Byron had tried to placate him – 'Now you can see *real* soldiers in place of terracotta soldiers!' Rudra had refused to be

placated. 'So we can't go to Shanghai either, or to Hangzhou...'
There was every chance that there'd be sympathy strikes all around
the country, every chance they'd be stranded wherever they went,
Byron had sounded the alarm – 'To leave China, Beijing is best.'
'Leave? Who's talking about leaving? We still have a fortnight to
play here...' Rudra had demanded the university refund their hotel
and plane fares.

'I'd be happy to be stranded...' Suppie sounded wistful. 'Stranded
on the Yangtze river on a floating junk, wouldn't mind the sailors
going on a strike.'

On their way to the Great Wall, Rudra leaned over to Byron on
the front seat and suggested a change in plans. 'Why don't you take
us to Tiananmen Square instead.'

'You mean...?'

'I mean where the action is.' He pointed at Suppie's camera, 'The
English prof wants to capture the tragic-comedy before it ends in a
comic-tragedy.'

'But it's forbidden for foreigners to...' Before Byron could discuss
the risk with their driver, they were caught up in a demonstration
making its way over to Tiananmen, sweeping them into its course,
leaving no time to make a proper decision.

Once at the square, they realized the risks. How does one go
from point A to B without getting lost among the millions, without
being swept off one's feet by wave after wave of marchers? The siege
was in full swing: a cordon of arms guarded the hunger strikers,
allowing just ambulances to pass through; an efficient supply chain
ferried bottled water to students who had camped out under the top
sun, and orderly queues had formed before the lavatories. An excited
Byron kept on translating the speeches that rang out over the
microphone. Rudra tried in vain to cut across the square to Mao's
mausoleum where the student leaders had gathered. It seemed they
were at the crowd's mercy to leave and rejoin their driver who was
waiting for them a mile away.

The trick was patience. One needed to plead with the volunteers
to slip through the cordon. Once past the throngs, they'd be able to
breathe freely, and with Byron doing the pleading, it worked quicker
than they had imagined. Soon they were on their way out of the
square through a dark tunnel following a growing mass of visitors
who were leaving, and entered an underpass crammed with jostling

bodies singing *The International* and desperate to reach the exit as fast as possible. Pressure had grown from behind and they felt trapped, as if they were close to a stampede. Clutching her bag, Suppie had hung on to Rudra – both stricken with panic. The exit was blocked by a passing column of marchers, and those emerging from the tunnel had to push their way past them, slamming and shoving, crashing against bicycles, almost trampling over others as they escaped the the tidal surge. Once inside their car, all three were numbed by the danger that had just passed. *What a lucky escape!* they had brooded on their way back.

Suppie and Rudra quarrelled that night. Sitting on the dark balcony, Rudra had made a face at the hunger strikers. 'They don't know what *real* hunger is…it's easy to talk about freedom and democracy with a full stomach. All they really want is to live like Americans…'

'What are you talking about?' Suppie raised her voice over the blare of a distant microphone.

'They want to forget their past. How do you say it in Chinese…enjoy the meat and curse the cook.'

'Why mustn't they? What's wrong with eating a bit better?'

'Don't be silly, Suppie…there *is* a difference between them and us. Fifty years ago they were just as poor as us, Indians. And now after…'

'What difference? Like between you and me?'

'You can't see differences, can you, just the whole world speaking English as a second language.'

'Really…what would you have them do then? Be like us and choke on their past?'

Clearing his throat, Rudra had stared ahead, wishing to put an end to the argument. They had fallen asleep, resting their heads on silk pillows, faces turned away from each other.

At the experts' residence, Carolyn had taken over, running a soup kitchen, relaying hot meals onto a waiting van that sped away to the square to feed the supporters of the fasting students camped under the sun. Handing Suppie a sack of vegetables to peel, she expressed relief that they hadn't left Beijing for their travels after all. There was nothing worse than getting stranded in China, she could vouch. A

German visitor told stories about sneaking out of Xian in a taxi with no Chinese or English. An Englishman had been taken for a spy in lovely Guilin and locked up for a week before the Embassy could prise him out.

Everyone woke and slept at odd hours, washed without hot water, milled through the campus in the evenings. The army was top of the mind for visitors and students alike. Twenty thousand troops had encircled the capital it was rumoured. A false alarm would have them rush out of their flats to see if indeed the soldiers had arrived to end the movement by force – to crush the watermelon. Would the People's Army turn on the people? What would they do if there were clashes on campus? The solitary payphone at the residence drew a long queue. Whom would they call for help? Suddenly, India seemed remote – their families and friends. They remembered the last time they were in a crisis – when Delhi was burning – each calling frantically to reassure the other.

One day the sky turned pitch black, rain and dust swirled over the grey buildings; banners and flags put up by the students flapped wildly in the wind. It was a sign from heaven, explained the night-guard at their residence. Rudra had started to plan a return visit, to fill the gaps from this trip. 'We'll be back in ten years. Then you can visit Xian and Shanghai, go on that Yangtze cruise. By then our Byron will have his single child family!' 'In ten years….' Suppie sounded unsure. 'Yes, to celebrate our diamond anniversary, as they say!' He kissed her drooping lips, 'You'll be right here with me, just like now.' She had gone to bed early as Rudra stayed up reading, then woken at midnight to horns blaring through empty streets.

Byron visited them next afternoon and rang the bell. 'See you later, Byron,' Rudra called out. Suppie hushed him with her palm. 'You must visit the Badachu temple,' he yelled and squatted outside their door.

'Why don't you take us to your hometown?' Suppie winked at Byron. He gave her a non-committal smile. 'You must, really…' She insisted. 'I must tell your mother to find you a nice Mongol girl!'

'What if he fancies a pair of round eyes?' Rudra egged her on. 'A golden haired maiden like his namesake?'

Bored by their touring routine, Suppie feigned a migraine. Rudra wanted to finish the *Red Chamber* and offered coffee, but Byron insisted on a trip to the ancient temple – 'They have a Buddha from India there. Plus you can taste lotus buns on your way over, the very best in Beijing!' By the time they managed to drag themselves over, the sun had set. After a walk around the stupas and shrines, they entered through a creaking door that led to a dark passage. A sure-footed Rudra led them past bronze statues lit by candles flickering through slits in the columns till they came upon a fluorescent stone wrapped in silk – the giant trunk of a standing Buddha. Devilish frescos surrounded his serene face. 'Why must the dragon devour the lotus?' Suppie's small but firm voice echoed in the hall, as she examined the green beast in the painting, shooting out from behind the clouds and strangling the flower in its grasp.

'The dragon is the sign of the noble Emperor.' Byron whispered.

'And what is she?'

'She?'

'The flower, what does she stand for?' Suppie kept on frowning.

'The flower stands for a flower, silly.' Rudra moved ahead. But she stood eyeing the lotus, a shadow on her face. Lush petals, pink as raw flesh, struck out from a jade-green stem. She saw a smear of blood where the dragon's fangs had pierced the bud. Byron sat on the floor, holding his head in his hands. She kept looking up at the dying flower, the shadow darkening on her face, the lotus pond shimmering in her eyes. 'I want to tell you something....' Her echo sounded faint among the stone columns. Rudra's sounded fainter still, 'I'm coming dear....won't be a minute...' She heard the sound of his humming, and the flurry of mice scurrying around the pillars.

He returned flushed with success, having discovered a secret passage that led to a dark crypt. 'What, Suppie? What did you want to say?' She didn't answer, kept looking at the shower of petals at the dragon's feet and the single remaining petal still clinging to the drooping bud. He gave her a hug. 'Still sad about your little lotus, aren't you, my dear? Still trying to solve the mystery?' With a sigh, she tapped Byron on the back, 'I guess we shall never know, shall we?'

That night they finished the *Red Chamber*. Still on the carpet, Rudra cradled Suppie and nuzzled her neck. 'What did you want to tell me....a secret?' They heard an explosion and he felt her stiffen. 'Ah! The famous Chinese firecracker!' She shook her head, 'Not a firecracker, a bomb.'

❧ ❧ ❧

On an idle day, the Embassy called. An evacuation had been arranged, a friendly Indian voice informed, that'd take them back to Delhi before the situation got any worse. As they packed their bags, Suppie wondered if she should tell Carolyn that they were leaving. It felt odd to go now, before they had seen the end. They'd have to watch it all on TV, find out about the students – whether or not the government accepted their demands, and what happened when the army finally arrived to do its job. They could imagine themselves eagerly waiting for news from Beijing once they reached Delhi, even calling their friend Byron to ask if the hunger strikers had broken their fast.

They rose early the day before leaving to visit Tiananmen one last time. Fortunately, Byron spotted known faces and hailed down a truck full of students, speeding up the twenty four kilometre trek. Letting go of their bicycles they had climbed aboard and spent an uncomfortable hour swaying from side to side, deafened by the chatter around them. It felt like a victory parade approaching the Forbidden City with the crowd cheering them on. Rudra wanted to catch a final glimpse of the fasting students. 'Must have my report ready for back home!' Gingerly, they crossed the avenue strewn with empty bottles and slipped through the cordons, Byron pleading with the volunteers to let them pass. 'I'll pretend to be a journalist from India! That must give them a kick.' Then grabbing Suppie's camera, Rudra strode confidently into the hunger-strikers' tent, leaving the two behind. Waiting outside, she asked Byron why... why he hadn't joined the students at Tiananmen, where he stood, what he'd do after they had left, if he'd return to his family in Inner Mongolia. She heard him recite...

> *The road belongs to him*
> *The dust belongs to me*
> *The dreams belong to them*
> *The blood belongs to me'*

Entering the square, they stood gawking like tourists. The place seemed quiet and emptier than before. The students were sleeping inside tents gaped at by visitors. The vendors had returned, selling balloons, popsicles and small wicker fans to twirl in the sweltering heat. Small groups sat listening to speeches; loudspeakers screeched and sputtered. Byron stopped to chat with a friend at the martyr's column and they were separated. Rudra still had Suppie's camera and tinkered with the lenses. She trailed after him, walking the entire length of the square down to the crowded market at the end. In her small but firm voice she said, 'I want to tell you something I haven't told you before.' A step ahead of her, he was pointing the camera at the Gate of Heavenly Peace. 'Go on, I am listening, Suppie...'

'I have a tumour....in my brain.'

A small crowd was singing *The International* around a white styrofoam statue; moneychangers sat bored, visitors peered at sleeping faces, shutters clicked.

When the phone rang in the middle of the night, he knew it was an international call from the crackling line. The operator asked if he'd accept charges. From where, he asked. 'Melbourne, Australia.'

'Hi! This is Byron, your friend from China.'

He was a student once again, doing a Masters in Economics, studying hard and speaking like Australians. Rudra could hear him laugh. 'I have to forget my English to understand what they're saying...!' He'd graduate soon once the thesis was finished and his Indian prof let him pass. Then go on to do a PhD, maybe in the States.

In five years his laugh hadn't changed. The same laugh that Rudra had heard from the back of the car, or flying over the heads of fellow cyclists on the road. Byron had gone home soon after the troubles in Beijing, but the grasslands were not for him. Many of his friends were leaving too, leaving China to study or work. But in Melbourne it felt like home. 'There are Chinese everywhere! Chinese restaurants even Chinese....'

'Do you remember Byron?' He drew his shawl around him to keep warm in chilly December. There was a pause at the other end. 'You mean the poet Byron?'

'Yes...do you still remember any of his lines?'

He heard a chuckle, could almost see their friend moistening his lips.

> '*Though the night was made for loving*
> *And the day returns too soon*
> *Yet we'll go no more a-roving*
> *By the light of the moon*
>
> *No more a-roving*
> *Though the heart be still as loving*'

Then he asked to speak to Suppie. Putting down the phone Rudra stared at her photo on the bookshelf – perched on a giant stone turtle – taken in Beijing during their honeymoon in China.

Snakecharmer

The desert was near. He knew it by the shapeless trees, and the way one looked up expecting the horizon. He felt it most at dusk when the swans left, churning the lake in their haste. Now and then he'd hear the splash of a return, spot a solitary bird turning circles in the twilight. During the day the fort stole his gaze. He'd stare for hours at the embankment and the comical turrets, or measure the moat from his steep angle. At night they were useless – gone like the swans onto darkness.

He saw her eyes on him. From across the room he caught the lean bend of her neck, the rash of mirrors on her embroidered skirt with a toe peeping out from underneath – watched her swish and turn as she strolled or leaned on the balcony.

On their seventh day together, she seldom stirred from her perch except to make her way from the room to the swing on the terrace – setting her scarf on wings as she took flight. Within moments, she'd be gone like the birds, turn into a speck in the sky. Then, just as suddenly, strike the floor with her heels and stop, eyes flickering with fear each time he made as if to disappear from her sight.

When the storm finally arrived, the lake blended with the moat. Twilight etched a frame around her tousled veil. A lightning flash bleached the two of them, the breeze sounding the panes like a flock of alarmed pigeons. For the first time since they had arrived at Lake Palace on their desert journey, she flashed her smile at him. Pointing up at the stormy sky, he smiled back, then reached for the gun on the floor.

How would anyone know why he was here, take him for anything but a tourist – Jacob Tsur, the Israeli-American professor, arrived in Delhi for his very first visit to India, hardly awake as he checked into

Lodhi Hotel? How could a sleepy face show all he had to put down on the form – his age of sixty, the purpose of his visit and his status as 'single'? He was no more than a suitcase and a body when he arrived, needing a cosy spot for a few hours before waking to the noisiest dawn of his life. He had been warned by others how it'd feel, how awful he might find everything at first sight. Flying over from Chicago he had expected things to be much worse; call into question his plan even before he had started.

Lodhi would be his home for weeks. It was easy to explain his extended stay given the full slate of lectures he had come prepared to deliver, hawking his miracle solar machine, doing what he had done each year since taking an early retirement to try his hand at business, teaching the world how best to harvest the sun. It was a way of life that made sense to everyone, including his three grown-up sons – mixing business and pleasure – taking side trips whenever he could, to Jordan's Dead Sea or Arizona's canyons, between lectures and demonstrations. How could anyone guess the real reason for his whirlwind travels, or how he spent his off-hours and hotel nights, if he slept well, if he had stopped grieving since the day he had turned single again?

India would be different, he had planned. It'd be the end of the whirlwind; here he'd settle his score with himself. But it'd start, he knew, no different from his other trips, rushing through meetings and keeping tour guides on their feet.

Within days of arriving he had become well known for his warm smile and friendly manners – appearing as a hot prospect for package tours or a massage by the pool. The hotel manager would steer him away from the hawks and offer advice, as would the charming receptionists, threatening to scuttle his plans with side trips. Piles of brochures stared at him from every corner – Bandhavgarh's tigers, Kerala's backwaters, the Himalayas... Fortunately, the manager spotted his camera and offered to pair him up with a photographer to show him Delhi's beauty spots. One isn't a photographer until one has photographed Delhi! Emphatic, he had introduced Jacob to Randhir Singh.

Good! He'd need an accomplice – a local who'd play his part and keep out of his way. A photographer would do just fine, one who was resourceful and had a nose for detail. In Randhir he had found both, plus the bonus of having a compulsive liar by his side. From the moment he knocked on the door of the studio and heard the photographer singing, he knew he had to beat the man at his own game before becoming his friend. He was the 'first Indian', Randhir told him within minutes of their meeting, to have covered the Golan Heights during the war of '78. 'Sixty seven,' Jacob corrected him. He boasted of his stint in Kashmir with National Geographic and offered to do a photo essay for Jacob on the Baghdadi Jews of Bombay. He was none other than Henry Kissinger's kid brother, Jacob had lied in turn, lighting up Randhir's eyes. Well, no more than Randhir was Cartier-Bresson in disguise! They had shared a laugh. He was really on a contract from Lodhi, Randhir had confessed, to shoot portraits of honeymooning couples and do the odd assignment escorting tour groups to the Taj.

Riding back with Randhir on his scooter, he knew he was lucky to have found his friend, just the right man for his special assignment.

Each night he'd empty his suitcase to reach the small envelope of photos tucked into a hard-to-reach flap. He'd lay them out on the bed and stare hard for hours at a stretch. Normally, his mind went blank as he scanned them for a faint sign of life. Just as he had on that frosty night in Chicago, he'd sit by her photos as if he was sitting by his dead wife. Even now he could hear the boys wailing among the mourners as he waited for her to break her silence and speak. He had wished simply to hear her voice again – telling him to ring her friend and call her over to their house; reminding him to give her a bath when he returned from the university; or to light up the shabbos candles for Hanukah. Even a sigh as she turned painfully over on her side to face the window as she couldn't bear to see him in tears. Each night up until her death, he'd return home to sit by Ofra and hear her whisper and sigh.

Early in her sickness, he would urge her to leave the basement. He'd plead with his 'foreign wife' – the desert woman from the Maghreb he had married, the one to have borne him his sons, remind her of their brief romance amidst the dunes and their journey down the Sahara to magical fortresses and nomad camps. Sitting in her basement shrine by the light of candles, he'd comfort her with faded photos from that trip; promise her a return visit as soon as she was well enough to travel.

Even now he could recall every word his wife had ever spoken to him during her long illness. He could see her becoming a cripple before his very eyes, lose hair, turn thin and bloodless, just the eyes left to stare back at her husband after her voice went.

He had returned to the desert a year after Ofra's death, scouted the souks like a treasure hunter, to catch a glimpse of the couple – he the Israel born and she the desert Jew – scampering their way past eager sellers in the maze during his visit twenty years ago. He had spotted the shop where he had bought dark kohl for her eyes and silver anklets. The taste of burning harissa still lingered on his tongue, and the foul tannery smell. At Essaouira, in the forest, she had agreed to become his wife and promised to bear his children as they held hands and strolled among the cedar.

The Ofra he had lost lived on in his whirlwind travels, sneaked into airplanes and hotels hiding inside his suitcase, kept him lovesick by day and awake at night. Away from her basement she was still alive, still capable of turning her husband speechless and misty-eyed as he held her photos in his fleshy palms. She was just a flight away, he'd pretend, in Chicago, waiting for him to return from his business trip.

How long would the photos hold her memory before they turned empty like her basement? He traced her hair with his fingertip, peeping out from a Berber scarf in a photo he had taken – his soon to be wife dressed up as a princess at the majestic sand castle that had become their playground for hide and seek. The lustre was fading – he could sense drifting sand moving in steadily to drown an ancient city. She'd be gone soon, leaving not a trace of grief behind.

'What does Tsur mean?' Randhir asked, puzzling over Jacob's last name.

'Village.'

'Ahh! I must take you to a village in the city.'

He took it for another one of his lies. His body ached after a whole day of riding pillion with Randhir on his scooter, stopping briefly at the beauty spots. With one look at the old fort he had waved his friend on – it wasn't his sort of thing – then hurried through the botanical show unwilling to waste film on the wilting exhibits.

Catching on, Randhir had sped past the traffic and landed him straight in Janpath Lane.

The village had greeted him with cheer – the women camped under a row of trees selling knick-knacks for tourists. Hard up for a living they had come from the western desert and made Delhi their home. It took courage to walk the stretch of shops, bullied to buy, the din of sellers making it hard to hear one's own voice. Jacob had looked around for bargains then taken out his camera to catch the haggling shopkeepers. He had spotted a young girl sitting under a canopy with other women, barely out of her teens, in a mirror-studded blouse – blazing in the sun. Before he could look away, she caught his eye and held up a golden scarf for Jacob to buy.

He thought the camera would frighten her. As he tried to take a quick shot of her face, she got the better of him, ducking under the scarf just in the nick of time. He tried again and missed. The women of the stalls laughed at their cat and mouse game, while the girl's brother sat on Randhir's scooter and admired the shining dials. A busload of Japanese descended upon them, blanking out her scarf and Jacob flipped through piles of souvenirs waiting for the rush to clear. Randhir came to his aid, fished out money from his wallet and started to haggle with the girl. She had lowered her guard then, giving Jacob the perfect shot of her face and posed brazenly afterwards knowing she had lost the game. As they left Janpath Lane, she flashed him a smile that read, 'Later....'

Her father was a snakecharmer, Randhir told him. He was as harmless as his snakes, and spent all day dozing under a tree, too drunk to notice his daughter's haggling. What did she ask Randhir about Jacob? She had commented, he said, about his grey eyes and asked if he was from the desert. She had given Jacob a gift too – an embroidered side-bag, as a prize for winning their game.

On their last stop at the cemetery, he had trailed behind Randhir. 'I haven't brought you here to show you a few tombstones' – his guide had declared, bribing the guard to let them enter after closing time. He had explained the meaning of Zenana Rauza – the graveyard for women, popular with the loneliest of men, the widowers. Among the overgrown shrubs, he had pointed at graves of daughters and wives of emperors, and recited a couplet in Urdu. Stumbling in the dark, Jacob had imagined a row of kneeling men – the poor husbands,

heads bowed over the gravestones. 'A lover's heart is never full....'
Randhir had recited another couplet and translated for Jacob, holding
him steady over the rocky path on the way out.

He had remembered his plan and asked his accomplice for a favour.
'A gun!' Randhir sounded surprised. He had had many strange
requests from his tourist friends, never as strange as this. Then he
burst out laughing, 'You mean an air gun to shoot the crows that are
keeping you awake, don't you?'

A gun meant to kill – Jacob had told him.

He had expected things to go horribly wrong in India, scuttling his
well-laid plans. The Delhi beat had sucked him into 'tourist mode,'
and he had all but forgotten his mission. Thanks to Randhir, procuring
the gun was simpler than he had thought, and he had given himself
a few days to steady his nerves before heading out to the desert. The
rains were due soon, closing down his window of opportunity – he
had read enough about messy monsoons not to risk his luck with the
journey. Back from his rounds at Janpath Lane, he'd sit brooding in
his hotel room, worried at his growing popularity with the women
of the stalls. In just a few weeks he had become their kind uncle,
starting to go all by himself without Randhir, between his lectures
and demonstrations. They didn't mind his camera anymore, didn't
even bother haggling if he offered a price too low, lowered their
price if his offer was too high. The young girl had become his friend
after he had helped her win over a group of hard-nosed tourists. He
had snuck up behind them and whispered into their ears: It was a
steal! Her offer was infinitely better than the one he himself had
foolishly accepted just moments ago. It had resulted in a quick sale,
and the women gathered around Jacob to praise him for his cunning
after the tourists had left. Counting the money, the girl had winked
at him; her brother thrust an ice-cold Coke into his hand. Jacob had
pointed at the wicker basket at the dozing snakecharmer's feet, mimed
him playing his flute. Perhaps he'd offer free entertainment to all at
the end of a successful day of haggling. His basket was empty, the
old man had smiled sheepishly; the snakes were dead, their skins sold
off to tourists.

Visiting Randhir at his studio, he found his friend unduly cross
over a missed opportunity. Terrorists had struck in a market killing

scores of innocent shoppers. Randhir had passed by the very spot moments before, armed with camera and film to shoot a marriage party. If only he had been a little late…. He rued missing the 'perfect shot' of a massacre. It was all about opportunity, he nodded wisely, a minute here or there could well turn a man's life upside down.

He didn't worry about Jacob's opportunity – visiting Rajasthan was a must for all tourists, let alone a photographer. He couldn't miss the desert even if he tried, or the flaming sunsets. 'They make even a fool look like Cartier-Bresson!' He confessed being a bit surprised at Jacob's choice, having expected his desert-born friend to opt for the hills or the sea instead.

As always he was slow to wrap things up – having a few final words with his business contacts and settling his bill with the hotel's 'rupee hunters.' The South Indian receptionist was crestfallen when she heard about his side trip. 'You should've chosen Kerala, sir….my mother would've made you appams….' On his last day in Delhi, he left with Randhir to catch up on a few last minute things like fixing a car and a driver to take him next morning to Udaipur. The photographer kept on his chatter, offering advice on how best to shoot the desert. 'Like a sea it'll invite you to plunge in, but you mustn't act hastily…choose the right moment…' Like the sea it was unpredictable too – made the novice look like a genius and the genius like a novice! He'd have come along with Jacob gladly had he not been occupied with the President's visit. 'The President?' Jacob showed surprise. 'Mr Clinton,' Randhir had smiled smugly.

At Jacob's insistence, they had stopped at Janpath Lane. He wanted to try his luck one last time with the snakecharmer and bid his friends goodbye. When they arrived the old man was dozing as usual, but Randhir came back with good news from the boy: his father had caught a snake and was back in business showing his tricks. By the time Jacob finished his Coke, the wicker box stirred with signs of life as the show started with the flute playing. Huddled among the throngs, they watched the snakecharmer play a little tune then lay his ear against the basket and go on to play another – appearing to hold a conversation with the snake. Children pressed against them, and Jacob saw the snakecharmer's daughter look on warily as her father brought out the hissing monster, holding it up by its throat for all to see. Then he let it go – leaving it to curl up with its hood raised inside the open basket, dart its eyes around and sway as he stopped his flute to look the snake in the eye and chant in a low voice.

'What's he saying?' Jacob asked Randhir as the old man kept up a nasal monologue. 'He's telling everyone why a snake bites a man' – Randhir translated in a low voice. 'He's saying that a snake bites because it has demons inside its head and wants to kill them...' Jacob looked suspiciously at the man, 'Demons?' Randhir nodded. 'He speaks to the demons with his flute, begs them to leave the poor snake alone. When they go away, the snake has no reason to bite. Not any more.'

The snakecharmer had called Jacob over, offered to drape the snake around his neck and have his picture taken. He could sell him a cassette of his flute playing for fifty rupees, or sell him the snake's skin for... The man had whispered into Randhir's ear as they were about to leave. 'He wants your help, wants you to take his son and daughter with you in your car and drop them off at their village near Udaipur.' Jacob frowned when Randhir passed on the request. His friend had seen him hesitate, and prompted his reply, 'It'll be good for you....they can be your guides, show you things you've never seen before.'

'When will you be back?' Randhir asked Jacob as he dropped him off at Lodhi. The hotel manager had asked him the same question – he'd have a room ready for him when he passed by Delhi to catch his flight home to America.

He saw her lying on the floral Tabriz. She was snoring under a light blanket, having chosen the floor over the palanquin. He saw the same pair of eyes as Ofra's, as lean a neck as hers, the same flutter in her lashes; a glistening bead at the edge of parted lips. She was old enough to be his daughter, the daughter he had always wanted but never had. Or the shy daughter-in-law married to one of his sons, who had entered the family as yet another 'foreign wife' come from the desert. They wouldn't have known what to do with her though, just as Jacob didn't when it came to his wife's strange moods – the fact that she was never really happy in America, as if she was simply waiting for her death to return home once and for all. As the blanket slipped, he saw more of the face – the dark kohl marking a lucky charm on her chin to ward off the Evil Eye. All the kohl in the world couldn't save his Ofra from the Evil Eye – he sighed.

What did she have against him – the foreigner, the master haggler, the kind uncle who generously plied her and her brother with cold drinks? What game was she playing with him now? Midway through their journey from Delhi, he had regretted taking Randhir's advice and bringing the Janpath girl and her brother along. He had scolded himself – it wasn't to be an outing with friends. For the most part her face was turned away from him, and all he could see was a rash of silver and stark white bangles coming up to her elbows. She was a blur in a perfectly static desert. The boy sat beside the driver and chatted away merrily, ignoring his sister behind them. They had gone through miles of ochre sand, passing villages with sun-baked walls guarding against sandstorm. Cowbells rang over the swish of the desert breeze and a steady stream of goats threatened to block their path, brother and sister reaching out of the window to fawn over the animals and share the herders' laughter.

After goats, they spotted blue bulls, grazing among clumps of grey trees shrouded with a yellow flower. The boy shot a glance at his sister, and Jacob had sensed her pulse quicken. The driver, speaking in pidgin English, had taken his permission to make a quick stop and they left the dusty roads to enter a village smelling of cow dung.

Following the girl, Jacob had taken off his shoes and stepped into an old haveli, his young companions leading the way up to a courtyard and inviting him to splash his face with water from a well. She had uncovered her head and shaken loose the curls, disappearing inside the mud-palace with her brother in tow. Waiting for them, he heard the sound of women clapping and singing, and climbed up a winding set of stairs to find a soiree on a terrace overlooking the courtyard. The girl had joined the dancers, skirts and scarves dazzling under the sun, striking and smashing earthen pots all around them as the music reached its peak.

The boy nudged him, pointed at his side-bag and made a sign for the camera – the camera that he had left behind at the hotel along with film, tripod and all his souvenirs.

Back on the road, his mind had once again gone blank. As on that frosty night in Chicago, a chill had spread through his limbs as if his own life had ended, the remaining years left to be filled with a dying strain of memory. Just as the desert reminded him of all that had been with Ofra, it struck him cold at the thought of enduring the long loveless years as he went about his whirlwind travels. A screeching halt had brought him back to the present. Out on the sand he had joined the others watching the flames of a funeral pyre leap up towards the fierce desert sun.

Jacob had sensed the moment approaching. His plan had started to come alive, like the snakecharmer's basket. He knew why he was here in India – to die by his own hand. The great ocean surrounded him and he had sensed a stillness before trundling away from his companions at the next roadside stop. The driver too had disappeared behind a shrub, the boy running around the car and singing while his sister perched on the bonnet with a faraway look in her eyes as if she could spot their village like a speck on the shimmering horizon.

Up on the dunes all by himself, he had reached inside the embroidered side-bag and taken the gun out, turned his back to the road below and raised it to his head, casting an awkward shadow on the sand like a scarecrow. The trigger felt cold. His heart filled with a final gulp of air then stopped. A peacock-blue sky blinded him; smoke from burning shrubs filled his lungs. He heard a squeal, and turning back saw the boy who had crept up behind him, covering his mouth with his hands at the astonishing spectacle. The squeal had broken that infinitesimal moment, bringing him back to the present in a flash – the flood of recent memory drowning out the deep memory of his dead wife. As he held up the gun in an awkward pose, he saw himself through the boy's eyes – an old man playing the fool – and felt suddenly embarrassed. Reluctantly, he had climbed down to the car and to the waiting girl who had witnessed the spectacle too. Her face had taken on a look that was never to leave her since.

From then on she hadn't left his side, hadn't taken her eyes off him or his bag. Even after her brother disappeared near their village, she had stayed on with him in the car, entered the hotel without an invitation. He had held out some money and asked her to leave, told the driver to take her home. She had stood with her head down behind him – like a child bride or a child begging to make up with her father. More? He had taken out three notes of five hundred from his wallet – more than he had paid for all his shopping in Delhi. With just five hundred rupees you could buy a baby cobra – Randhir had told him. No? She shook her head, still standing, then followed him to the reception, waited till he had finished his business and sneaked up to his room under the gaze of an amused bellboy. After Jacob had finished tipping him, the young man had served him the smirk reserved for dirty old foreigners.

Now alone with her in the hotel room and waiting for the first drop of rain on the lake, he switched off the brass chandelier. For a split-second he lost her. Unlike previous nights he didn't hear the swans and searched for them from the balcony, catching instead the nervous moon hiding in the clouds like a thief. He heard the breeze trapped inside her veil – the flutter and tinkle, friction and purr – as if she stood at the storm's dead centre. She woke with a start as he made a move towards the terrace, darting her eyes to spot him in the darkness, fixing her frightened gaze on his bag as if it were a basket of snakes.

It had become their new game – her eyes following every move that he made, watching him closely should he dip his hand again into his bag. Without a word exchanged between the two, it seemed as if one animal were stalking another in the forest. He felt trapped with her inside their room, unable to slip out without bringing on a howl as she rushed up behind him, pleading with her eyes for him to stay. For two straight days and nights he had had to order in their meals, the girl eating on the floor with her hands while he occupied the plush sofa. They hadn't seen anything of their hotel – Lake Palace set like an iceberg in Pichola Lake, full of opulent interiors with paintings of maharajas. Nor stepped out to view the forts and palaces or to lose their way in bustling lanes full of miniaturists clamouring to perform their miracle for foreigners: paint an elephant on their thumbnail. They might arouse suspicion, he feared, might even be taken for fugitives or worse – someone might contact the Embassy in Delhi and he'd be asked to furnish details of his 'affair.' It took real cunning to bring her out of the suite, holding up his bag and leaving it conspicuously on the bed.

Out of the hotel and into the lanes, they seemed like ordinary tourists, rather a tourist and his local guide, one more excitable than the other, easily distracted from her companion as she stooped to admire glass bangles in the shops or swooned over warm jalebis long after Jacob had marched ahead. She appeared like a village girl come to a fair for the very first time, unable to stop gawking. Then, suddenly aware of his absence, she went tearing through the crowd till she spotted him on an elephant leaving for a palace tour with other tourists.

She waited till the elephant returned, then nudged Jacob towards the jalebi shop. With her in the bazaar, it felt like a side trip, almost like his early visits to Janpath Lane. She'd find her own sort in Udaipur and leave – he thought, still puzzled by her behaviour. Was *she* the fugitive – fleeing from her family, unwilling to let go of her sugar daddy? Maybe she'd meet a village uncle in these alleys and disappear like her brother. He thought he had succeeded in losing her at the artists' lane, as he slipped into one of the numerous studios. He didn't want an elephant on his thumbnail, but the artist insisted on painting a flower instead – a sign of his 'friendship' with Jacob. Within moments he was deluged with albums of emperors and courtesans, hunting scenes and court scenes. Just as he had managed to extricate himself, the artist sprang his 'special' Kamasutra album, trapping him for a few more minutes till he spotted the girl spying on him through the shop's window. Leaving in a huff, he had broken free of her and threaded his way past the shoppers, arriving breathless at the hotel only to find her waiting at the grand entrance – looking sheepish under the glare of the doormen. They'd have thrown her out if Jacob had arrived any later. He had considered throwing her out himself, grabbing her by her frail shoulders, resisting the urge for no good reason.

Sitting on the terrace swing at their suite she had resumed her intense look, darting her eyes about if she saw him fidgeting with his bag; as if she read his mind perfectly and saw through his plan going right back to Ofra's death. Each time he stretched his arm to pick up his matches and light a cigarette, she gave a start as if she saw a gun instead, held in his fist and aimed at his temple. She would bang on the toilet door and let out a howl if he was late. Coming out with a drenched face he'd find the room turned upside down in her search for the bag, then calmly point at it under a pillow. Even when she sat on the balcony and ate from the tray with her hand, she'd glance back at him every now and then, dropping her veil from her head.

Why did she want to stop him? He was no more than her customer. Why couldn't she simply let the stranger die?

Only the creaking swing reminded him of his chance, swaying gently in the breeze as she slept on the floor. He'd have a few moments to collect his thoughts and reach for his gun before she woke and fixed her gaze back on him.

He had called Randhir to ask yet again for advice. 'You mean the girl's still with you!' He could hear the photographer chuckle. There was a moment's silence, then Jacob heard his lying voice. 'Maybe she really likes you! Go on, don't be shy....India is giving you a second chance, my friend!' He had hung up.

At this rate he'd have to go ahead with his plan, ignore her presence. He could shut himself up in the toilet with his gun when the girl was sleeping. Or do his job when she went to wash up. He could face her fair and square and splatter his brains all over the pink marble floor as she screamed in horror. Maybe he could even teach her to shoot, then tempt her to take aim at his bald head!

He felt Ofra was watching him through her eyes. As long as they stayed fixed on him, he felt like a prisoner. He didn't want to die before her just there and then as Ofra had died before him, couldn't bring himself to inflict as much pain as he had suffered over the years. What if the girl were to fight him, if she tried to wrestle away the gun; or raised an alarm and had the staff banging on their door?

'Are you enjoying your honeymoon suite, sir?' The bellboy had smirked.

What if he lost his will and made up with his travelling companion? What if he took her home to Chicago and shocked his boys?

He dreamt of Ofra and woke up weeping. He was begging her to die and end the curse of death. The trial was draining his blood, he could hear himself pleading. *A lover's heart is never full*.... How could he fill such a long life simply dreaming of her? He felt her breath in the dark unable to see beyond the glow of the moon.

Only death – he heard himself whisper over and over – could end his desert journey.

The storm brought silence. Like invading cavalry it came tearing and flapping over the horizon, then lost its voice at the edge of the fort. Within its dark plumage, a kernel of light doused the cenotaphs with the brightness of noon. Like a giant reflector it whitened the lake, etching the swans in strands of grey and silenced the cackling and cawing. A curtain of light blanked out the marble palace. Then, suddenly, it was dark again – the kernel vanishing into a dark hole.

Sitting on the balcony, he heard the storm and made up his mind. With or without the girl, this would be the moment, he couldn't wait any longer. Like Jacob himself, she too must remain a witness to the spectacle of death. Like him, she'd have to live with the demon then pass it on to someone willing. Cross-legged on the floor, he had reached for the gun and raised it to his head, felt the cold metal on his temple.

She called him over with her eyes. He had risen and lumbered to her perch on the terrace as if he was in a trance, followed her gaze out to the lake. Through the haze of flickering lamps waiting to be nipped by the gust, he saw an undulating centre lit by a silver beam and a solitary bird turning circles – its last languorous turn before death. Only a slight frown played on the foreboding calm on his face. She had looked into his eyes with the eye of a snakecharmer and for a moment his mind had gone blank as on that frosty night in Chicago, the gun slipping from his hand and dropping below with a splash.

She had laughed then. Not her usual 'see me buy my stuff' half-childish laugh, but with her veil rising above her head – tinkling, swishing, rustling, meshing metal with metal – silencing the roar. She had stormed off the balcony and left the suite, running down the corridor out of his sight.

Long Live Imelda Marcos

W e knew exactly when Mary fell in love. As we were watching the news in our flat overlooking Hong Kong harbour on a breezy October night a few years ago, there was an explosion. Firecrackers – we thought, bursting all over Manila as the reporter jostled with the crowd that had come to cheer the ex-First Lady of the Philippines being led away from prison after her release. We watched her beaming face as she waved to her supporters, looking regal in an aqua-blue dress amidst bursting crackers and chants of *Long live Imelda Marcos*.

The explosion turned out to be in our kitchen. We found Mary, the only witness and the sole survivor, crawling on the floor as she reached under the oven to recover a Salmon head that had scattered when the simmering pot had overturned. Half-cooked tomatoes lay among the debris; the sink was splattered with lentil soup. A whole jar of garlic pickle had been dislodged by the impact and perched precariously on the edge of the shelves. Luck had saved three heads of cabbage from falling on the chopping board, having them sit in a straight line on the floor like balls in a game of skittles.

In life, as in a work of art, it's the accident that reveals more than the plan. With Mary, it had revealed everything about her, as she managed to capture the fish-head that showed signs of life and threatened to slip out of her hand, then stood up to examine the result of a sudden quickening of her heart. Her face was radiant, and catching sight of us, she sighed – not the sigh of dismay, but of ecstasy.

Seeing her thus, it seemed she was someone else. Not our Mary – our bun bun, our very own feiyung, the yaya to the child that we were expecting – not a Filipina maid who had messed up her employer's kitchen, but a young woman who, at that very moment, had fallen rapturously in love.

It seemed quite out of character, although until then we weren't sure what her true character was. Outwardly, she was perfect, utterly incapable of making mistakes. Ever since she had stepped into our cramped-for-space flat for dual-career expats that was tailor-made for domestic help, she had seemed like God's answer to chaos. Gone were the manic moments – the phone ringing in the middle of ironing, or bleeding the colours by mistake during a hurried wash – and the inevitable compromise one needed to make with odour and dust simply to find time for the crosswords. Mary was chaos-intolerant. Watching her in the flat was like watching a virtuoso performance. With her in charge, nothing seemed impossible – cooking, cleaning, dusting, ironing, even nursing the lost-cause houseplants to life. Like a great performer, she gave her audience no clue to her aching limbs or a throbbing head, needing gentle reminders to stop, lest the 'all-too-perfect flat' embarrass its less-than-perfect residents.

Clearly, she had a habit of overdoing things, like pestering us for a ladder she could use to clean the ceiling fans every week, or visiting three markets instead of one to get the best price on chicken liver. We had even caught her one afternoon hanging banknotes with clips to drip-dry on the clothes line, and she had defended her action by citing the questionable hygiene of the clerk who had slipped her the money over the counter. She dressed primly even in the kitchen – never a curler in her hair, nor appeared once without matching slippers. But it was her performance in the kitchen that drew the greatest praise. Within a few short months she had become the keeper of our taste buds, having addicted them to adobo chicken in coconut milk, to pancit noodles and sinigang soup. We learned to tell halo-halo from dinakdakan, and reached a point where the very mention of karekare – oxtail stewed in crushed peanut and rice sauce – would make our mouths water. Kaya pala! – we had adopted her favourite expression, coming home to find her smiling her impish smile and surprising us later with our favourites. 'Kaya pala!' – So that's why….!

The fact remains that we had almost lost her, almost chosen Lisa over Mary. Both were 'superior products' marketed by the hiring agency, superior to Sri Lankan and Indonesian domestic workers, both 'first timers' – unspoilt by the bad habits of previous employers. It was hard to choose from the long list – page after page of passport photos alongside the vital statistics: age, education, marital status, religion and body weight. *Weight*? The agency manager had offered her explanation, 'A plump woman tires easily, a skinny one hides from work.'

Lisa and Mary were identical in terms of their vital statistics. We were both struck by the pair of round glasses on Mary's face that gave her a thoughtful, almost 'intellectual' air. She'd look the part at least, we thought, among our friends – pseudo-intellectuals, each and every one of them.

If sometimes I call Rita, my wife, 'Tita,' it's because Mary called her so – Tita for aunt. She called me 'Mang' – Mister – not 'Tio' for uncle, or 'Manong' for elder brother, although she'd act as if she were indeed my younger sister. Rather, act as my younger sister when Rita was in one of her moods, and as her niece during mine. She had lied just once on her application form – she wasn't a 'first timer,' but a veteran, whose first employer was a 'dragon.' Mrs Wong had met Mary at the airport when she had flown in from Manila and taken her straight to a barber, the kind of place where old men go for a haircut. She told Mary that she couldn't work properly with her ponytail and had ordered a man's cut. She was forbidden to wear makeup, nail polish or perfume. Short skirts weren't allowed, or tight jeans – just a nurse's uniform. She had prayed for a kinder employer, and worked illegally for months after Mrs Wong had terminated her contract because she spent 'too long in the shower.' Mrs Wong to Mrs Chiu, then a string of other mistresses had brought her no closer to the El Dorado she had dreamt of in the Philippines – bringing her closer instead to the Inferno of dirty dishes, wailing babies, grumpy grannies, lecherous misters and their jealous wives. She had learned the maid business the hard way – how it felt to sleep on the floor of a hot attic, listening to the purr of the air conditioner in her employer's bedroom; cleaning her master's car for free; to being called a 'member of the family' and treated to leftovers. But it was the curfew that had made her flee back to the Philippines, the weekend restrictions that prevented her from meeting other Filipina maids – her friends – at Hong Kong's Central District. She had gone home after working abroad for four years, but the usual bad luck had brought her back.

We didn't probe her bad luck. All we knew was that she had wanted to be a dentist when she was growing up, and her mother had taught her to be a good wife – darn, sew and cook for her husband. Her dead granny was her guardian angel. She kept the old lady's photo in a frame at her bedside and her fiesta gown, which she had inherited, in her trunk.

Living with us, Mary had no restrictions. We were the restricted ones. It wasn't possible, for example, to step out of the shower naked and dry oneself in the living room while watching television. There were limits to how long we could stay out at night, without waking her up to open the specially made safety locks. Given the clear view from inside, making love on the open terrace under the neon beams of the city was out of the question. We'd tiptoe reluctantly back to our bedroom, although the walls weren't strong enough to absorb the tell-all cries. Mary, of course, must've known everything, sleeping on her single bed in the guest room. After a period of shyness, we had given in to her presence, taking just the obvious precautions to guard our privacy. It felt like living with a relative or a long-term visitor. This is how it will be when our child grows up, we thought – three months pregnant, Rita had been quick to bond with Mary in a way mothers bond with grown up daughters.

Despite being older than Mary, we had allowed her to slip into the role of a guardian. We were both forgetful, and she was our memory, never failing to remind us to take along car keys before leaving home, or to tip the doorman before Chinese New Year. She took the blame for our failings, made up excuses for our absence from neighbours' parties, and felt more tense than we did if we left late for work. We, on the other hand, knew very little of what was on her mind, what made her frown or purse her lips as she dusted the bookshelf, whether or not she felt homesick, what friendship meant to her – and love.

Almost unconsciously, we had started shedding friends – those that employed Filipina maids. It was a defence mechanism. There had been times when we were stung by their callousness and cruelty as they discussed their bun buns, rubbishing a Dora or a Lisa, a Christie or a Martina. It felt as if they were rubbishing our own Mary.

'She likes to negotiate, our little Susi…!' The hostess at a party was regaling her friends with stories of her maid. 'She refuses to wash the car, it's not in her contract, she says….won't wear an uniform because it makes her look like a maid! Won't sleep in the attic because…'

'How would your daughter feel?' Rita had blurted out, 'If she had to sleep on an attic floor?' Our hostess had looked puzzled – her daughter was on her way to the States to do an MBA. We wondered how many of our friends were 'dragons' in disguise, if there was one among them even who had employed Mary in the past.

'And she fears the vacuum cleaner, won't have anything to do with toasters and coffee makers, dehumidifiers and....'

'I have electrical nightmares too.' I tried to squash that, before someone brought up the myth of the 'sex-starved Filipina.' 'You've seen how they sit in buses, haven't you....with legs spread out like this!' – one of the guests had stretched his middle and index finger apart, and smirked.

We didn't know if Mary was sex-starved, didn't know much about her true character till that explosion in our kitchen at the very moment when supporters of Imelda Marcos were celebrating her release from prison.

'She has a lover now.' Rita whispered to me in bed, a few days later.

'Well...?' I had assumed, irrationally, that it was our Chinese doorman, who was married but looked the type who'd never give up playing the field.

'His name is Yusuf, and he's an Indian.'

Mary had met him on a Sunday, her day off. Yusuf had saved her from Kowloon Romeos who chased after Filipinas eating ice cream on the boardwalk. He had come between her and a drunken man who was hell-bent on giving her a kiss, then escorted Mary and her friend Angie to the nearby subway stop. Like a true gentleman, he had left without giving his name, or making any demands on the girls himself.

'Mary on Kowloon's boardwalk at night?' It was hard for me to accept such indiscretion from someone as level-headed as Mary.

'Why not? What's wrong with girls having a bit of fun?'

She had met Yusuf again later, purely by accident, at a busy crossing on Nathan Road where he was handing out advertising fliers to pedestrians for the tailoring shop where he worked. He hadn't offered Mary a flier as it was a shop for gents, but she had snatched one right out of his hand.

'She's been seeing him now for over a month...'

It was easier for me to imagine Mary at Central District, spending her Sundays with the giant flock of birds that filled every lane and alley, park bench and pavement – Filipinas from the whole colony come there to laugh, talk and eat; to braid hair and polish nails; buy pirated tapes and comic books; to gamble and to cry. I had gone to Central on a Sunday afternoon to meet Mary and retrieve our house keys from her, having lost ours on a shopping trip. It was Mission Impossible. How was I to find her in the colony of birds – on which street would I begin my search, under which tree of Chester Gardens, on which of the many parking lots turned magically into fiesta grounds? From the singing that could be heard from miles away, it seemed a grand wedding was underway where the guests had arrived in great numbers, pouring out of the hall into the streets. Queues had formed before mobile photographers who were charging a small fee to shoot 'studio portraits'; evangelists sought donations of 'love money' in exchange for the Pope's daily sermon. Ghetto blasters played Belafonte's *Brown skin girl stay home and mind baby*... A few love-struck Western men slunk around trying to look normal, as if they had stopped by simply to taste the karekare sold by an elderly matron, scooping out rice from her tiffin carrier. The green mats that the women had brought with them to sit on had turned the asphalt roads into fields of lush paddy.

Which Mary was I looking for? Mary Igloria, Mary Gomez, Mary Hidalgo, Mary de la Cruz..... Ah! Mary Villanova from Leyte! One of the women unzipped her phone-pocket and took out her phone to call a friend in Leyte province in the Philippines, who confirmed what she knew already – the Leyte girls were to be found picnicking behind the black statue on Statue Square.

I had returned to a flustered Rita an hour later that Sunday after a haircut, a lunch of karekare, and a lesson in basic Taglish, armed with a bag of ripe guava presented to me by the friendly barber, and our house keys.

One would normally find the lovers further away from Central in the waterfront parks facing the piers – the young women sitting on their fiancés' laps to avoid wetting their bottoms on the rain-drenched benches, watching a swarm of pigeons peck away at a half-eaten apple. We had never spotted Mary among the lovers during our walks by the waterfront, and against Rita's nosiness she had always offered a stolid defence, 'Maybe I find a boyfriend in Leyte when I go...'

Where did they go in the evening after the fiesta, I had often wondered. Some were under strict orders to return to work after sundown, Mary had said. Some of them crowded around Karaoke bars. Those with American boyfriends filled up internet cafés, while a few drifted off to Kowloon's boardwalk to take in the bright lights and flirt with sailor boys who were as far away from home as they were themselves.

'What does *seeing* mean?' I tried to judge if Rita was overreacting. Perhaps it was nothing more than a passing phase, brought on by the restless monsoon that somehow stirred the Asian soul just as it wrought havoc in the fields.

'Exchanging sms messages, making calls….meeting on the boardwalk for ice cream, shopping at Causeway Bay. Last Sunday they went to Lantau Island in a boat.' Rita didn't think twice before betraying Mary's confidence. 'She doesn't want anyone to know yet, not even her friend Angie…'

'Has Yusuf told her anything?'

'He has asked her to consult with her heart,' Rita sighed, obviously moved and puzzled at the same time.

'Consult with her heart! How stupid of him! What does the heart know about the problems of a Catholic Filipina marrying a Gujarati Muslim?'

'Do you think he could be married already, just playing with our Mary while…' I could see worry beads on Rita's face.

'How would *I* know if he has a wife back home?'

'Men can tell these things, can't they? Know when a man is double-crossing a poor girl?'

'For all you know he might be a perfect…'

'Predator?'

I was about to tell her that only a woman can tell if a man is honest – from his kisses – but she seemed to be overwhelmed with her suspicions. It was left to me to visit Yusuf's shop and either confirm or allay her fears. 'You must judge if he's right for Mary.'

A Force Ten typhoon had been announced and when I left for the gents' tailoring shop on Nathan Road on a Saturday afternoon, rolling mist had swept in from the sea and turned the city into a Chinese scroll painting. This is how the island would've appeared to shipwrecked sailors and fleeing Taiping rebels from the mainland as they glimpsed their future home for the very first time. Hurrying past the famous Peninsula Hotel, I felt like a colonial sod forced out of an opium den to attend to something he was utterly clueless about.

As I sprinted across the Salisbury Road junction to beat the evil traffic lights that took fiendish delight in turning red at the wrong moment, I fretted over Rita's words – how deftly she had turned something that was none of my business into something that was. 'You need a new suit,' she had said, and Yusuf – if he knew who I was – might even offer me a discount.

Mr Mohabbatwallah – the shop's owner – welcomed me inside with a look of disbelief. A dozen tailors crowded the patch on Nathan Road, and winning a customer involved gladiatorial combat as the ushers fought each other to guide a curious onlooker through, whispering like a lover into his ear. Bearer of a name that was curious even by Indian standards, Mr Mohabbatwallah, the 'seller of love,' seemed stunned by his luck as I slipped past the ushers into his shop. 'What do you want, sir?' he said, clearing his throat, taking me for a no-gooder who had entered his shop only to seek directions to the nearest loo.

'Unfortunately, we are unable to offer you an urinal…' he started to say, before I could utter the word, 'suit.'

'A *suit!* Oh….'

Recovering quickly, Mr Mohabbatwallah drew immediately on his vast repertoire of charm, pointing at the mannequins in the shop window.

'A suit isn't just a suit, but a suit by someone special. Like Giorgio, or Hugo, Valentino, Ferragamo….whose suit did you have in mind, Mr….?'

'Sanyal.'

'Ah! A Bengali.' He seemed relieved. Bengalis weren't known for their bargaining prowess, unlike Punjabis and Gujaratis. He read my confusion and stepped in quickly, 'I suggest a Giorgio Armani for you, sir, it's just the right one for artists and intellectuals.' Having stroked my vanity, he barked out rapid orders to fetch a Coke for me, keep the toilet door firmly shut to stop crafty tourists from sneaking in, and for Yusuf to start taking my measurements.

For the next few minutes, I stood speechless with curiosity – not at Yusuf, but at my measurements. It had been a while since I had had a suit made, and found it hard to agree with the measuring tape as it was lassoed around my waist, or hung like a limp stalk down to my ankles. Plus, there was the added discomfort of being measured so openly by someone I had come to size up.

How does one tell from a man's face if he's honest? I wished I had the skills of a trained interrogator or that of a mind-reader to turn the young man inside out in order to discover how much of his soul was given over to our Mary. Yusuf looked calm and qualified enough to announce the measurements in an unfaltering voice, and seemed to command Mr Mohabbatwallah's respect, who let his judgement go unquestioned. After he had finished, I wrote down my address, paid a deposit but forgot to ask for a discount and left, promising to be back in a week for fittings.

Rita was waiting anxiously, and I told her everything I had seen in Yusuf: dark eyes shaped like almonds, a trim beard, and just the hint of a smile.

Into the second trimester of pregnancy, Rita and I had our own worries that kept us from worrying too much about Mary and Yusuf. But it was always there in the back of our minds – the fear of something going wrong. Some days, Rita would play the critic and I the believer, then we'd reverse our roles like ebb and tide. Out shopping for our little one, I was gripped by a sudden panic as I imagined a half Indian-half Filipino child abandoned by its parents crying its heart out in a baby cot. *What if....*

'What if he gets her pregnant?'

'Who gets who pregnant?' Rita frowned.

'Mary...who else. What if...'

'She isn't pregnant.'

'How do you know?' I was prepared to challenge her callous attitude, as I walked away from the baby cot and paced the aisles.

'She hasn't missed her period yet.' Rita hurried me out of the shop, 'Come, you must be hungry' – drawing the ridiculous conclusion that an empty stomach was the cause of my anxiety. 'She's Catholic,' she said quietly in the car, 'Catholic girls don't give in easily...'

It's not as if we didn't trust her; we didn't trust the crazies that were out there. Those who took every narrow-waisted golden-skinned girl to be a flower waiting to be plucked. Those that rolled down their car windows to scream at foreigners. In a way it comforted us to know that she might be with Yusuf – her knight in shining armour – when she was out in the streets. We thought of asking her to bring Yusuf home when we were out at work. That way they'd be safe, and have their privacy as well. This is how it'll be when our child grows up…we mused, stroking Rita's tumescence that held the object of our future worries.

On her part, Mary had become truer to her character ever since the explosion in our kitchen. That she wasn't fastidious by nature was clear, simply quick to learn from her past mistakes. If she spent a good hour scrubbing the bathtub for no good reason, it was because she had already run through her chores and the plain act of scrubbing helped her to daydream. Her speed was her asset, and a roving imagination that lay carefully hidden under fluttering eyelids and a gentle twitch of her lips. Ever since that evening, she had shown herself to be a risk taker – learning to cook the Indian way from Rita, then trying her hand with confidence. 'She's getting ready for her in-laws!' – we'd smile and wink at each other. She'd borrow glass bangles from Rita, to wear on Sundays when she'd be out with Yusuf; she learned to speak simple phrases in Hindi, and would stare wistfully at the Taj Mahal framed on our bedroom wall.

Like a friend, she had started to drop her guard, taking just a few months to confide in us the 'real' reason why she had left home. It was true her family needed the money, and she had promised her mother that she'd pay for her sisters' higher studies. But she had left their hovel in the Philippines to forget her father – the one she loved most of all – who had died in her arms when they were too poor to take him to a hospital. In a few sketchy words, she had let us into her private well of sorrow. She thought of him every day before she went to sleep, counted her rosary beads without fail to wish him well in heaven. It was his smiling face that had kept her on track as she slaved through tests and interviews to be chosen for a 'plum' job in a foreign country, had made her bear the many disappointments during the years spent abroad. 'He's taking care of me now, just as I took care of him when he was dying…' She thought nothing of hiding her disgust at her mother who simply wanted more from her – more for her two siblings, one ugly the other lazy. Like a friend, she'd show us her impish streak as well, pulling my leg over my forgetfulness – hiding my shoes and socks then surprising me with her 'discovery.' She liked to listen to her favourite love songs and felt at home turning up the stereo's volume as she hummed along in the kitchen, more than ready to defend the mushy oldies against our jibes. 'What kind of music does Yusuf listen to?' Rita had asked Mary. He was still a shadowy figure about whom we knew precious little. She had made a face, 'Hindi, Hindi, Hindi....!'

We wondered if the two were planning to get married soon. Yusuf would have to go home and convince his mother, Rita confided. He'll go soon with a photo of Mary dressed up as an Indian girl. Mary had already told her mother and sisters – she was seeing a certain Joseph, she had told them. Joseph for Yusuf! How smart of her, we had laughed. What Catholic would oppose the marriage of Joseph and Mary?

'They've been here...' Rita murmured one evening as we stepped into our flat after work. She sniffed the air, and announced confidently, 'They've cooked, watched TV, and...'

'And what?'

'Made love.'

'You mean right here...?' I glanced suspiciously at the sofa.

'Could be here, or on the terrace, in the kitchen, even in our bedroom.'

She had promptly dismissed my doubts – 'women just know these things' – then discovered burnt biryani in the garbage. Maybe he had cooked for her, or they had both started to cook then forgotten all about the biryani.

We didn't know if we should be pleased at the bond that seemed to be deepening rapidly, if we should advise her to be careful as we would've certainly have done had she been our daughter, if we should scold her for almost setting the kitchen on fire.

It'd be better, we decided, to invite Yusuf to come over and meet us, end the hide and seek once and for all. We'd be happier having our Mary as a careless daughter than as a perfect maid.

The fortune teller had told her she'd be married soon and away from Hong Kong. It was the same man Mary visited every Easter and Christmas on Temple Street, a stone's throw from Tin Hua Temple. He read palms and tarot cards, sitting on a stool under a kerosene lamp, and she had immense faith in him for predicting that she'd return to Hong Kong when she was on the verge of leaving for good. He had predicted her mother's cancer and her friend Angie's miscarriage, and had assured her that she wasn't born to be a maid for life, that she'd leave her job one day but only after she had served the kindest people on earth. He could well be right again, Mary had beamed. It felt like a prediction that was destined to come true, well, almost true – Mary was yet to meet her future husband, the old man had said, making probably the rarest of mistakes, then blessed her for her marriage.

When Yusuf arrived at our flat, the party was in full swing. He might feel embarrassed meeting just the two of us, we had thought. It might even seem that we had called him over for a grilling. The presence of others would make it less awkward for Mary as well – I could imagine her sitting across from us, Yusuf by her side, her nose up in the air to mind her unfinished business in the kitchen. Let's all mingle, Rita had said – businessmen and vagabonds, bun buns and tailors.

It turned out to be a bad idea. He arrived with a gift – a kilo of dried fruits in a brown paper package – and promptly disappeared into the kitchen to be with Mary. Throughout the evening we tried several ploys to coax the two out, succeeding only in ensconcing them firmly, as they helped each other stir the pots, pop champagne, and fill trays turning water into ice.

He's shy, we told Mary when she asked for our opinion after the guests had left. 'He's not shy with me,' she said with a proud smile. And what did he say about us? 'He said I was lucky to have such a kind master and mistress.'

Master and mistress!

We knew she was sad when Yusuf left Hong Kong to visit his home in India. She had made ginataan for him – a pudding of rice flour – but he couldn't take it with him on the plane, and ended up finishing the whole bowl at the airport as she looked fondly on. He carried Mary's photo with him, and a letter she had written to her future in-laws, drawing heavily on Rita's drafting skills. Yusuf had worn a white suit for the journey – one that he had tailored himself – and Mr Mohabbatwallah had presented him with a matching tie. We too had passed on our sending-off gift – a rose for his buttonhole.

We felt sad knowing that Mary would leave us soon. It was simply a race against time, waiting to see which came first – our baby or the Catholic wedding that Mary's sisters were planning to hold in Leyte. Given our situation, it wouldn't be possible to go over, we knew, but drew comfort from the fact that she'd be returning to live with Yusuf in Hong Kong. From being our maid, she'd become our friend. I could imagine us out on Kowloon's boardwalk eating ice cream. Maybe Yusuf would join us too, shed his shyness finally and enlighten me about the trick his measuring tape had played around my waist.

As in classical love, in which parting brings on incalculable yearning, we could see how much Mary missed Yusuf. She'd come back from her outing early on Sunday evenings, even stay home all day scrubbing the bathtub or scraping off mould from the fan blades. Her fastidiousness seemed to come and go without notice – we'd return, for example, to find a squeaky clean flat without a trace of food in the kitchen. Her friends too were nowhere in sight, when she probably needed them most. It'll take time for him to convince his mother – I could hear Rita comforting Mary in the kitchen. She'd throw a fit at first, then come around slowly. That was the way with Indian mothers – *all* mothers. No, he couldn't possibly forget Mary and marry a bride that his mother had chosen for him. The fact that he hadn't sent her many messages since he had left, wasn't necessarily a bad sign. Things could easily go wrong in India without a warning, lead to unforeseen delays, like strikes and monsoons. She shouldn't worry…good news always arrived suddenly, didn't it?

After a fortnight had passed, I went to see Mr Mohabbatwallah. This time it wasn't Rita but my own counsel that prompted the visit. I should get a progress report, I thought, on how things were going in Gujarat, that might help to relieve Mary's worries. There was a flickering doubt as well, the kind that men feel towards other men when it comes to their sisters and daughters. An expert mind-reader, Mr Mohabbatwallah knew that I hadn't come for another suit but to talk about Yusuf. Ordering his assistant to bring me a Coke, he took out a photo album and started to turn the pages slowly. 'Let me show you the picture of Yusuf's uncle,' he brought his face close to the page as if to read the piece of paper the elderly man in white was holding in his hand. 'It's the certificate he received from the President of India for his role in the freedom movement, and the years he spent in jail.' The photograph was taken in Sabarkantha, his home district, not far from Ahmedabad. Sipping my Coke absentmindedly, he moved on to the next page. 'And here's his brother, Yusuf's father.' The family had fallen on bad times after Yusuf's father's sudden death, and the boys had to leave school to learn to work with their hands. One of Yusuf's brothers had become a signboard painter, another a carpenter. 'If he was lucky, Yusuf could've become an engineer, but now all he does is cut cloth for foolish people who can't tell a fake Giorgio from a real one.' He looked a touch embarrassed at the obvious meaning of his comment. 'I have met Mary. She's a fine girl. I've given Yusuf a letter for his mother, my own sister, telling her not to be stupid, not to worry about religion, but accept Yusuf's choice.' Mr Mohabbatwallah had looked me straight in the eye, speaking as man to man – as the groom's uncle to the bride's elder brother. When did he think Yusuf would return? He should've been back by now, Mr Mohabbatwallah had scowled, and blamed the kind of trouble that always came out of the blue and delayed things.

Mary had gone out that evening, and the two of us felt like celebrating. She was in good hands, after all. Yusuf came from just the right stock – honest to the core and earthy – even though his suit hadn't quite lived up to my expectations. We thought of carrying our celebrations over to the boardwalk's ice cream shop, where we could sit and flip through the list of prospective maids the hiring agency had sent over, to find a replacement for Mary. Like experts, we'd scan the photos and once again spot the right one – a good employer always finds a good maid, Rita had announced, and I was in the mood to agree with her.

A long-tailed boat stood motionless before us, perfectly framed by the harbour lights, enjoying a moment of lull before it revved its engine and sent a wall of waves crashing to the shore. The gulls had perched nearby, waiting for the unlikely generosity of a visitor throwing them a little bit of something, and even the policemen were in a jolly mood as they chatted with the Romeos. We spotted Mary sitting on a bench all by herself. She was dressed in jeans and black leather boots, straight hair down to her shoulders, and wearing a light windbreaker to keep out the February wind. She looked like a bedraggled little bird that had lost her flock, shivering all alone by the pier. There was something about her that stopped us from calling out. We couldn't see her face properly, but it seemed troubled as she kept peering intently at her phone as if she was expecting it to ring any minute or flash her a message, praying to the dark sky to send a fluorescent gift into her palms.

That night, we realized the obvious difference between us and Mary. She *was* our maid, and we her master and mistress. Despite the fondness that had grown quite naturally, it was impossible for us to become true friends – share her deepest feelings, her pains and her dreams. It was true we lived under the same roof, but as employer and employee – a truth that all the kindness in the world couldn't erase. At best we could look helplessly on and wish her well as she hopped from one home to another, settling perhaps for good with Yusuf. Maybe he was her final perch – the home of her dead father that she had left behind.

'Yusuf will be back as soon as the troubles are over…' I told Rita, comforting her with Mr Mohabbatwallah's words.

Back in our flat while tidying up things, I found a music disc snuck under the sofa – one we hadn't played in a long time. It seemed odd for it to be out there – a collection of old-fashioned love duets in Hindi.

> *Tere been sune nayan hamare*
> *Waat takat gaye saanjasakaare*

> ….my eyes are blind without you…

The man with almond eyes played it, I was certain, for Mary before they had made love for the first time in our flat.

A day or so later, as we were watching the news there was an explosion. It was on the screen – bombs bursting on empty streets, ringed by flames from burning homes all around. A frantic reporter, running along beside a news van and clearly out of breath, was shouting into the microphone as he ducked the hailstorm of brickbats flying around him. Gujarat was burning, he was saying. Rioters had gone on a rampage, killing innocent men, women and children – Muslims – setting them on fire, raping, hacking their victims to pieces, burying them alive. The orgy had gone on for three days while the police watched in silence. Every city, town and village had been affected in Sabarkantha from where he was reporting. Not a single home had been spared by the killers, not a family remained who hadn't lost a member, not a…..

'Where did you say Yusuf's family was from? Wasn't it….' Rita's voice had choked. Coming out of the kitchen and standing behind us, Mary had watched it all, her hands firmly holding a boiling pot as her eyes scanned the rows of coffins that had been brought to the graveyard by the survivors.

❦ ❦ ❦

She had left suddenly that very week, without giving us the month's notice that had been agreed upon at the start of her employment. We returned from work to find the flat empty of her things, not a trace left behind of our Mary. A card on the guest room's dresser announced her departure – *Dear Tita and Mang*, she had scrawled in her girlish hand, *may God bless you and the little one.* Saddened as we were, there was nothing to be gained by informing the employment agency about the breach of contract. It was clear that she had left us for good, perhaps left Hong Kong as well, and we didn't wish to sully her record should she ever plan to return and become a bun bun again.

We heard from Mary next about three years later. She had sent us a photo of her family, and the very fact that it managed to reach us halfway around the world bears testimony to the goodwill of neighbours and the persistence of postmen, those we are most likely to blame for errors not of their making. The letter had come redirected from Hong Kong to New York, where we lived in a flat overlooking the Hudson River – Rita, I and our little girl. It was a photo of Mary's family in the small vegetable garden of their home in Leyte. She looked just the same with her round glasses, wearing her dead granny's fiesta dress. Sitting next to her in a wicker chair, Manuel, her husband, strummed a guitar, while their young son, Joseph, sat solemnly on his lap – a lovely boy with a full head of hair and perfectly shaped almond eyes.

The Accountant

*B*esides being a clever man, an architect must be a mathematician and an artist, a historian and an engineer…. Mr Ray looked up from his book and cleared his throat as if to read aloud to his wife, then turned his gaze back. *…He should be a good writer worthy of conveying his plans in minute detail, a skilled draftsman versed in geometry and optics, possess a good ear for music and show no ignorance of the motion of heavenly bodies…*

Sitting on the bed, Mrs Beena Roy continued to fold dry laundry, which took up almost the entire evening after she returned from work at the income tax office – buttoning up shirts and matching the sleeves, pressing her palm down over the ugly bumps of a starched sari, folding napkins into bunny caps or slapping the pyjama bottoms to rid them of ungainly static. In the end, they lay in neat stacks before her, a chastened bunch, requiring no ironing. It was a routine as well as an excuse to withdraw from the pointless chitter-chatter of long married couples that added less than pepper and salt to plain evenings with television and occasional incursions by neighbours. She was used to living quietly without children after twenty childless years of marriage and without pets after a Maltese had triggered her husband's asthma.

Mr Ray read silently, waiting for the nightly news to quicken the evening's pace – the flurry of dinner, washing up, making up the bed and selecting items from his wife's neat pile for the next working day. After twenty years in the same job there wasn't much to discuss about work, although he made a point of promptly disclosing any rise in salary so that his wife could duly report it on their joint income tax returns. Barring a tiff or two over visiting relatives, there was no hint of the type of 'marital troubles' his peers routinely discussed, and he was proud to have a wife who didn't overspend or gossip with neighbours, embarrass him in public in any way or burden him with sickly in-laws. She was as indifferent to his reading as he was to her folding. Even when they were younger, each had been mindful of the other's routines and shied away from upsetting the even pace of an easy life. The only oddity that he had noticed was his wife's refusal to spell her last name in the same way as he did – not Beena Ray, wife of Bimal Ray, but Beena *Roy*. She had avoided the 'anglicised Ray' as the only mark of discord – the nameplate on their South Delhi flat puzzled the neighbours and prompted postmen to ask a few questions before a parcel for Ray could be delivered to Roy or that for Roy to Ray.

Mostly, he read for self-improvement – manuals and refreshers with the occasional 'path-breaking study' thrown in, that his boss demanded every employee read, offering words of encouragement to the half-willing and threats to the rest. Mr Ray, of course, needed neither threat nor encouragement, simply fodder for his evening routine in the company of his silent wife. It wasn't exactly true that he never shared his readings with Beena, but limited them to taxation matters that could help her improve as well. On these occasions he'd clear his throat and begin reading, as if his wife expected him to do so, often going over a paragraph twice for emphasis. Hands parted to take in the full breadth of a bedcover, she'd listen with her face hidden behind then offer her comment after folding the piece to perfection.

...He must perform both manual and brain work for which he should be free of disease and disability... Mr Ray laid down the heavy volume on the stool before him then started to read aloud. 'An architect must be free of the seven sins; he must not have excessive desire for gain and be generous to the point of forgiving his rivals...'

Mrs Roy frowned, threading her fingers to bunch together the mosquito nettings – the most difficult of all items to fold properly – and cast a quick glance at the TV to check if it was indeed her husband's voice she was hearing.

'Geography will tell him if the chosen land is suitable, astronomy guide him in setting the building to the right proportions, physics will inform him of the conduct of rivers and lakes that may surround his creation, theology advise him of its proper role among men. Besides being a Jack of all trades, an architect must be accurate.' Mr Ray shut the volume and wet his lips ready to conclude his reading, 'Above all, he must be a devil for detail.'

As she put away the neat stacks into the linen closet, Beena Roy glanced suspiciously at the volume on the stool, *A Guide for Architects in Medieval India*, and offered her own conclusion, 'Just as an accountant like you.'

He woke promptly at two, at the exact hour he had woken every night during the past month. Sitting up on the bed he wondered if he should wake Beena up and tell her everything. His gaze slipped through the open window and crossed the boundary wall of their gated colony, into the deserted roads and sleepy shrines. Then on it soared over the national highway, flying straight as a crow through the dustbowl of Northern India. It skirted the Yamuna on its way down the plains and came to rest on a flat bed beaten out of the alluvial soil where the river changed course from south to east. Agra! Mr Ray felt he had arrived, yet again, at the very spot he knew only too well. He sensed a familiar rush of excitement as he saw a much younger man who bore him a passing resemblance stride past throngs of labourers assembled on the flattened riverfront, struck with frenzy just as an event was about to unfold. Words rang in his ears…*Mimar! Mimar!* that followed the young man.

Mimar….the architect. He could understand everything – greetings, complaints, even a sly request for a leave of absence – muttered in a dozen tongues, knowing instantly that he had arrived at the Taj, not one of the world's wonders as it is called today but the wonder that it was even as it was being built more than three hundred years ago by a team of clever architects. Mr Ray felt certain that *he* was the Chota Mimar – the young architect arrived from Persia at the call of Hindustan's emperor. A shudder went through him as he closed his eyes and realized what he was thinking. Ever since these strange things had begun, starting always in his dreams and lingering on even when he was fully awake, he had had to pinch himself to see if indeed the recollections of his past life were as real as commonplace memory – the memory of his move to Delhi from Calcutta twenty years ago or that of his marriage to Beena. He was worried that he had contracted some kind of rare disease, perhaps of the brain, that was turning him mad. And he couldn't even begin to imagine what would happen if any of this were to become public knowledge. Who would believe him, the successful accountant with decades of uninterrupted service and a steadfast marriage now claiming to remember his past life – not just any life but as the Taj's architect –

trust what he saw and felt every night, the flashes that inexplicably reminded him of who he once was? Rubbish! He himself would've thought so, nothing but hocus-pocus. Yet, he couldn't bring himself to deny the thrill, the secret pleasure of dipping into his memory, that drew him to the edge of his bed every night as he woke to relive his dream.

It was the first urs of the queen's death, the day of union of her soul with the Eternal. Mr Ray smiled sadly, knowing what was to follow. He, the Chota Mimar, had heard rumours in Agra – the body had already been dug up from the makeshift grave in the Deccan where Mumtaz had died. Her corpse was on its way, accompanied by her lady-in-waiting and the second eldest prince. She'd be given a second burial at the western garden of the riverfront terrace that afternoon and a small dome would be raised over it quickly to shield her from the eyes of a thousand labourers building her final resting place, the Taj Mahal.

He could even remember the precise date – 1632, the first Wednesday of the month of Zil-Qa'da. All those assembled were sulking under the Agra sun – nobles who had arrived on their horses and elephants, pious men who had come armed with the Koran, scholars and traders along with the high and low of the empire gathered in tents fitted with fine carpets and awnings. The labourers had withdrawn to their quarters for the day – the masons and stone cutters, carvers, inlayers and their masters – but the team of architects was still present led by Ustad Ahmad Lahori. *The Great Pretender!* Mr Ray could hear himself snorting under his breath as he stood beside the Lahore architect who had managed to crawl his way into the Emperor's sight without even an ounce of talent, ushering in his cronies as well who couldn't tell a stable from a tomb, a rauza from a simple garden. Had it not been for the Emperor's father-in-law, himself a Persian, there wouldn't be a place for the Chota Mimar in Agra. Didn't the queen's mausoleum deserve the very best? Its plans drawn not simply from Hindustan but from Isphafan and Constantinople, Kabul and Samarkand – from the whole world? And where else but in Persia would one find the best of the best?

Everyone, including him, understood the Emperor's grief. Catching a glimpse of the widower Shah Jahan sitting crestfallen beside his father-in-law, he had mistaken him for a fakir – eyes sunk into deep hollows, hair turned grey, counting a string of rosary. He recalled bazaar gossip – the Emperor has stopped listening to music, given up wine, shed jewellery. Unlike his ancestors, the loss of a wife has meant more to him than an absence of hawa-i-nafs – the games one enjoys with a perfumed body – an absence no embrace could ever fill. He could hear sniggering voices around him…*if he goes on like this, poor Mumtaz will be forced to give up the joys of paradise and return to earth…!*

He thought he had sneaked away from the assembly to share a laugh with his Persian friend, the artist Mir Sultan, and a puff or two from the opium pipe carefully hidden underneath his ceremonial gown. No…it couldn't be so, Mr Ray corrected himself. His friend, the scoundrel, was still asleep, as he learnt later, hung over from the night before.

There was a commotion, he recalled, as Shah Jahan rose to distribute alms to a group of beggars assembled in the terrace. By the time the coffin arrived, many had fainted from the heat. Then the Emperor started to recite the Fatiha, the very first and the briefest verse of the Koran….*In the name of God, the Lord of Mercy, the Giver of Mercy!*

As he took a gulp of water from the glass beside his bed, Mr Ray sighed, wondering why he had recalled such a tragic scene in great detail. He felt sad, just as he had felt in his past life – the Chota Mimar's heart turned heavy at the sight of the poor husband cradling the coffin like his bride; the Emperor – the Shadow of God – reduced to a mere shadow of himself in grief.

Yet, in his early days in Agra, he the young Persian architect had felt nothing but contempt for the Mughals. Building a house on earth to resemble the queen's palace in paradise! He had taken Lahori's instructions with a grain of salt. Like the other garden tombs of the city it was to have a marble mausoleum flanked on either side by a mosque and a guest house, a Khorasani garden up to the great gateway along with a forecourt, quarters for the tomb attendants, a bazaar and a caravanserai. The youngest among the architects, he had broken into peals of laughter when shown the design of the mausoleum's dome.

'It looks like a guava!'

'Shh….' A fellow architect had covered his mouth, cautioned him against speaking his mind. The Emperor himself was the master architect, the real ones charged simply with drawing up his dictates on paper.

It was a hodgepodge, the Chota Mimar had concluded after careful scrutiny. The gate stolen from Constantinople, the garden from Kabul, the minarets from Arabia, even the dome was a vain imitation of Jerusalem's Rock. They were Mughals after all, he had thought – upstarts. One needed to visit the tomb of their great ancestor Timur in Samarkand for proof – that obscene blue dome sticking up into the sky as if to rival heaven itself! What else could they do but steal from others? In the early months, he had had to console himself – it was just a matter of time before the Taj would be built and he'd make his way back to Persia. Turning over on his bed and listening to Beena snore, Mr Ray wondered why his rich memory didn't offer a hint of his past life spent in his native land, why he remembered nothing about his Persian parents, his brothers and sisters. Not a trace remained of his journey to Hindustan, only the years he had spent in Agra, as if his life had started and ended there.

An Agra native, Mr Mehta, his boss, knew and cared little about the Taj. 'It cost half a million rupees to build and generated a yearly revenue of just twenty thousand from the mango trees!' – he quipped flippantly after Mr Ray had delicately brought up the matter. The office peon was better equipped, entrusted with the duty of delivering sensitive documents once a year to their sole client in Agra, always ready with bus and train timetables at his fingertips for the 193-kilometre journey. Mr Ray wasn't starved for facts, simply desirous to dwell on the subject every now and then in the same way as one dwells upon one's hometown or a place visited long ago. The very mention of a familiar name might, he hoped, help him keep silent about his past life, give him strength to resist the urge to reveal everything and make a fool of himself. Keeping his head down over annual reports and balance sheets, he could imagine the shock and the daily dose of sniggering that'd inevitably follow should he succumb to a moment of weakness.

He had started to leave the office early, secretly by the back, an excuse ready on his lips. If asked he'd say he was on his way to meet a client or to hand over a report to the Auditor General's office. If his boss were to catch him, he'd lie about Beena, confer some terrible disease upon her. He was leaving to take his wife for a consultation, he'd tell Mr Mehta.

Following his instinct he went first to the local library and then to the National Archives. It didn't take him long to lose his shyness asking the librarian for books he'd never had any reason to consult before. The more he read about the Mughals – their gardens, tombs, fortresses and palaces – the more he sensed the architect within himself. He'd grasp unknown facts with ease; nod in agreement with passages no accountant could possibly fathom, or argue with an invisible author who he knew for a fact to have committed a careless error. Nothing, of course, excited him more than examining the plans of the Taj – its architectural drawings preserved under layers of dust in the Archives.

Ah! The Hast Bihist! Sitting all by himself in the dark reading hall, Mr Ray could hardly contain himself. Hast Bihist – the eight chambered paradise that was to serve as a model for the queen's mausoleum. He traced the lines of the perfect square on the crumbling page lovingly with his fingertip. Four simple lines divided the square into nine parts, suggesting a domed chamber at the centre, forehalls in the middle of the four sides and Baghdadi towers at each corner. From experience he knew it to be typically Persian with Byzantine ancestry. Lit by the setting sun, the plan glowed in his hands. Mr Ray felt he was gazing not at a piece of paper but at the completed mausoleum set amidst the gardens of Agra. Even so, his face hardened as he recalled the fate of the plan drawn up by the Taj's architects. What was the use of presenting the Emperor with the Hast Bihist when his pen would flow freely over it, cutting open a terrace here, inserting an arch there, replacing towers with domes, just to please a pair of mortal eyes? *Allah!* He bowed his head over the desk.

'Tea…?'

Mr Ray jerked his head up, the spell about to be broken by the voice of the Archive's assistant. He was a young man, ordinary looking, a smile to cover his disappointment at holding such a lowly job, unlike most of his friends. Must've fared poorly in his exams to deserve this, Mr Ray thought, wiping his glasses as he returned to his office-beaten self. The two of them had struck up a rapport – the shy assistant taking the middle-aged visitor to be a scholar working on his next book, or a hobbyist with time to kill. On arrival, Mr Ray would find the oversized folios waiting for him neatly arranged on a desk by the window. The assistant would bring over a moist sponge to wet his fingers should the pages prove to be too dry to turn, a pair of gloves if too brittle; he'd supply a magnifying glass and offer tea when the closing hour approached.

He was tempted to tell his secret to the young man. Grinding his teeth at Lahori, the wimp, he thought of narrating the incident when Shah Jahan had all but fed him to the lions. Snatching the pen from the head architect's hand, the Emperor had smeared ink all over the plan while showering him with the choicest of abuses. The design of the mosque, grim and overbearing, had sparked his anger, as it risked distracting the viewer from the centrepiece – the queen's tomb in the mausoleum.

The Turks and Afghans among them had frowned – at this rate the plan would forever remain incomplete, although none were brave enough to raise their voice in public. Lahori himself, Mr Ray remembered with glee, had nodded violently in agreement to save his head. The Persians in the audience had winked at each other – the Emperor after all was no more than an ordinary lover!

The assistant had looked at him in wonder, seeing his eyes fill with tears – tears of joy as he turned the pages of Shah Jahan's imperial chronicle, and arrived at a painting of the durbar that showed the Emperor signing an important decree. Only he, Bimal Ray, among the living, knew it to be none other than the plan finally completed. Standing behind a pillar on that day in court, he had seen Shah Jahan gaze lovingly at the roll of paper as if it was the face of Mumtaz he was holding in his palms. A cry had gone up as he raised it to his lips to kiss the seal of approval.

Mrs Beena Roy treated the books her husband had started to bring home and his reading outbursts with suspicion. Privately, she had expected it to be much worse, his midlife crisis, believing what she heard from her friends at the income tax office – men of fifty taking up with young maid servants; hiding whisky bottles under the bed, or developing a prostate problem. No stranger to his reading habits, she had expressed only a mild suspicion in the beginning, giving him the benefit of the doubt. Perhaps the government had asked Mr Mehta's firm to check the accounts of the Taj as part of its anti-corruption drive. She had reacted woodenly when quite out of the blue her husband had suggested visiting the Taj Mahal on their 23rd anniversary.

'Are you suggesting a second honeymoon?' She had replied, using a measuring ruler to beat down a cotton-filled blanket that bloated up every now and then on account of humidity.

'Second…?'

'Don't you remember the first one?'

He did remember his first visit to the Taj, *their* first visit, a good month after their marriage. Mostly, he remembered the journey – no less tortuous than in the Mughal times – plagued by missed buses, un-ladylike ladies toilets and an overbearing urge to return to their Delhi flat as soon as possible.

'You can take Keya and her mother if you want to go again.'

Looking up from Sir Thomas Rowe's account of the Mughal court, Mr Ray gave Beena a searching look.

It had been years since he'd met Beena's niece, Sutapa, and her daughter Keya, then eight years old. He remembered the mother as pleasing and outspoken, almost as playful as her daughter. Separated from her husband and on the verge of divorce, she was planning a trip north from Calcutta to get away from it all. There were grounds for worrying, he felt, having to save his secret from another adult who'd share the same roof. What if she asked him awkward questions?

'History is my favourite,' Sutapa had declared, going through Mr Ray's books borrowed from the library. Just as he had feared, she had asked one awkward question after another soon after she arrived at their home and tested his knowledge to the full. Keya had played her part too, replacing the evening's reading and folding with a lively Q&A.

'Why didn't they build the Black Taj?'

'Black?'

'Yes. Didn't Shah Jahan wish to be buried in a black tomb?'

'No, no…' Mr Ray shook his head.

'How do you know?' the girl persisted while her mother frowned, and Beena waited for him to answer sitting before a pile of unfolded linen.

There was never a plan to build a Black Taj or anything like that, he knew for a fact. The Emperor was then mulling over a new capital in Delhi. Why would he have wished to be buried anywhere else? Mr Ray exercised extreme caution, pulling back from his reminiscences to offer a piece of archaeological evidence – the rumoured spot of the black tomb had been dug up many a time, but no trace of any building was ever found.

Then again, he had to refute the story of Shah Jahan blinding his architects after the Taj had been completed so that they could never build anything so magnificent. He controlled his laugh....*he should've blinded that impostor...would've stopped him from using his rotten eyes and swollen head ever again!*

'We must go on a full moon,' Sutapa had taken charge of the planning, mildly surprised at her aunt's refusal to come along but thrilled at the prospect of having an expert all to themselves as guide.

'We never saw the Taj at full moon.' Breaking her silence, Beena had reproved her husband. 'At least one of us will have the chance to now.'

It was pointless, he knew, to quell the 'full moon' fever. Who'd have seen the Taj at night in those days? Besides the guards, no one was allowed to even cross the forecourt let alone climb up to the mausoleum. The row of chinar trees too would've prevented Peeping Toms outside the walls from having a peek. Yes, Shah Jahan could've entered the complex if he'd wished to. But then, it was common knowledge that the Emperor went to bed promptly at ten.

'It's nothing much...just a trap for tourists...' he had tried to assuage Beena's disappointment.

'How would *you* know?' His wife had refused to be soothed, adding her own expertise drawn from her friends... 'In any case it's better to go now before acid rain drowns your Taj in a year or two...'

Mr Ray had turned up the TV to bring the evening's Q&A to a close.

On the day they left for Agra, the day after the twenty third anniversary, Mr Ray felt buoyant on account of what had happened the day before at the Archives. He had gone prepared, armed with Keya's school geometry box full of pens, compasses and callipers. The reading hall was busier than usual and he didn't have the assistant's undivided attention. But that hadn't stopped him donning the frayed pair of gloves and turning the folios' pages.

For days now he had felt it necessary to correct the mistakes in the plans. He blamed the archaeologists – British and Indian – for the inaccuracies, mixing up the Mughal gaz, for example, with their modern feet and inches, metres and decimals. There were glaring errors in the dimensions of the grid on which the Taj sat. Pen in hand, he had started to cross out the offending parts and insert the facts as he knew them to be true, unmindful of the hovering assistant and other visitors. He felt like the Emperor, correcting the draft plans presented to him by the head architect, and adding the finishing touches. How was anyone to know what was what in the seventeenth century, and he was proud to supply an eyewitness account. It took him much longer to finish than he had imagined, and by the time all the folios had been corrected the assistant had left for the day without the usual invitation to tea. As an afterthought, he had gone back over the plans and inserted the names of the architects too at the bottom, just as artists would in miniature paintings, starting with that of the rascal and ending with his very own Persian name.

Their plans changed within moments of arriving in Agra. Mr Ray had taken charge as they jostled through the bazaar's congested lanes within sight of the Taj complex, surprising Sutapa with his intimate knowledge of the city. He knew the quickest way to the perfume market; which turn to avoid as it would invariably lead to a blind alley; and how best to slip past the pesky vendors by escaping to the banks of the Yamuna.

'Aren't we going to the Taj?' Keya pouted, about to break into tears. Once they had pulled into midstream, the Taj appeared in full view, sitting still on the flowing river, and turned them speechless. This was the garden city he had glimpsed, arriving by boat three hundred years ago! Not just travellers, but the natives themselves went by the river to visit the tombs – the Ram Bagh or the Chini-ka-rauza. He smiled to himself – even after all these years he hadn't forgotten the best way to view the Taj.

'Wish I was there then...' Mr Ray caught Sutapa mumbling wistfully to herself. On his part, he wished to be a crane nesting on the dry riverbed, or a water buffalo left to roam on the banks by its owner, feasting his eyes on the Taj all day. Even he, the fastidious Persian, was astounded, he remembered, seeing the completed mausoleum, fooled by the guile of the upstart Emperor. Where Akbar, the Emperor's grandfather had used white marble to highlight the red sandstone, he, Shah Jahan, had reversed the colours. In place of the typical geometrical patterns one found on Persian and Arabian tombs, he had used flowers – honeysuckle, lilies, tulips and roses – and made the audacious move of inlaying marble with gems, like the Florentine pietra dura. *Who would've thought a wild red flower had such power to capture a suffering heart!*

They were taken for a family of three – a middle-aged man with a somewhat younger wife and a late issue. Inside the tomb chamber, he taught Keya the echo trick – a word uttered at the right pitch would hold its sound for half a minute. Trying to draw Sutapa's attention to the marble screen around the cenotaph and the ninety nine names of Allah inscribed on it, he caught her rooted to the floor before Mumtaz's tomb, eyes shut, as if she was praying to the dead queen lying with her head pointing north and face turned west towards Mecca.

'Is it true a dewdrop falls on her tomb every night?' She asked him, opening her eyes. Mr Ray didn't know the answer to that question.

'How do you know so much about the Taj?' Sutapa asked him as they sat on a garden bench with Keya playing around them. He smiled weakly.

'You must have a very good memory to remember all these things from your school days.' She gave him a conspiratorial look, 'I remember some too as history was my favourite.' She sighed, almost inaudibly. 'Sometimes I feel I was here during the olden times, working perhaps as a tomb attendant at the Taj….couldn't have been much better than that, could I…?' Then she broke into her childlike laugh, 'I thought you were an accountant, but…' Her thought remained incomplete as Keya arrived to drag her mother off.

He woke that night with memories of another Agra. He, the Chota Mimar, would escape from their official residence full of quarrelling artists and architects, and reach the bazaar's back lanes at dusk to clear his head and let blood flow to where it mattered most. He'd prowl the dirt roads and the thriving brothels searching for the special face that had caught his eye in the very first year of his stay in Agra. Even now Mr Ray could feel his temples throb as he re-enacted the moment in his mind. It was Rajab, the holy month. He saw himself standing on tall scaffolding, holding up the mausoleum's plan and shouting instructions to the labourers when a sudden breeze arrived to blow it away from his hand. Looking down he could see it floating like a butterfly. He had caught her eye then – the Hindustani, wearing the typical blouse, skirt and veil, carrying a basket of sand on her head – looking up at the butterfly.

On nights like this he'd search for her in the labourers' camps along the Yamuna and at the bazaar. If she was a Rajput, she'd be married to her stonecutter husband; if the wife of a captured soldier from the Deccan, she'd be sick with Agra's fever; if a slave girl, she could be starving. His eyes would glow as he peered into cages of women brought from the length and breadth of Hindustan for Agra's pleasure.

Sitting alone in his room at the lodge, Mr Ray heard strains of music. Was it the rebab they were playing, or the rudra veena? He could hear sounds of celebration coming from the lanes below. It was too late to knock on the adjoining door; he rose and dressed quickly, leaving his room on an impulse.

Smoke from the burning pits got into his eyes and he stumbled along till he found the musicians. A wedding party had spilled over and taken up the whole bazaar. Men danced with groups of singing eunuchs, clouds of coloured dust hanging over them. Firecrackers set off squeals and shrieks, a few made-up faces peeped through the windows and blew kisses at the passers by. He was taken for a reveller, dragged aside and made to share sweets and drinks with the rest. Someone pushed him into the circle of dancers and before long he became one of them – face streaking with colours and sweat.

He had crept back to the lodge long after midnight and turned on the bathroom tap to run on a trickle in order to avoid waking his neighbours. Washing away the colours from his face, he was relieved that Beena hadn't come with them. It would've been worse, much worse... Tucking the blanket around himself, he had sighed...*Beena would never have come out with him just like that....*

Mr Mehta had called on urgent business, his wife informed him, the moment he returned to their flat after seeing Keya and her mother off at the station. From her face he knew she was worried about the 'business,' but unwilling to speculate. Before he could show her the knick-knacks he had bought in Agra, the phone rang again having him rush off to his office without even a proper shave. His heart had leapt to his throat at the thought that somehow the business about his past life had reached his boss's ears. Might Beena have guessed...? Leaving Mr Mehta's office he felt dazed. A grievous error had been made, he was told, on a report prepared by him. An error that'd shame even a novice. If discovered, as it was certain to be, the client could sue them for a hefty sum. In his typically nosy way, Mr Mehta had enquired if he was keeping well lately and if all was fine between him and his wife. He had stopped short of accusing Mr Ray of wilful mischief. Given his twenty years in the job, he wasn't fired immediately, but shown the courtesy of a forced leave and asked to stay at home till the matter was sorted out and a decision taken whether to keep him in employment or not.

Everyone at the office seemed to know except the peon who greeted him warmly as he stopped to collect his personal belongings, and passed on the 'good news' heard last night on the radio – the new train that'd halve the time between Delhi and Agra was soon to have its first run. He left by the back, needing no excuse any more but out of habit and set off for the Archives, head swirling with the events of the past few days up to the last hour. A part of him wished to go straight to Beena's office to inform her that the urgent business had ended. But then he hesitated, wondering if it wouldn't be better to tell her in the evening when she had more time to think things over between her folding.

He found the reading hall closed for repairs. 'For how long?' he asked the sleepy doorman, but failed to receive a proper answer. 'Repairing what?' – he persisted with his enquiries without making much headway. How could they shut down such an important place without advance notice, he fretted, then asked to meet with the young assistant. The doorman pointed to the closed shutters and waved him away.

Back home he collapsed on the bed, exhausted from travel and the day's troubles. Almost instantly, he retreated to Agra – to a nightmare: a labourer had entered his room to steal and he saw guards lead him by the neck towards him, sitting at the caravanserai with his friends after the day's work. The thief had broken the trunk's lock where he kept his precious mementos – a clutch of jewels bartered from nomads, a saddle presented to him by the grateful owner of the caravanserai, his portraits drawn by his artist friend, and a fine veil of pearls that he had been saving for his bride-to-be. Blood streamed down the man's face as the guards kept beating him then made him kneel on the ground before him. The artist Mir Sultan had drawn his attention to the veil, tied like a pair of handcuffs around his wrists. *Kill him, Chota Mimar!* Onlookers had egged him on and he had drawn his sword, about to chop off the thief's hands, when he saw her – his temptress, the face he had glimpsed from the scaffolding – held back by the guards as she reached for her kneeling man. A thief's wife! She had broken through the cordon of arms and flung herself on the ground, the two writhing together, embracing, kicked and bludgeoned by others. He had thrown away the sword and dashed madly at the couple, screaming to their tormentors to let them off, before his friend had caught him and wrestled him away from the ugly scene.

He woke with a start, a cry throttling his throat and soaked in sweat as Beena held him firmly and patted his chest.

'I thought you were having a heart attack,' she said that evening as she finished darning the tablecloth before folding it away. 'Maybe you were agitated after what happened…' He nodded. He *was* agitated by what Mr Mehta had told him. His pride as an accountant had been wounded. What was the use of twenty error-free years, if a single one could lead to such a disaster? But the closed Archives had agitated him more. He had felt thwarted from checking the plans once again. While at the Taj he had had an inkling of further mistakes that he wished to correct on the crumbling pages. He had hoped to see the assistant's smiling face welcoming him to the reading hall.

He missed holding the folios in his hands, breathing in the pages – the dust, the insecticide – that reminded him of the Chota Mimar, scurrying past the labourers in the half-built mausoleum with a rolled up plan under his arm. At home, he avoided re-reading the books, worried about an onslaught of unpleasant memories. Would the thief reappear in his nightmares – hung from the gallows as his poor wife watched in horror? Would he see himself sword-fighting the guards to win his release? Or thrown out of Agra by Lahori for sheltering a whore? As days went by he tried in vain to block out his past life, shut the southern window to keep out the howling – his own – down the alleys as he banged on doors in search of the thief's wife.

Beena suspected a link between her husband's unexpected error and his architectural readings, but it was too great a mystery for her to solve. As a whole month of enforced leave went by, she tried to distract him by cutting short her evening's folding and reading out her own manuals brought home from the income tax office. As an accountant he might be interested to read what mockery was made of accounting, she thought. Perhaps it was time for him even to start thinking about early retirement, at least a change that'd take them out of Delhi. She had flickering doubts about her young niece after a postcard arrived from Calcutta bearing a photo of the Taj at full moon with 'Next time!' scrawled across it. She had hidden it from him, following her friends' advice not to fan the flames of his mid-life crisis.

She had thought nothing though when the doorbell rung one Saturday morning, and she had to explain to their visitors once again about Ray and Roy. The three men were from the Archives, and she had left them to her husband while she went to make tea.

Mr Ray recognized the young man and flushed. Improbable as it seemed, for a moment he thought they had come to inform him of the reopening of the reading hall, reasoning to himself that it'd be easy to find his address in the visitors' book that he filled meticulously during each visit. He felt light, almost light-headed after a whole brooding month.

'We have reason to believe you have tampered with our records, Mr Ray,' the oldest of the three, the Archive's director said, drawing out a file. He continued grimly. 'You've falsified the official records of a national treasure...no,' he corrected himself, 'of a world treasure...the Taj Mahal.'

'Falsified...?' Mr Ray could only repeat the incriminating word. The young man kept his head lowered; the third, balding member of the group held a steady gaze at his confused face.

'Beyond doubt it is a punishable crime...'

'What authority do you have changing the Taj's plans, Mr Ray?' the balding man, the expert, started his interrogation. 'By what *historical* authority, I mean. Can you prove that these are wrong?' He gave a sarcastic laugh. 'Prove that the Maharajah of Jaipur who was the first to draw up the Taj's plans was a fool? Was Lord Curzon, who saved those plans, a fool too?' With a quick glance at the director, he went on, 'The Archaeological Society of India is no fool either. You've written down the names of architects even, when no one really knows who they were. Might've been a Turk, or a European even...' He ignored Mr Ray's frown. 'How can you claim to know more than anyone about these architects?'

The director changed his tone as if scolding a schoolboy. 'Even children are taught not to scribble in textbooks. At first we thought it was a security issue, that the Taj might be at risk. Someone perhaps was studying the plans to plant a bomb inside.' Mr Ray could see

Beena standing behind the curtains with the tea tray waiting for a suitable moment to make her entrance. The director shook his head, 'In the end we thought it was nothing but an act of…'

'Madness.' The expert supplied the missing word.

The file was pushed in front of him, opened at a letter written by Mr Bimal Ray to the Archive's director giving him his undertaking never again to set foot inside the reading hall or face the consequences, and he was asked to add his signature.

Beena received Mr Mehta's call just as the visitors had left. Cupping the phone with her palm, she had passed it to her husband. From his boss's voice he couldn't tell at first if he was calling on routine business or to convey news. In his usual manner he had gone on about this and that then brought up the report. It was all right, he chuckled, the client had glossed over the error and ended up praising it to high heavens! It was one of those things – a sheer stroke of luck. 'Come back from your holiday!' He could feel Mr Mehta slapping his back as he rung off.

He sat by the southern window after the sun had set. It was the best hour to view the Taj – the saddest. He heard nothing, just the silence of the completed mausoleum free of labourers and architects. Not a leaf stirred in the garden, the river still like a mirror. The bazaar and the caravanserai were empty, not even a beggar stooped for alms before the mosque's closed door. The Emperor had left with his soldiers on a campaign far from Agra.

He saw the Chota Mimar crossing the mountains on a mule as he returned home to Persia, stopping every now and then to cast a look back at the queen's tomb – glowing in the dark like the heart of an angel.

Tiger! Tiger!

When you see a tiger swimming in the river, chances are it's a female, a tigress. Nine times out of ten. A pregnant tigress in search of protein for its foetus – human protein. And it has a nose for its prey, prowling in the spiky mudflats to spot the right village with thinly scattered huts along the riverbank. A village where children equal goats in number, making it hard to spot a missing boy or girl gone swimming in the creeks. Stalking in silence, sometimes for hours, it expects a quick kill – overpowering the victim and severing its spine or simply smothering it to death. Rarely would there be an exception – a short chase through the mangroves, running the risk of being spotted by alarmist monkeys on treetops. Even then, the game would only be half over. The tigress knows it must obey the river's whim – start and finish the hunt before ebb turns to tide, lest the crossing be strenuous with a baby in the belly and a corpse in the mouth.

When Rowena Hawthorne had her first glimpse of the Royal Bengal tiger, it was neither dead nor fully alive. A roar had brought her out of the lodge that she had rented for her research visit to the Sunderbans, poised ideally on the banks of Matla – the 'Mad River' – and looking out towards the forest. Not a tiger's roar, but the crowd's – she found the whole village gathered at Canning's jetty and gawking at a passing cutter. Cries went up at the sight of the tigress, tranquilized and lying like a docile cat at the feet of the forest officer, Captain Singh.

It was the time of the autumn floods. The half-eaten body of the blind beggar who played his harmonica at the bazaar had just been found, rotting on the banks. 'Serves her right for killing a blind man!' The villagers bayed for blood, demanding the culprit be thrown overboard. 'Let her drown…' 'Feed her to the crocs!' The forest officer was called upon to play the shikari – shoot the beast right there and then.

She saw her friend Anwar in the crowd – the master poacher – the subject of her research. He was the big fish, a chicken farmer by day and a killer by night. Rowena had known of his reputation ever since she'd arrived from England, even before she had become his friend. His knife was sharper than a chicken's beak – sharp enough for deer and fox, even tigers. She wasn't afraid to go and meet him alone in his hideaway, the little boathouse among the mangroves. Most days she'd find him taking an afternoon nap. He told her about men who'd kill a tiger for less than $20; clean out its hide and claws, bones and whiskers, only to pass on a greater profit to the middlemen – killing with poison and traps, bullets, or laying out live wires in the forest and waiting for a thousand volts to strike a bolt of lightening into their prey. It paid to poach, she was assured, paid more than selling women or turning into tigers to feast on the weak. When it came to the *real* poachers, Anwar kept mum. Despite her probing, he had refused to rat on the businessmen who ran the empire of animal parts.

As she stood on the jetty, she thought she spotted a tinge of regret in the master poacher's eyes. A whole tiger, powerless to escape or attack, carried away lovingly to the forest, when he could've had it dead in his shed and harvested properly for an all too willing buyer.

'Do you know how much it costs to keep a tiger alive?' Rowena asked Anwar as they broke free of the crowd. He eyed the rolls of sari draped formlessly around her and smiled, 'Much more than it takes to kill it!'

The forest officer wasn't his headache, Anwar had confided, but the breed of younger men who didn't care for anyone, not even the police. He'd appear old and soft compared to the new poachers and their ways. Why bother with traps or poison – stalking a tiger for hours and returning empty-handed, when you could set the forest ablaze and shoot the animals like sitting ducks as they fled to the riverbank? Why worry about giving the forest patrol the slip when you could blast them away with guns smuggled across the border? It didn't take much to get them involved in risky business such as killing a tigress and capturing her litter to be smuggled to Nepal where they'd be sacrificed to the gods. Surrounded by the mangroves and sipping freshly cut coconut, Anwar had lamented his failure to talk sense into his own men, preventing them from giving in totally to the greed of the traders.

Cycling back to her lodge, Rowena watched the jetties spilling over with giggling youngsters boarding ferries to return home; fishermen clambering out of boats like brown-legged spiders; slipping and sliding tourists anxious to reach the crocodile farm before feeding time. As she trundled along the muddy lanes of the bazaar, she could pass for a local – of a fair variety – in her sari. It was no mystery to her who the poachers were – the smiling fishermen, paddy farmers, honey collectors, witch doctors and cockfighters – the fathers and brothers of snotty sloe-eyed kids all too willing to pose for her camera as she made her way through the villages.

That made the two of them – the foreign girl and the old fox. The villagers didn't make much of the two spending their afternoons in the mangroves. Not like the other two who kept their tongues wagging all afternoon.

From her eatery Amina had spotted the cutter, caught a glimpse of the Captain brandishing his gun like a shikari. Her husband Anwar had told her all about the new forest officer after the 'accident' that had brought them face to face. In the rush of noontime customers – visitors and fellow shopkeepers who were her regulars – she had missed the newcomer, serving him fish and rice when she noticed him finally. 'Eeeek....!' The shriek had made her drop a full pot of boiling water and nearly caused another accident. Shoving past the throngs that surrounded the tall man, she had seen him rise from his seat and roll his eyes in agony.

'It's a bone stuck in his throat!' She regretted even now just as she had regretted then, serving him fish-heads full of sharp bait-like bones rather than the soft flesh of the stomach. How it must've stung him – the tangy sauce drawn saliva to the tongue just as the intruder slipped stealthily past the molars and lodged under the gullet. He was pointing at his trembling lips and gasping for air like a strangled duck.

She had parted his jaws just as fishermen part a dead crocodile's to scoop out the fish inside, sticking in her thumb and index finger to wrench the blood-tipped bone free. His heart was beating fast like a scared animal surrendered to its captor.

He was in her power for a few moments. Then he had turned his face away and spit blood, fish and saliva onto his plate before he had marched out with giant strides. He was from Bihar, she learned when the whispers resumed, the new forest officer. *A Bihari eating fish! He probably doesn't know what a fish looks like!* Whispers had turned to laughter and she had had to wind her way past her regulars to clean up his mess.

The accident was the beginning and when later he'd stop by at noon, she'd avoid the fish-heads swimming in golden curry, bringing him his own plate of safe Bihari food she had hidden in the back of her kitchen. She remembered too the grateful look on his face as she served him dry home-made bread and lentils.

There'd be gossip, she knew, about the forest officer frequenting her stall and the special meals she cooked for him. People would've noticed how he looked at her when she served his lunch, how his eyes followed her as she fanned her stove, stirred the pot of fish-heads; how he lingered on long after he had finished eating, lit up cigarette after cigarette to while away his time till all her regulars had left and she was alone in the eatery with him. They must've heard his humming and whistling as he strutted and preened like a cockatoo in heat. On days when he didn't come, she'd wait to eat her lunch way past the normal hour, wouldn't be sure and steady as usual – dishing fish curry on a customer by mistake or dropping a jar of pickle on the floor. She'd be late cleaning up and closing down, and sip a glass of rice wine behind her shop as she gazed out at the river hoping to catch the streaking beams of a speedboat.

Poor boy…. She felt sorry for the forest officer, so far from home and among those who didn't even speak his tongue. He was her husband's enemy. 'You should've left the bone where it was!' – Anwar had laughed when he heard about the accident. 'Should've shoved it down and blocked his windpipe!' What chance did the Bihari have against him? 'He's young,' Anwar had muttered under his breath. He had made a bleating noise with his tongue – to tempt a young deer into entering a rifle's range. She had felt a shiver go up her spine. *His muscles were useless in the Sunderbans*… It took far less to kill a man here – a knock on the head at night, a witch doctor's spell, even a gentle nudge to land him in the crocodile pits at feeding time.

Days after she had seen him with the tigress, Rowena spotted Captain Singh, the forest officer, from her ferry while returning to Canning after a trip. He was riding his speedboat on Matla, cruising the shores like a playboy, sunglassed and sporting a flaming red lifejacket. *What business did he have in the forest*...she'd fume whenever their paths crossed. She saw him often at the bazaar, a pair of roosters slung over his shoulder, looking much like a shikari himself, on his way no doubt to a feast with his fellow officers. She wondered if he knew anything at all about poachers – what went on inside their heads, about their wives and snotty children, and the invisible masterminds who played them like a set of cards.

'They are foreigners.' Captain Nawal Kishore Singh sounded dismissive when Rowena brought up the subject of poachers in their first meeting in his ugly barracks-like office.

'Foreigners?' She frowned, pen poised on paper.

'Yes, from Bangladesh. You don't know how porous these borders are, do you? One push of the oar and you've crossed over....phew!' He mimed heaving a boat, then brushed off her concern. 'We have a problem of illegal immigration here, not of poaching.'

'You mean to say everyone on this side of the border is clean?'

He ignored her question, and started to lecture. 'Of the 102 islands of the Sunderbans, 60 percent are in a foreign country. But tigers don't apply for visas! Neither do poachers who cross...'

'Why don't you catch the illegals then?'

'That's for the border patrol to do.'

'But I thought you.....'

'I am the forest officer,' Captain Singh had smiled like a playboy and showed off his hairy chest.

Was *he* a tiger? Stalking the women she met on her rounds – dusky and full, ripe like melons stacked high in the bazaar. Has he struck a deal with the poachers – exchanging their prey? Despite his muscles, he seemed soft compared to the men she met in the Sunderbans – men who made it their business to survive droughts and flash floods, tigers, corrupt officers, diseases and simply the rotten luck that comes with living on the edge. It had surprised her when Anwar's men brought news of the raid while they were chatting one afternoon in the boathouse.

She saw a flicker of doubt on her friend's face. 'Raid?' The messengers blabbered nervously. Captain Singh had arrived at Anwar's chicken farm with his men and was going around threatening to arrest everyone unless he was shown where the treasure was hidden.

Treasure in a chicken farm! She had taken it as an example of the Captain's foolishness. Leaving Anwar, she had pedalled as fast as she could to catch the action before it was too late.

The streets were empty. Word had spread of the raid, drawing everyone to the circus. Men who played cards all day in the temple grounds were gone; the husking mill was closed, and barking dogs ushered her to the farm fenced all around with barbed wire. Standing behind the wall of onlookers, she watched the mayhem – Captain Singh stomping around the coops, kicking the rubble and smashing the eggs as the chickens scattered under a cloud of feathers. Half a dozen or so farmhands stood before a shed, hands on their heads, encircled by the raiders. A bullhorn sounded every now and then, warning the villagers to mind their own businesses and stay out of trouble. Rowena watched in amusement as Captain Singh made a mad dash towards a flock of birds, as if he was giving chase to a band of poachers. Some of the larger birds tried to lift off in vain, struck the barbed wire fence and got stuck – their squeals and shrieks rising over the Captain's barked orders. The few that did manage to fling themselves over the fence, landed in fox-traps and were pinned to the ground by their wings. With the sun beating down, it looked like a battlefield.

What's he looking for…? Rowena couldn't help wondering as she stood among the ashen-faced villagers. A chest buried underneath the soil, hiding deer hides and tiger pelts? Snake baskets dressed up as haystacks? Eggs of rare Pacific turtles mixed up with those of the chickens? She heard Captain Singh let out a whistle as he kicked open the shed's door – the crowd straining to catch what was inside – then watched him come out holding up a giant wooden beam for all to see. Sundari! – the most precious tree of the Sunderbans, illegal to fell no matter how much the timber fetched in the black market. A shed full of poached wood! – Rowena saw Captain Singh smile the smile of triumph.

How did he know…? There were spies everywhere, just a few rupees enough to turn poacher into spy, spy into poacher. Rowena's heart skipped a beat as she saw Anwar enter the farm – bare chested and wearing a sarong, looking much the chicken farmer – and make his way over to the shed. He was strong enough to take on the forest officer. Just a call from him would be enough for the spectators to break free and charge towards the raiders. He could outnumber the

Bihari's men with his own men, and turn the tables if he wished. Instead, he came over to the shed and joined the farmhands without a fuss, looking no different from them. Her face half-turned from the scene, Rowena winced at the Captain's curses. He had his gun out and pointed it at Anwar, made him kneel on the ground with his hands on his head. She saw her friend hold still at the Captain's feet; like the sleeping tiger, he made no attempt to answer his charges. *Surely, he can't shoot a man just for felling trees!*

From behind the onlookers, Amina watched the shikari brandishing his gun at her husband. Sunbeams danced on his muscles, mouth frothing from all the cursing. She saw him lock his gaze on her when he left on his Jeep at the end of the raid, cranking up the siren. Not a sound reached her ears, just her own beating heart.

The raid had changed the bazaar talk in Canning. There were mixed views. Some called it foolish, brash and unnecessary. As long as there've been trees on this earth, haven't men felled them for food? It was a master stroke from the master poacher, those who claimed to be in the know winked at each other. Anwar himself had planted the rumour about the logging and led the sniffing hound to his chicken farm while the *real* treasure boarded the trawlers in full daylight and sailed lazily away. A few tonnes of wood in exchange for a rich bounty. Others grudgingly praised the Bihari's guts – never easy for an outsider to take on the locals. When was it last that they had seen a forest officer who couldn't be bribed with money or women? The officers were the poachers' best friends – wasn't it commonly said in the Sunderbans? Perhaps it *was* about money, the feud between Anwar and Captain Singh. Or was it about the woman....?

Voices fell silent inside Amina's eatery. She was known to be tough, wouldn't stand idle gossip inside her shop. Younger than her husband, she was the busier of the two – up at the crack of dawn to buy fish from the fishermen, she bustled about all day feeding half of Canning, then put it to sleep with the rice wine sold from the back of her shack after sundown. She didn't spare the drunks if they smashed up her stall, not even her husband, or if his men demanded a free drink before they went hunting in the forest. She was a partner in his crime, even though he was too old for her, too old to fill her womb.

She had hastened back from the chicken farm to her empty stall, waited for the circus goers to wake up to their appetites. The day had passed without much talk about the raid, and she had left after closing up to sit by the riverbank with a jar of rice wine hidden in her sari. As on other nights, she peered into the darkness to spot the forest patrol, circling the islands on their speedboat, waiting to nab the poachers as they paddled out of the creeks into the open river. Both sides had guns, each prepared to kill the other to stay alive. As storm clouds gathered on the horizon, she felt drunk. Her body exhaled her night-scent, and she threw the empty jar into the river. The absence of a flashing searchlight made her anxious; she didn't wish to return home yet and face her husband – the mighty Anwar reduced to a chicken farmer and a petty thief. She blamed the foreign girl, fluttering hither and thither like a butterfly, perching on her husband's shoulders to chat for hours and turn him into an old blabbering fool. She'd be happier if he were out there with his men, heaving the oars, returning to her at night smelling of deer blood. Her heart turned cold as she spotted a dark and silent form making its way over to the landing without searchlight or the fishermen's lantern.

The forest officer jumped ashore from a fishing boat and made his way up the muddy slope, slipping and sliding – bare chested, with his khaki trousers rolled up to his knees. *Why has he come....? Did he know she'd be waiting? Has he come to beg her forgiveness for insulting her husband? Or to claim for himself what was now duly his....?* She shuddered in the breeze, waiting for him to scramble up a bit closer, then spotted an ugly gash on his forearm, cut by the barbed wire of the chicken farm. He stopped and stared at her – a pair of eyes glowing in the dark. With the same instinct that had made her pluck out the bone from his throat, she reached forward and caught his arm, drawing him towards her. Then she started to lick his wound, covering it with her saliva, tasting the dry and crusted blood. She threw him down on the muddy banks and throttled him with her weight, the spiky roots of the mangroves sticking up like knives and opening up many more wounds to their flesh. As the storm broke, the tide rose to drown the mudflats, dragging the two into its currents. They turned into crabs, clinging to the shore and to each other to save themselves from drowning.

❦ ❦ ❦

From then on a gossiping village wouldn't stop her, nor the fear of being caught by Anwar. Shutting her eatery, she'd make her way past the emptying bazaar and leave the village behind to enter the brick kilns – the feared nest of cobras and vipers. The Bihari would be waiting for her. The afternoon sun played on them as they slithered on the rubble or pressed up against columns of baked mud scattering junglefowl and pecking parakeets. On other days she'd have her neighbour mind her stall while she ran by the drooping mangroves and splashed into a creek beside the moored speedboat. Her lover would pull her up, their heaving and rocking threaten to keel the boat over. There were nights when he came looking for her in her village. She'd see him outside the window and pretend to be asleep, then give in – slipping away from her husband's side to enter the granary, ready to silence a nosy neighbour with her sickle.

'What fish did you cook for him today?' Anwar would ask yawning, after he returned from the boathouse.

'Fish! I'd be damned for killing a poor man!' Her husband was too sleepy to notice the bites and scratches – she'd be relieved, thank her barren womb for saving her from disgrace.

The young poachers were winning the war. No longer happy to slink away from the forest with a jar or two of stolen honey, or playing hide-and-seek with an otter to sell it for peanuts and stay up all night in fear of a raid. The sight of Anwar kneeling before the forest officer had changed everything. From now on, they'd have to take matters into their own hands. Like the rest of the village Amina had heard of the daring events that had taken place just days after Captain Singh stormed the chicken farm. A shoal of Gangetic Dolphins had been trapped with mechanized trawler nets, and shipped off to an unknown destination. A gang had descended on the crocodile farm and slaughtered dozens of crocs to skin them for profit. And even Anwar had been awestruck by reports of the forest patrol's speedboat being hijacked and its searchlight trained on a horde of wild boars before they were shot. They'd be after the tigers next, everyone was certain, wouldn't mind taking on a troop of forest rangers if it came to that.

Sitting by the river, her punctured bicycle sprawled by her side, Rowena too worried about the big raid that was rumoured to be on its way. She heard a tinkling bell – Captain Singh looking almost plain without his red life jacket. He offered her a ride on the narrow seat behind him. She hesitated for a moment before accepting. The roads were rough, in places there weren't any roads at all, simply a track through the bushes. What if she lost her balance and fell…what if her driver rode recklessly and dumped her on purpose?

'Tell me what the scoundrel is up to.' He threw his words back at her over his shoulder.

'Who do you mean?'

'Your friend. You two seem to get along quite well.'

Was he spying on her…? Did he sense the storm that was about to break? The bazaar talk must've reached him by now; he'd have heard about the restless men planning to upset the balance of power in the forest. They wouldn't stop at anything, it was rumoured – even burn the Bihari's speedboat if necessary.

'I think you've got it wrong, horribly wrong.'

He slowed down to take in her words. 'You mean Anwar has fooled you too! I thought you foreigners were smarter than us.'

'He's no more than a pawn.'

She seemed to have upset him as he got off the bike and started to pace the banks, hands stuffed inside his pockets, spitting out his words at the river. 'Tell me who *isn't* a poacher here. You can't round up a whole village, can you?' He glared at her.

'Have you tried….'

'You don't mean the doctors, do you?' He interrupted her rudely. 'Those who'd have a tiger killed to cure a toothache?' Holding up an imaginary nozzle, he started playing the doctor. 'What do I see here? Ahhh! A swollen tonsil….well, eat a tiger's paw then! What do I see now? Gout in the knee. Eat a tiger's tongue! What do I….'

'Wait, don't you know…'

'What do I see now? A limp mushroom… Oh my god! Eat a tiger if you want a cucumber instead!' He crooked his index finger and held it over his crotch. 'See…?'

For the first time, she saw Captain Singh in a different light – almost nervous underneath his cocky exterior. Had he sensed the big push that was coming, was he afraid of losing to the poachers? Did he fear for his life?

'Why don't you ask Anwar to help us?' He whispered to her. 'No one will know and he can leave when the job's done…disappear wherever he wants to, take his chickens with him.'

She looked at him puzzled. Did he really believe that she, Rowena Hawthorne, the foreign researcher, could broker a deal between two deadly enemies?

'We need to break their backs now. Once and for all. With Anwar on our side, we could clean up the rascals.' He looked her in the eye, 'otherwise it'd be the end for tigers.'

She shook her head. It was naïve to think it'd be as easy as that. Kill a poacher and another will spring from his blood! It'd be foolish to show her hand to Anwar – he wouldn't take kindly to her talking with the Bihari.

'No?' His jaw hardened as he stopped pacing. 'What good are *you* then? Pretending to be a Bengali in your sari, going around and chatting up a few men? Why don't you visit the crocodile farm and go home like the rest of your…'

Later, lying under the mosquito net in her lodge, she brooded over the Captain's words. It was foolish of her to accept the playboy's invitation. He had hurt her more than she had imagined. Busy researching the poachers she had all but forgotten the poor animals. As much as she resented Captain Singh humiliating her friend in public, she knew Anwar was guilty. Guilty as any other man who had played a part in the extinction of the rhinoceros from these forests, that of the swamp deer and the wild buffalo, and soon perhaps of the tiger. There were only 274 left. The new army of poachers would see to that, she was sure. It was up to us, she thought, to stop them as quickly as humanly possible.

Arriving at Amina's eatery, Rowena found it shut. It was still early for an afternoon nap. She felt disappointed standing before the bamboo shutters, wondering what to do next. It'd be foolish to go looking for her in the village and risk running into Anwar himself. She'd have to return and catch Amina soon while there was still time, before calamity struck. On the verge of leaving, she heard whispers inside the stall like purring cats. A stifled moan blended with cooing doves, making her spring back in surprise. Was this where Anwar hid his jungle catch – in his wife's shop? She imagined traps full of rare birds, imagined baby otters and snake baskets, and kept watch from behind a tree. Moments later, Captain Singh emerged from the shack, blinked in the sun and left on his bike.

When Rowena entered the stall it was empty. She heard kitchen sounds from the back till Amina came out and gave a start at seeing her. She ordered tea, held out a few coins and settled down facing the cold stove. From the corner of her eye, Amina watched her. What did she want from her? What did she know about her and the Bihari? As Amina brought over the tea, Rowena caught her hand. Your secret is safe with me – she told Amina. As safe as between two sisters. But she needed to know the other secret, the bigger one.

Amina had wrenched her hand free and run back to the kitchen. What secret? Cleaning up in a frenzy, she didn't notice the foreign girl come up to her and whisper into her ear. What would she rather have – a dead husband or a dead lover, Rowena had asked her. The way things were, they could both be dead. She needed to know when Anwar would go hunting in the forest next. Not for deer or boar, honey or wood – but tigers. How did it matter to her if both died – Amina had snapped back. She had seen the hurt look in Rowena's eyes. It took them some time to settle down, before they could start to speak to each other. It was all about power and cunning – the forest officer's power and the guile of the old fox, they had agreed. Between them, they could fix the poacher army. What'd remain in the end? They had kept looking at each other without an answer.

As the monsoon arrived, they met infrequently, Rowena opting to stay indoors to avoid the bloodsucking leech. The number of passengers who travelled by the ferry fell as usual, causing the bazaar stalls to shut early and the entire harbour bore a deserted look in the afternoons. It was the time when fishermen turned farmers, and the fields were busier than the river – the time when the mangroves grew by a foot each month fed by the salty sea water. Every now and then there'd be rumours about poachers, but even they seemed to have left the flooded shores of Matla for drier grounds, making Rowena all the more sceptical when word came from Amina about a raid into the forest. On the night of a new moon? She didn't believe her. The narrow creeks would be dark and full during tide, making it hard to spot a tiger even if it swam right before one's eyes.

Her instinct was to go over to Anwar's boathouse. Instead, she pedalled off to the forest office and demanded to see the Captain. A sentry blocked her entrance and asked to see her papers. Giving him a piece of her mind didn't help – Captain Singh was absent from his desk. *Out for his midday sport….* Rowena fumed. *Might have to catch him at Amina's eatery and break up their session*…. For a fleeting second she regretted that she hadn't betrayed the playboy to the master poacher. Anwar would've cut his neck like his chickens. There'd be another forest officer then, one that could be trusted to act in a crisis. Turning back to leave, she heard Captain Singh's booming voice across the compound where he stood half-shaven with an open razor in his hand. 'Bring me Anwar.'

Anwar, Anwar…. Finding Amina's stall shut, she sat in front of it and started to compose a note to Captain Singh, an SOS to prompt him into action. She took care not to divulge her source but didn't mince words about the poachers' plan. It'd be a big night, Amina had told her, with dozens of men arriving in trawlers and tugboats to outnumber the forest patrol. They'd do what none had done before – cordon off a few of the forests' islands and land the men like an invading army. Fishermen had been alerted to stay away from the river if they wished to avoid being caught in the crossfire. Gallons of petrol had been stocked in secret warehouses, and firearms smuggled in. Businessmen had promised huge rewards for the night's haul, and rumours of tiger sightings had raised the tempo to a fever pitch.

She had visions of herself standing alone on the riverbank, facing down an armada of poachers. Then she realized her mistake. How silly of her to have relied on the forest officer. The job was too big for him – his speedboat no match for the trawlers, his small band of men certain to lose against the poacher army. She needed to warn higher ups. Dashing off towards the bus stop she knew she'd need all her luck to meet the District Magistrate and persuade him to come down and take charge of the forest.

The night had taken everyone by surprise. When village elders met later to go over the events, they'd scratch their heads unable to explain how matters could've come to such a pass. Few had any clue of the horrible things that were to happen, the grim reports that made headlines in the papers and brought shame unto them all. It was true that they had seen ominous signs in the weeks before, and most had thought it wise to retreat to their homes to weather the events from safe quarters. Canning had looked like a ghost town. With nightfall, they had sensed the activity on the river, heard the low drone of approaching trawlers, followed by chugging tugboats. The more adventurous among them had stepped out to watch the giant flares that had lit up the sky, brighter even than bolts of lightning. It was a night of echoes – gunshots ringing across the river; calls of alarmed animals; and a muffled bullhorn sounding like a mad dog barking in the lanes. Sleepless, they had imagined a burning forest, bonfires lit up on the banks and men cheering as one mighty tree after another was hacked down and fell rumbling around them. They imagined the animals fleeing – the monkeys, the cleverest of them all, splashing into the river and swimming for their lives, leaving behind the hapless deer, the mongoose and the jackal. The birds probably fared better, just their nests smashed under the fallen trees, and the reptiles as well, although the monitor lizard wasn't perhaps as lucky, forced to leave the burning mangroves and come out into the open only to be shot for its skin. The crocodiles of Matla must've had a field day like the poachers, as they swam close to the forest's edge and waited to drag away a struggling civet or otter, rewarded handsomely for their patience.

And tigers? The poachers, of course, had carried off their kill and it was impossible to know how many tigers had been killed. Only a new census could tell by how much their number had dropped.

When Rowena Hawthorne arrived on the spot riding the District Magistrate's cutter, there was calm. The river had receded after its assault on land, and she saw the ravaged forest – smoke rising from various parts and a blackened shoreline. Circling kites had scared the gulls away and she heard the trees rustle in the morning breeze. News of the night had reached her while she was away, having her return with a heavy heart. As she came upon the stretch of mudflats next to the forest she could see a man building a funeral pyre, chopping wood and laying it out by the bank. A woman sat with hands on her head. Anwar and Amina. It didn't take long for him to finish his job, the wooden cradle lying still like a marooned boat. Then he disappeared behind shrubs to bring out the corpse on his shoulders, dragging its long legs over the mud. Breathing heavily, he took longer to raise it over the pile of wood; then sat down to wipe his head and light up a strand of wild grass.

Captain! Rowena let out a gasp.

Winning the race with tugboats but outnumbered by the poachers, Captain Singh had led his men as far into the forest as possible, stayed out of the enemy's firing range and waited for the poachers to come through the clearing. He had chosen his targets carefully, got as close as possible before he took aim, stepped back from rolls of live wire and snapped them with his pickaxe. The animals were all around – swaying from the branches, leaping over forest fires or lying in blood-spattered heaps. His men had used bullhorns to warn the poachers, but the Captain had stopped them. Better killed than warned; better to settle it all here in the forest. There were early celebrations among their enemies as flares lit up the forest – blind bats flying through the canopy of light and smashing into tree trunks. He was losing the battle, he knew, and caught a flash of golden light just yards away from where he sat crouched. A flash of deep yellow with black markings. *Amina!* He thought he saw her in her yellow and black striped sari, hiding in the bushes just like him. *Amina in the forest…!* Dropping his gun, he whistled to her, calling her over. He saw her move quickly, vanishing behind a tree trunk, just as fleet of foot as he knew her to be. Maybe she had sensed the poachers closing in on them and was trying to lead him away to a safe spot. He followed her, followed the golden flash that showed through the tall grass. *She must've come to pass on a secret…* He took off his shirt and quickened his pace, ignoring the flares that kept bursting over his head, afraid of losing her. They could both be within the poachers' firing range, both killed by a single blast. Panic struck as he imagined her bloody corpse and called out to her, the cry echoing in the forest, then stepped into a clearing ready to break into a run to grab her and fold her into his arms.

The tigress had struck him then. Rolled him over on the ground with her yellow and black paws and smothered him with her weight, just like Amina. He had smelled her strong musk – the smell of love – her love bite snapping his spine in two.

From her cutter, Rowena watched Anwar come over to his wife and raise her to her feet. Then he looked hard into Amina's eyes, a look which only she could fathom, and passed on the burning stalk to have her light the funeral pyre – give the dead her last and the most intimate gift. She accepted without a word, then held the flame at the corpse's lips. Rowena watched the two of them circle the burning logs and perform the last rites of Captain Nawal Kishore Singh, as they would in his native Bihar.

Father Tito's Onion Rings

He stood with his violin on the church's balcony as the 'Lords of Kidderpore' considered the newest arrival – the padre at the port's Catholic Mission. Unlike the lot of Father Johns and Father Pauls – Kerala Christians from the deep south – he resembled a white whale beached overnight by the river. 'Name the sucker!' yelled one of the drowsy hellraisers, basking in the lazy morning full of flies drawn by the smell of human cattle and rotting rubbish by their tea shop. As they called out to their favourite dogs and threw them ends of sweet jalebis, the naming game started and kept going all morning over fits of hysteria.

'Madan...!' They rolled with laughter. Indeed, he looked like a Madan, a fool, marching into the whorehouse last night looking for young boys to sing in the church choir. Lata's mother, the owner, had eyed him coldly... 'We only have girls here.' 'Bhoot,' they toyed with the idea of a ghost after his pale skin; and 'Jumbo' given the hulk. It didn't take long to dispatch 'Sahib'; he wasn't the usual English, but from some strange country. 'Let's just call him Jisu' – someone squawked, naming him after the poor sod nailed to the cross. But his fleshy neck and bare skull reminded them of just the opposite – the executioner; or even wrestlers who came looking for work at the port and ended up as thugs, resembling their thin-limbed pot-bellied victims by the time the dogs felt safe licking their faces as they lay sprawled out in the gutters. Would he become like them? Sleepy in the morning, alert at night, always feverish, a customer at Lata's mother's? He smiled at them from the balcony, and they had occasion to judge his whitish brows, the pronounced cleft on his cheek – like a quick incision – false teeth, and red ears that seemed to have been stuck on to his face. The dogs looked up, stopped chewing on the jalebis.

'Where's he from?' There was a moment's silence.

'Jugoslavakia,' the youngest of them announced. They looked at each other, then burst out laughing. 'He looks like a Nepali.' 'No, you idiot....it'd take half a dozen Nepalis to come up to his prick!' 'Well, call him something...' the jalebiwalla grew impatient. Then the youngest piped up again, 'We'll call him Tito' – recalling a chubby man who looked like a film star, beaming down from a frayed poster, in the company of gun-toting soldiers. 'Yes, Tito!' They confirmed in a chorus; the dogs yelped for more.

In a firm voice, Father Tito read out his prayers. Then he kissed the string of rosary beads and rose from the altar. It was six and he felt hungry. Crossing the church's compound he saw his shadow on the pond – green like the algae. The port's siren sounded faint under the rustling cranes coming in to share the groves with a talkative owl, a team of brilliant parrots and a million fireflies – fill the void left by the departing bats. This was the moment which reminded him most of home. Hurrying along, he checked the padlock on the gate that was his only guarantee of a good night's sleep, and reaching his modest quarters called out for Lata – the rustic Bangla syllables flowing smoothly from his Slavic tongue. But the kitchen was quiet. He tiptoed past the room that held his priestly belongings and peered through the doorway, catching sight of an oil lamp beside a neatly arranged setting on the floor – plate, cup and a platter full of golden brown onion rings. Smiling, he rolled up the sleeves of his tunic, and sitting cross-legged delved into the puffy fries – still tangy as freshly cut onions.

Father Tito had left Yugoslavia the first time to escape the Nazis; the second time for the love of onion rings. Dipping the fries in the red chutney that was Lata's specialty, his mind returned to those frayed memories, to his first evening in a Bengal village where he had arrived as a fugitive in 1942 after the German occupation of Belgrade. He remembered being struck by the dusk, which reminded him of his very own Banja Luka abuzz with fireflies. Relishing the delicious onion rings with his new neighbours, he had looked back in horror to those he had left behind. Here in Bengal, he had gradually forgotten Hitler and the guns booming across the Danube. As the head of a small parish at the mouth of the bay, he felt he had returned to the peaceful land of the South Slavs, protected in the north by the Alps and at heart by the Holy See. His pale skin had blended with his parishioners from whom he had picked up his Bangla, and the waft of the troubadours on his violin. By the time the Wehrmacht had been dealt a death blow by the Allies and the Yugoslav partisans, he had gone fully native, convinced of the virtue of onion rings – the ecstasy they brought to the senses and to the soul.

As he polished off the chutney, he called again for Lata, then made his way to his room grumbling at her absence. Taking off his white cambric robe and slipping into a comfortable sarong, he looked every bit the troubadour and the executioner rolled into one. The rare cool of a December breeze seeped in through the cracked window, fluttering the grey Zagreb poster hanging precariously on the wall. Father Tito made no attempt to straighten it, and stared instead at the buildings leaning over like the Tower of Pisa, the horse-carriages riding upside down as if they'd been blown to bits by the Luftwaffe, and the distant chimneys belching smoke just like in Kidderpore. And he remembered his second departure from a free Yugoslavia – no less anxious than the first.

Returning to Europe after the war, he had witnessed the horror – droves of survivors trudging through morgues and cemeteries looking for their dead; scrounging the ruins for treasure; settling scores in mock trials. He was unable to look his friends from the seminary in the eye – those who had stayed back to see the war years through. Everywhere he saw deceit and a quick defacement of memory. In Zagreb, he ran into a fellow musician, Kidric, known to have been close to the Archbishop of Sarajevo. He had asked him if it was true – that the church had stood by the massacre, even applauded and goaded it on. 'It wasn't the hour for music…it was the time to live as wolves!' his friend had boastfully replied. Father Tito had felt a deep loss in the land of his birth, and a longing for his land of exile.

But returning to Bengal was more difficult than he had thought. On his way to Belgrade to plead his case before his superiors, he had slipped and broken a leg. Working through the dark corridors of the Church, it took him two more years to arrange a foreign mission. Why India? – he was asked repeatedly. Wouldn't he rather go to Kosovo – the tiny Christian enclave among Muslim Albanians? His war years came under scrutiny, and threatened to delay departure. Until he finally managed to slip through the divine crack as replacement for a Belgian who grew cold feet on his way to Calcutta. He left Yugoslavia just as Tito was breaking up with Stalin.

He woke up as Lata was about to pass his room, her head wrapped in a shawl, just as brazen as she was after Father Tito had finally managed to convince her mother that the church posed no greater threat to her character than the brothel. It was a tenacious argument. Treating the white man with suspicion, Lata's mother had gone for the jugular – 'What if she marries a fool and runs away? What if she gets a belly…?' She eyed his hulk accusingly, dismissing the padre's offer of a maid's job to her youngest. 'What if she becomes a nun…going about like a shaved chicken…always praying, never marrying, kissing lepers…?' He had smiled at her with his false teeth…. 'What if she becomes a whore like her other daughters? What if she's picked up by some policeman and locked away?'

'What if the Padre wants to marry me?' Lata had shrieked in amusement. In the end, he had his way with Lata, just as with the boys who kept their neighbours painfully awake on Sunday afternoons.

As he dozed in spurts and listened to Lata singing in the kitchen, he was at once suspicious and happy. In two decades, he had done what the Church least expected him to do – not just stay on in India but spread the gospel in ugly places, ending up in Kidderpore, the ugliest of them all, of his own free will. A successful man, he felt assured by what he had – a spot of peace at the edge of madness, a delicate balance that bore testimony to his continuing faith in fellow beings. Like a responsible parent, he suffered bouts of anxiety at Lata's periodic escapades, but more than keeping his word – raising her as an honest maid – she seemed to be related to that balance; the fate of Kidderpore's Catholic Mission resting on the daughter of a whore he had named Lasta – the swallow in his own Croat, one that twittered less than she crowed.

He had to settle for an orchestra instead of a choir. The boys scuttled his plan, descending with glee on the cello, horn, accordion, cymbals, drums and violin hidden under their prim covers behind the altar – a parting gift from the port's Anglo-Indian stevedore, who had left a few years back for Australia. Starting with unexpected gusto, the seven musicians and their conductor whipped up a frenzy of rehearsals delighting the water fowls wintering on the nearby pond, surprised everyone by their tenacity and revealed the most extraordinary talents that earned just a single rock through the stained glass window. After a morning's work at the tea shops or simply fooling around with the dogs, the boys dutifully assembled at the Mission in the afternoons, bare chested and barefoot in the beginning. Walking up the staircase to the balcony, they paused to inspect the row of marble saints, ran their grimy fingers over Latin verses etched on the busts, and stole a dahlia or two from the garden on their way out. Throughout winter they coughed and sneezed on their instruments, till Father Tito was forced to lay out a table of syrups and pills, going as far as to quarantine a hapless musician, forcing him to sit downstairs and nurse his cold while listening to others play. Within a short while, the neighbours grew accustomed to the seven musicians as they trooped to the Mission in blue uniform, sporting neatly combed hair and dry noses. Their parents, or whoever they lived with in the shanties, stopped noticing the oversized books bearing strange notations that they carried around under their arms. 'What do you play?' The tea shop owner asked the boys from time to time. 'I bet he's teaching you Christian songs...' He'd look suspiciously at the balcony and lower his voice, 'Did you see Lata with her Muslim lover inside the Mission today?'

He had started with the devotionals, then infused them with his mountain spirit. His pupils rose to the challenge, abandoned caution and pounced on the fantastic. Nothing seemed beyond their reach – the eight year old Ganesh bit his lip as he waited his turn on the cello; or Manik, just as at ease with the drums as he was scaling walls or diving to the bottom of the dirty river. They thought he was partial to the accordion, allowing Dulu, the eldest of them, to carry on unrestrained. In fact, he was most critical when it came to the violin – his favourite; but there wasn't much to complain about the violinist – his real protégé, the buck-toothed Abu. At times, he'd stop to correct Abu, his eyes lighting up as he realized his own mistake. It didn't take long for the boys to master the scores, till he stopped flapping his white limbs comically out of his white tunic, sat on the balcony and listened to them play.

The boys were his. He had bartered his life and the Mission to have them. As he visited them in the shanties – to tend to a sick child or to intercede in a family dispute – it brought him closer to the port's gang leaders and labourers, ferrying scrap and disappearing into ships' dark and sooty holds. Voices called out to him over the clatter of machines to share a cup of tea, squatting over rusty metal, encircled by drums full of rivets and bolts – like chopped liver – as he skirted the piers on his way in or out. He met the migrating birds – peasants and fishermen fleeing their dark groves – and surprised them, speaking in their own tongue. Strangely, the port reminded him of Zagreb in the aftermath of war – armed bands stalked their rivals; shadow lines of enmity sparked like streaming bolts from a welder's rod. As he returned to the Mission through the winding lanes, he'd come upon a burning hut or a gutted tea shop paying the price of foolishness or betrayal. He'd hear reports of each catastrophe from Lata, as she merrily boiled water for their morning tea. She lacked sympathy for the victims, but kept herself well informed. 'They caught a thief last night....kicked his balls till he spoke the truth.' *Smacked, burned, gorged, fucked*... Her voice rose and fell like water in the kettle. He avoided the gossip, tried to keep her occupied with the Mission. She scolded him for his indifference, 'Your violin won't die of dust... Wait! Let me finish telling you about the thief...'

'Why?'

'Because he was *both* a thief and a swindler who…'

'What use do I have for a swindler?'

'Padres are swindlers too...!'

He laughed, told her to remind the boys not to come for their rehearsal – it was Easter. In a guarded way, he asked her about Lateef. In a roundabout way, she told him to mind his own business. Was her mother badgering him, she asked, raising a broken eyebrow – and did he believe what she told him?

'Yes.'

She made a face and told him to return to *Juggia*, or wherever he had come from. Suddenly tender, she asked him what was the difference between a Hindu and a Muslim – or a Christian even?

'He's just like you...' She sighed, finishing her tea.

Tuning his violin, Father Tito rose to leave. 'Yes I know, you've been feeding him my onion rings.'

Lata told him about Adhirbabu – the 'gentleman from Calcutta' – and his plans for the port. Unlike those who came from the city and palmed out rupees in exchange for votes, he was a businessman who spent his time holding meetings at the shanties, presented residents with bluish-white rolls of paper full of pictures – neat houses stacked up like sweetmeats inside a confectioner's shop; gleaming neon-lit avenues thronged by gang-men in hats and boots, and children in school uniform. 'He'll do for *all* of us what you've done for just seven,' she declared spitefully.

'Will he teach you to sing too?'

'He knows *everything* about you.' She scowled, then shared her secret – 'He wants your boys to play on Independence Day.'

He clutched the wet pillow, waking with a start as a ball of sweat rolled across his cheek like a scurrying ant. Once fully awake, he could see the port's giant cranes holding up an empty sky – a passing cover to the emptiness beyond. And he listened to the growls that came from the lanes of infinite curvature beneath the balcony.

Father Tito thought he heard a jackal among the dogs, and peered down to see if he could spot a golden back and greyish tail feasting by the gutters. How did it manage to find its way here? He wondered if it had boarded a rice barge at night and escaped to the city; or had been brought over by a peasant mother as a pet for her child, now left to fend for itself, breeding as it pleased with its canine cousins. Perhaps they were *all* jackals – joined by blood, simply putting up with their jalebi munching masters out of kindness.

A ship's siren brought his thoughts back to the Mission and to Lata, sleeping downstairs in her quarters, and he listened carefully to check if there were one or two strains of snoring. He worried about her, just as her mother worried over her lover. The two were inseparable – just a matter of time before seeds of love spawned the seed of a life.

He knew they'd have to come down their balcony one day. Pleasantly surprised by Adhirbabu's invitation, the orchestra went into top gear. A solemn Abu suggested the opening score – the National Anthem – that he had heard on the radio, prompting others to rattle off their own favourites. 'Wait! Surely they won't let us play all evening, will they?' Father Tito tried to restore order. There'd be speeches, and a film show at the very end.

As the musicians assembled on the makeshift stage by the whorehouse, they seemed like seven spring-toys ready for action, encircled by the crowd that had closed off all exits. Sitting on a stolen bench behind the throne reserved for the chief guest, Father Tito waited with the others for the speeches to begin, and bouquets to be given out. He was used to delays, and gestured to the boys to keep their instruments tuned and pull up their sagging ties. He looked around for Lata, and just as he spotted her carrying a lavish bouquet, Adhirbabu arrived. On cue, Abu started playing the National Anthem but a young man sporting a bandanna strode up on stage and silenced the orchestra with a sweep of his arm. First, he said, there'd be important announcements about the port's 'model city'.

Father Tito thought he heard gunshots at the back, and lusty cheer. Turning around, he looked past the hull of a fishing trawler and saw the clock tower of a medieval European hamlet – heard marching feet on cobblestones. Bugles played on the streets of Banja Luka, and he saw himself cheering. A shudder passed as the maze of coloured streamers unfurled in the breeze. He smelled hazelnuts. Trying to spot his friends from the seminary, he saw them playing in the band in the town's square, bent over their strings and horns. As he pulled his gaze back, Adhirbabu rose to wave at the crowd and beamed at Father Tito, 'I've heard you've become a Bengali!'

It didn't take long for the boys to recover from the interruption, then weathering the last of the speeches, they followed Abu's lead and deftly played out the National Anthem. By then the ink-blue sky had deepened to the colour of the chimneys' soot and encroached upon their stage like the river in tide. The seven played their chosen songs, first to moderate applause, then as Manik struck out on the drums, the crowd broke free of the cordon in a mad rush. Firecrackers rained on them like confetti. Father Tito closed his eyes and heard a sortie flying low. He could see hats thrown up in the air, and loosened his collar. Just as they started to play the last number, he felt a thrust on his flanks and landed in the circle beside the boys.

Waking from his trance, he saw Abu holding out the violin. Everyone was chanting his name, and for a moment he was puzzled...*Tito? He can't be here in Belgrade....must be hiding from the Nazis in the south...* Then, recovering quickly, he smiled through his false teeth, and asked for the accordion instead. Arms cradling the bellows, he surprised even his fellow musicians, going over to the gypsies... 'Me Ham Motto...Me Ham Motto...' *I am drunk!* He sang in Croat with his eyes closed – in a voice as deep as they could imagine.

✤ ✤ ✤

Next morning, he woke to Lata's mother. She hadn't come alone, but with her friends from the brothel to inform him that her Lata had disappeared yet again. She blamed Lateef, the Mission's gardener, for putting the devil in her daughter's belly and mentioned a secret marriage that stood to damage her honour. 'You must find her, Padre,' she shook a finger at him. His first impulse was to deflect the whole matter. How could she be sure? Maybe her Lata was sleeping late, as usual, at her aunt's after a long evening full of brawls. How did she know what was in her belly?

'Show me her blood, Padre!' She raised her voice. Her friends demanded to see the scoundrel's room by the garden. He walked them over to Lateef's hut. It was locked. His gardening tools stood by the fence. Entering with his spare key, he stumbled on a pile of bulbs saved for the spring and sat down on the coir bed. Then he offered his second line of defence. What made them think they'd be here? 'Because you've encouraged them, Padre.' The small room came alive with voices. 'It was happening right under your nose'; 'you should've thrown the bastard out a long time ago'; 'the girl would've been safe with her mother.' And, 'Did you make Christians out of them both before they escaped?' He thought of leading them back under the church's high ceiling where he could breathe, but a shadow blocked the way out. He heard Adhirbabu at the back of the crowd, 'Good morning, Father Tito!' He entered the room smiling and bade others to leave with a flick of his head, 'I didn't expect you to be busy so early…'

Back at the Mission's office, he offered tea, and waiting for the water to boil, wondered what the businessman wanted from him. The milk jar was empty. He searched under the cabinet where Lata hid her nest eggs, but there was nothing there except a jar of rancid lime pickle. Raised to be master of his own home, he felt like a stranger in Lata's kitchen. He was still breathless from the morning and started with an apology, 'Lata would've made you a better cup, but…' Adhirbabu glanced up from his newspaper but made no mention of the morning's events. Instead, he told Father Tito about the model township that he was planning. He spoke with a slur and the cast in his eye made him out to be older than he was – resembling more an elderly priest than a businessman. It was important, Adhirbabu said, to 'believe in the future and seize the moment rather than wait for the heavens'. He smiled at the obvious reference, then charged right ahead…. 'The Mission must play a role too…' He went on about serving the people, about give and take and not giving in. Just as he had in his speech last night, he rephrased the same question twice, the second with a farcical twist. It was fortunate that the port's bosses were on his side, but the battle wasn't over yet. There were enemies everywhere, and he knew who they were. 'You'll meet them soon, Father,' he fixed him with the gaze of an inquisitor. Unsure of his enemies, Father Tito reached for Adhirbabu's cigarettes laid out on the table in open invitation. 'Smoke?' 'No, no…' he withdrew his hand quickly. Ready to leave, Adhirbabu rolled up his newspaper like a baton and waved it at Father Tito. His smile gave nothing away.

The visit reminded him of his time at the seminary, of his superiors at the church. He didn't know why Adhirbabu had come, made such a dramatic appearance and saved him from the pack-wolves, didn't know if it was giving or taking.

But for days, the model township took the backseat to the story of Lata and Lateef. The shanties waited for them to return, the whorehouse held its breath, the tea shops spun one yarn after another. Evenings saw Lata's mother cursing the lot who 'prayed five times a day but thought nothing of spreading their filth to the innocent'. Her screams frightened the dogs, sending them leaping over the drains like racehorses. Lateef's clan – the Muslims – offered silence, tempting bystanders to peer over the mud-walls to catch a glimpse of the 'praying culprits'. Her vulgarity drew the gang-men returning from the port. They crowded her door in the hope of catching a glimpse of the brothel girls, cheered her on and added their two-bits, until a rock landed at her feet causing the crowd to break. Then she took her battle onto the streets, charging in and out of the lanes – squawking, wailing, heckling, and goading the weak-hearted to shed their impotence and rise up. Watching her from the tea shops, the 'Lords' were charmed as well, and spent the whole evening engorged in heat. Not a day passed without someone adding a new twist to the tale….the two had been spotted in the city…her belly was the size of a cow's! Others supplied details of their intimacy – at the padre's Mission. Eyes would turn towards the church's stained glass, blackened by the night.

❦ ❦ ❦

He remembered the last time he had prayed at his village church, just days before leaving. Thoughts of exile gnawed at his heart. The pain would never pass, he knew – the pain of deaths and the loss of everything he loved. Like the absent birds, his departure would further denude a land charred and maimed. It would've been better to die with fire on one's wings, if only it'd pay for their sins. Sighing, Father Tito recalled the last days – digging up and filling the graves to save the corpses from rotting.

Yet, as Dulu came charging into his room one morning, he was unaware that the pot had finally boiled over, that Lata had returned alone the previous night and made her way over to her mother's. Down with a touch of cold, he hadn't seen the ugly sight of men wielding arms marching through the lanes. Lata had confirmed the gossip about her belly, but not the culprit. Along with her mother and her brothel sisters, she was waiting for the public trial to begin – to punish the guilty and bring matters to a close.

His head caught in the tunic and he struggled before Dulu helped him slip it on. Wiping sweat off his bald head, he looked in the mirror, noticing his ears – the only survivors of the tropical sun, still red after all these years. Once they had arrived at the clearing by the whorehouse, he squatted with Dulu behind the ring of men, his head rising above them all. Glare from the church's windows made him blink and he looked around for a spot in the shade. The din had suddenly dropped, and an elderly man was reciting the basics. He could see Lata staring at the speaker.

For a good hour he coughed and sneezed, gurgled then swallowed the gluey spit tasting of raw tea. As he reached for his sash to blow his nose, his watery eyes made him look scared. The refrain rang clear through his buzzing head – *betrayal, cowardice, honour, justice….* Old men – fire leaping from their bulging eyes – raised their voices over the crowd's noise; whores pointed fingers and blamed everyone they knew; the young circled their enemies like wrestlers. And he saw Lata's mother watching him across the maze of weapons held in sweaty palms. After the harangue, eyes turned to the kneeling form before them – at the victim. *Give us his name!* They spurred her on as she rose to her feet and stood before the crowd – the swallow shorn of her feathers.

He was reminded of Palm Sunday – the day the sky had filled with glittering planes flying low over Belgrade. Fireballs rose where the bombs fell, a carpet of smoke spreading as far as he could see. Flames streaked from the cathedral, the spires snapped like carrots and screams could be heard through the terrible drone. Machine guns strafed women and children, corpses lay in heaps along the streets – among them a bride and a groom from a wedding party caught by surprise at the church. Looking past the firestorm, he saw the fascist Ustasha gangs swooping down on mountain villages....Osijek, Karlovac, Sisak, Knin.... forcing men and women to dig their own graves, hacking down a son before his father's eyes. Breathing in spurts, Father Tito followed priests as they hunted partisans, arm in arm with the murderers, hurling them into ravines or hanging them in the pine forests. He met them again at Mostar, their tunics splashed with blood, filling wagons with corpses. *Lord, turn thy eyes from heaven…* whimpering voices rang through the woods. Stopping to catch his breath, he entered the main square of Borova on the Danube. Where he had once heard bugles and firecrackers, he heard prisoners forced by their assassins to confess their crimes. At Siroki Brijeg, he had to cover his eyes; in Glina he shut his ears and ran. Just as he was about to blow through his clogged passages, the smell of burning flesh caught him in a vile fit of coughing. Holding on to Dulu, he strained his watery eyes and saw a gazelle freed from the bombed zoo roaming the streets – a frightened angel in the land of death. On a sudden impulse, he rose, pushing his way through the wall of men before him and on reaching the heart of the circle stood, his hulk next to a frail Lata, facing the crowd. In the same voice with which he had stunned his audience with his singing, he began to speak.

In spring, they came for the dogs. Riding an open Jeep and cranking up a ferocious siren, men from the pound arrived like an alien army trailed by urchins. A cloud of dust covered the port like carpet-bombing. Coughing and swearing, the residents watched the hunt from their shanties and tea shops, wondering which of their fawn-eyed, dull-witted, jalebi-chewing pets carried the deadly saliva of rabies. Crowded on rooftops they cheered the dog-catchers. Boys set off crackers to scare the monsters out of hiding.

Within minutes the traps were set. Moving from lane to lane with electric prods and bleaters, like quick-footed rangers, they searched behind garbage dumps, culverts, even the brothel's roof where the girls were known to hide their pets. It didn't take long for the victims to fall into their nets, trapped and wailing in the cage at the back of the Jeep. Leaving, they spread cheer all around and spurred renewed calls for tea.

Then it came out from its hiding place behind a tea shop – shy at first, before it started to wag its tail at the lip-smacking, petting and nuzzling. The Lords of Kidderpore threw bits of jalebi to Tito, the newest arrival – the mongrel they had named after a strange padre who had closed down the Catholic Mission and left a year ago in disgrace. They remembered him well – standing up like a fool before everyone in his white tunic and confessing that it was he who had given the belly to their poor Lata.

Miss Annie

At the age of twenty one the scales of fortune are even. So she couldn't blame dumb luck for failing to find a whoring job in Japan. Her agent, biting his nails, had suggested Sochi on the Black Sea then withdrawn at the hissing and hooting. His dollar paying clients expected to wait at tables, dance at bars, offer massage, and sleep with foreigners for foreign money not lousy roubles. In Bryansk – in all of Russia – there weren't too many like him: a kitchen-table agent with a flair for grabbing contracts and plucking foreign visas from thin air. A decent man, he urged the young ladies to be patient. Their future was bright – from New York to Bangkok, the world was waiting for Russian beauties. In truth, she didn't care much about the world, staring at the frayed lot of Aeroflot posters at her agent's office with scenes from Ulan Bator. All she knew was – Asia was cheap. But her untimely rheumatism made her refuse *The Goldfinger* – a massage parlour in Phuket. The agent had failed to convince her: the pain would dissolve in the ocean breeze, he had reasoned. Plus she could meet the wealthy Japanese there. She was too young to go to India – he had pleaded like a caring uncle. But at twenty one the scales of judgment are snagged, and she arrived in Calcutta for both a good reason and a bad.

The officer at the immigration desk frowned at her passport, then called out to others – 'Anna Pavlova! She's here.' Everyone eyed her like a celebrity, but their tone was mocking. 'It took her fifty years to return!' And, 'Where's the rest of the Bolshoi?' The man gave her a serious look and asked if she knew who Anna Pavlova was. Taking pity at her silence, he stamped her passport and mumbled... 'Poor things, they don't even know their past.' She knew then there was something strange about the city.

Fortunately, she was met by Ibrahim at the airport. He was part of her agent's chain of contacts, and in his own words, 'handled

everything' – lodging, business deals, and bail – 'in case there's trouble.'
With an eye on the road, he hastened to add, 'Don't worry, Calcutta
is safer than your Russia.' He looked as pious as his counterpart in
Bryansk: neatly cropped silvery hair parted in the middle, a long
white sherwani coat that reminded her of Afghan POWs, and
hawk-eyes shimmering with a thin film – like tears. And he spoke
calmly, never probing, peeling the onion with deft fingers. First, he
informed her of her illegal status – she'd be working in India while
on a tourist visa – and politely asked to keep her passport. Pointing
out the dangers of carrying cash, he recommended converting her
savings to gold, and his cousin – an honest jeweller in Bowbazar. As
they moved slowly past a column of sheep headed towards the
slaughterhouse, he showed her the cemetery where his wife lay buried.
In a roundabout way he spoke about doctors, a church that she might
want to visit, and the police. 'They are reasonable here,' he grinned,
then broke into a laugh: 'Not like the Middle East! No lashes for
showing flesh!' In a bid to keep her awake, he stopped briefly before
the city's incinerator and the foul smell woke her up with a start.
'Garbage!' he looked triumphant. 'The biggest dump in the world!'
They rolled along dusty avenues full of scavengers – ragpickers, pigs,
and mating dogs. 'Afraid?' Ibrahim asked, eye on the road. 'No.' He
told her about foreigners like her who thronged the city – Russians,
Italians, French, Americans – for business or pleasure. She'd need
just a touch of Hindi to go with her pidgin English – 'Calcuttans
understand *everything*' – and knew of a man who could help her,
offering once again his extended family. Then he spoke to her
about *Venus*.

Stopping at Ibrahim's office – only a touch larger than the agent's
in Bryansk, and cramped with desks – Anna slumped on a couch.
Someone brought her tea and her appetite, dulled by the shock of
arrival, returned to life. By then, Ibrahim had busied himself with
Hajj pilgrims sporting white caps, and glanced at her from time to
time with a reassuring smile. Men stared at her. A breeze came in
through the half-shut window and she rolled up her hair in a bun to
feel the damp air. Still in a trance, she gave Ibrahim her passport, and
received funny looking banknotes in exchange – her 'pocket money.'
An assistant brought her a plate of fries and an omelette. Seeing her
race through the omelette, Ibrahim stood up to apologize. Then he

brought her and her red-and-white vinyl suitcase to *The Terrace*. Falling rapidly into the first of many mid-morning naps, she thought she heard church bells.

In her dream, the flight returned to Bryansk. Stepping out of the empty airport, she glanced up at a peeling billboard welcoming visitors to the City of Seventeen Sisters. In dreamy steps she climbed the overpass and gazed at seventeen ugly smoke stacks rising from the flat earth like an obscene gesture – a counterpoint to the northern Urals. The crumbling fence of one of the seventeen model factories, now abandoned and overgrown with the dry shrub of late autumn, stared her in the face, its silence broken by the clip-clopping of a solitary hammer stripping away the last remains for scrap. Scaling the fence out of habit, she stood facing the barracks where the workers once lived, then kicked open the canteen door scrawled over with the drawing of a skull. As she sunk a shade deeper into her dream, she could hear herself singing; see her beaming friends in the crowd gathered at the barrack's canteen that resembled a bomb shelter. The band was egging her on, her friends cheering her to take the floor, and she smelled the smoke swirling around the gyrating bodies. Someone pressed a cold white pellet into her palm, and soon she was rising above the crowd, hovering like a bird over the party goers, till a scream at the back of the hall brought her crashing down.

Turning over on her side, her eyelids fluttered briefly. Then she started to float again, clutching her broken heels as she left the canteen, limping past her neighbours' hard stares into an ugly flat she shared with her mother. A flickering TV lit the dark room, and she saw her mother rocking on her favourite chair, staring at the black and white screen, at the familiar face of a dying man – a set of cruel eyes framed by a monk's beard. Strangely, he stared back at her over her mother's shoulder, and drawing on all her strength Anna tried to remember the name of this man she had seen countless times. Then she woke with a start at the strike of a match and found a bearded man sitting before her cross-legged on the floor. 'I am Ramakrishna,' the man said. Instantly, Anna knew who he was – the dying Tsar from the film they'd see over and again on her mother's TV.

'And you are our Annie, aren't you?'

'Annie?'

He laughed, and she fell back instantly into a deep dreamless sleep – her first since she was handed her ticket to Calcutta.

Looking back on her first day, she remembered her dream and the church bells. She'd hear them later on busy mornings as well. But the source remained elusive even after a month at *The Terrace*. Trooping around her neighbourhood, she heard their resonance in stairwells awash with light, clinging on to damp ceilings like peeling plaster. Everybody she knew heard them too, but no one could lead her to a church. The rest of Ibrahim's pointers were accurate enough: the fruit seller Rahim at the corner of Sudder Street delivered her weekly pocket money without fail; she got her Hindi from the boy who picked up her laundry; the frightening man at the hotel's bar sent her drinks to her room. In the very first week, she visited Dr Lama – sitting behind a doorplate that read 'V.D. Specialist' – for her cramps. He listened to her with a look of disbelief and advised her on a bewildering range of germs she was bound to catch sooner or later. She stayed clear of other Russians, and hung out with assorted Europeans at *The Terrace's* bar. They told her about Kathmandu, hashish, Mother Teresa, and exhilarating tales of theft and assault in Moscow. A girl from Sweden offered to teach her massage, but she refused on account of her rheumatic fingers. Within the month she had her first 'visitor.' After an elaborate introduction, Ibrahim had left her room, and lying under a whirring fan she had made out with her very first Calcuttan, filled with wonder. In the interim, her purse was stolen on a hot and busy day when the city suddenly filled with chanting crowds marching towards the central parade grounds waving red flags emblazoned with hammers and sickles. 'Why?' She asked her Swedish friend. 'Because they are communists, just like you!' Squashing a fly, she tried her meagre Hindi – 'Bakwas' – bullshit!

Then Ramakrishna took her to *Venus*.

Within the month she had told him everything. Sitting on her balcony overlooking Rahim's fruit stall, she confided the collected episodes of her twenty one years. In the end, he knew more about the city of seventeen sisters than anyone else in Calcutta, more about her deal with the agent in Bryansk than even Ibrahim, and her 'real' birth date. 'You are a Taurean,' he said, peering at her horoscope, sitting cross-legged on the floor in his favourite padmasana. He told her that her father was dead, that the woman she called her mother was really her aunt, that she had three siblings. 'No, two!' she protested. The third must've been stillborn – he was adamant. He confirmed her bone problem and wondered how she'd manage to dance in his new play, set to open soon at *Venus* with Anna as the swinging, bopping, and baring sensation the city had been waiting for. 'Dance?' she was taken aback. Ramakrishna nodded. The owner of the theatre had asked Ibrahim for an American girl. He in turn had offered a Russian... 'They too were a superpower not long ago.' Besides, a Russian was cheaper than an American – he had clinched the argument. Then, in a reverential tone, Ramakrishna had walked her through the hallowed walls of *Venus* – Calcutta's favourite theatre, where the plot of the play mattered less than the dancing girls who performed their burlesque shows at curtain call, giving the audience its money's worth. 'That's where a man goes to watch a woman who's not his wife do naughty things!' Ramakrishna smirked, then sobered up noticing Anna's pout.

'But I want to *sing*, not dance!' She made a face, wondering if she should call her agent and go over her contract, or visit Ibrahim at his office. Dance to what, dance when, dance in a dress or without....? She needed to know more. Singing was out – Ramakrishna was firm; just like the other dancers, she'd have to dance to film songs. Hadn't she heard them before? Then he startled her, launching into a fantastic bout of yelping and writhing that brought tears of laughter to her eyes.

At *Venus* she met the dancers: Jyoti, Lilly, and Kajal – Miss Jamie, Miss Lilly, Miss Katie. She got the drift and introduced herself as Annie in a spirit of camaraderie. They called themselves 'cabaret artists.' 'Stage-hussies!' Ramakrishna remarked before he was shooed away. Walking her around a half-lit stage strewn with props, the dancers offered Anna pocketbook versions of their lives. Mixing her Hindi deftly with gestures, she extracted the basics: Jyoti's rise to fame after she was discovered by the theatre owner – a strange bird with a strong nose but a weak appetite for public revelry. Like a true veteran, she reeked of smugness, despite the years that had rubbed off on her charms. Shaving her legs, Lilly was less open. She, undoubtedly, was the show's centrepiece. Half-listening to Jyoti, she kept staring at Anna, shooting off her questions. Could she dance? Could she jiggle her boobs? Sucking in her breath, Miss Lilly rolled her shank to demonstrate, till they all burst out laughing. Then she asked a grinning Ramakrishna about the new girl's role in the new play.

'That of a cultural imperialist,' he replied gravely. 'Corrupting the East with the disease of the West.' 'Bakwas!' they yelled in a chorus. Only Kajal was subdued. Somehow, she reminded Anna of Bryansk, of the canteen dancehalls, and she offered her a cigarette.

Parting the curtains, she stood facing the empty theatre – three hundred wooden chairs, and the standing fans with faces turned away from each other like quarreling lovers. She smelled stale smoke, a pungent urinal, and the burning coil of an arc lamp glaring down at her from the ceiling. She noticed Kajal smoking her cigarette, legs dangling from a raised platform. She offered lunch, but Miss Katie shook her head. It was Ramadan; she was fasting. In the afternoon she listened to Ramakrishna's play reading, with Kajal translating for her. Once again, Lilly asked about Anna's role. This time, a serious Ramakrishna fixed her with a frown and just like a real playwright kept them guessing for a moment. 'A whore. She'll play a concubine, a kept woman, a .....' He didn't mince words. And she could dance just as she pleased, style her own costume – play the alien at the shrine of vice. Relieved, Anna exhaled deeply. After all, she wouldn't have to worry about funny dresses and jiggle like Lilly.

Sitting in the cab on their way back to *The Terrace*, she asked Ramakrishna about the play's ending. What's the use if a whore remains a whore? Why doesn't she cut her losses and run from her pimp, the scoundrel? She asked him if he fancied any of the 'Misses.' Staring out at empty streets he seemed to have heard her, yet about to answer a different question. Eyes seeping with a pathetic kindness, he asked her if she had read *Crime and Punishment*, if she had heard of a certain Dostoyevsky, and if she knew what happened to Rodion Romanovitch Raskolnikov. Then, as if in a trance, he started to recite.... 'What if man is not really a scoundrel, man in general, I mean, the whole race of mankind? Then all the rest is prejudice, simply artificial terrors, and it's all as it should be...'

Anna sat bewildered, wondering why this strange man was telling her about dead Russians.

Truly, she surprised her worst detractors. By the time the new play had run its first season, she was an old hand. Ibrahim had stopped pampering her and moved on to minding his Hajj pilgrims. *The Terrace* was used to her late breakfasts, and she herself had fashioned a door sign – *Door Hato!* – commanding silence during her mid-morning naps. She reserved the afternoons for walks, lazily eyeing fake pearls at the nearby New Market, or browsing through fashion magazines. As *Venus* took more of her time, she saw fewer visitors, slipping invariably like the rest of the city into an endless string of excuses. Ramakrishna would come in the evenings, and three nights a week they went in a cab to her show.

Still, on her first night she had panicked. Waiting for her turn, her rouge had started to run. She worried about the lights; about the music. The crowd had been cold to Jyoti, pelted Kajal with catcalls, and taken off their shirts during intermission. She eyed Ramakrishna nervously across the wing, wondering why she had given in to this dancing business. Then, at the roll of drums, she emerged swaying, arms raised for maximum thrust. At first the crowd kept silent, taking in her light skin, golden hair, and blue bodysuit – three hundred ghostly faces ogling her. Halfway through the act, there wasn't even a whisper and she feared the worst. Then a paper dart came gliding in from the back row and lodged in her hair. Paralyzed for a moment, she hissed, 'Shit!' breaking loose all hell. As she stopped in her tracks, stunned, somebody blew her a lewd kiss; she turned her back to the crowd and screamed… 'Kiss my arse….!' They roared in delight. Every curse drew a louder cheer than the one before, and she ended her routine hands on hips under the bright beam in typical burlesque. Kajal embraced her as she entered the green room. Crowding around her, the cast beamed at their new star. Like a grande dame, Jyoti slipped off her ring of fake pearls and placed it on her finger. A courteous Lilly held the door open and whispered something naughty into her ear. Taking off his comical straw-hat, Ramakrishna bowed like a ballerina…. 'Salaam, Anna Pavlova!'

From then on, she became a known name. Even Ramakrishna was intrigued by the curious appeal of the cussing and swearing. There were rumours that the shy theatre owner came to every show and many recognized his voice in the repartee. In her success she didn't forget her agent. Converting her savings to gold, she wrote to him to confirm that his promise of a golden future had indeed come true, and that she was on the verge of discovering her *real* talents. Bored with herself on one of her free days, she took a chance on a bunch of raucous Australians, and after a long while had a cold white pellet pressed into her palm. Waking up a day later, she almost missed her show, stuck yet again in another flag-waving procession. She resolved to move from her lodgings to a proper house, but was persuaded against it by Ibrahim. *The Terrace* was lucky for her. Within the spell of a short winter, she fell in and out of love with Ramakrishna. He taught her yoga and predicted a long life full of twists and turns. Then her fellow performers went on strike, closing down *Venus* just short of their one hundredth performance.

It was a case of industrial dispute, she was told. The owner, buoyant at his success, was dreaming of greater fortunes – selling off the dilapidated century-old building to a land developer. There were plans to replace the theatre with an air-conditioned shopping mall. The man had all but sealed the deal, they were informed by insiders. Lying on her bed, she heard Kajal prattle on. She had brought the bad news, and nervously asked Anna for a cigarette. They were planning a strike, she said. A shutdown would cost the owner dearly. 'You, Annie, must tell him what to do.'

'Tell him what?'

Kajal bit her lip. 'The theatre has a future, doesn't it? He could make all the money he wants keeping us here rather than throwing us out.'

Anna frowned, 'You mean…?'

'What if there was a new play every year, a live band, and…'

'Stop!' She silenced Kajal, then gave her a suspicious look. 'Why me? Why must *I* tell him all that?'

Kajal had fallen silent. Then she looked at Anna, eyes full of despair and pleading. 'They said you're a Russian…. you *must* know more about these things.'

Dumbfounded, she played with her pearl ring, twisting it on and off. Secretly, she was amused. She thought the troupe viewed her as a lightweight, as a transient with a flair for gaffes. She was their diversion from tedium, a partner in pranks, a generous plier of cigarettes. Despite the effusion they left her out of the real stuff. At best she was their distant friend, an equal sufferer to stifling evenings under the arc lamp. Suspecting that Kajal was overplaying her hand, she asked pointedly – did they want her to simply stop working, or meet the owner in person.

'We want you to stick it to the jerk, just as you do in the shows.'

When the entourage of the four Misses and Ramakrishna showed up at the go-between's flat to meet the owner, he had all but dissolved under the dark shadows of a brass lamp. Face downcast, he looked like an errant schoolboy. A book lay open before him with the page marked by an evening's pass to *Venus*. His glasses seemed a touch too shiny, casting a strange mask-like quality on his oval face. And he was busy with his nails – cleaning and polishing them, frowning at an imaginary stain on his milk-white shawl. Right up, Jyoti played the historian recalling decades of tradition. Lilly fidgeted with a glass paperweight till the owner calmly retrieved it from her hands. Ramakrishna recited the basic economics in favour of the show, and stole Anna's lines, or so she thought. Unusually radiant, Kajal sat next to her and flashed her Lolita smile. Meandering through a lifeless hour, they seemed to have reached a dead end, when Anna spoke up and demanded to know why the owner was 'screwing everyone's happiness'. A cigarette delicately poised between her fingers she asked him if he had ever watched the show. If he knew what it took to blow three hundred heads all at once? His delicate eyelids fluttered for a moment, then he gave her an innocent smile and asked why she'd be bothered. Wasn't it true that her contract with her Russian agent would soon expire? That she was but days away from her trip home? He asked her about her return ticket, then went back to polishing his glasses in the ensuing silence. Instinctively, she had turned to Ramakrishna, looking for her missing line. The glow of cigarettes seemed brighter than the brass lamp, and for a moment she was reminded of her mother's flat lit by a flickering TV. Only Kajal kept staring at her, while the others looked away. Blowing out blue smoke through her lips like a comet's tail, she had finally made up her mind and locked gazes with the owner – 'Well, if I can fuck half the city, I can fuck my ticket too.'

At twenty one the stakes are at their highest; and so as *Venus* reopened for the one hundredth time, there was talk about a young Russian stealing the show with her outrageous Hindi and pidgin English.

Waking to churchbells, she read Ramakrishna's Dostoevsky, labouring her way through the story of Raskolnikov – the poor young man who had murdered his landlady. She wasn't impressed, and wondered about the ending. Recovering his *Crime and Punishment*, Ramakrishna asked her if she had understood Raskolnikov's torment – 'Should he confess his crime or keep mum and go scot-free?' 'Yes, yes...' she yawned, 'It's the same old Russian story....called screwing oneself!' More than her answer, he seemed keen to reveal a plan. Eyes dancing, he asked her to leave with him to meet three 'unknown' men. She was surprised, wondering if Ramakrishna had taken over Ibrahim's role of finding her clients. Abruptly, she told him to stuff it. She could find her own men and had no use of Ibrahim or him. Besides, she was on her period. 'These men aren't afraid of blood!' he told her. Together, they left for the Coffee House. Inside the dark hall packed with men, a curious niche separated each table from the rest, guarded by its own cloud of smoke. A team of waiters scurried from one end of the hall to the other. They recognized Ramakrishna and pointed to a corner. She felt she was entering *Venus* once again for the first time.

The three unknown men were waiting for them. In a hushed voice Ramakrishna introduced her as Miss Pavlova. They fell into an uneasy silence over their coffee, and Anna looked around for the loo. Then Ramakrishna provided the crucial opening line – 'She's from the Soviet Union.'

'Ex...' One of the men corrected him, then asked, 'Why is she here?' Ramakrishna smiled in reply. That was enough.

Soon they opened up – the three members of the Bolshevik League, whispering her into their secret world seething with 'class struggle' and 'guerilla warfare.' Ramakrishna nodded in agreement. Observing her cast darting looks around, they reassured her: the Coffee House was safe, safer than *The Terrace* – 'even Russia!' Over a brimming ashtray, they asked her about the 'ex-Soviet Union,' about 1917 and 1977 – the revolution and the counter-revolution. Like excited pupils they recited a full list of names – Lenin, Stalin, Trotsky, Molotov, Bukharin, Breznev, Gorbachov, Yeltsin. They quizzed her on the 'left' and the 'right,' then charged right ahead... 'What was the Red Army thinking now?' By then, her jaw had dropped and she drew in the table's smoke.

She wondered why Ramakrishna had brought her here, tried unsuccessfully to draw a link – between his play and the revolution, between *Venus* and the Coffee House. Feeling the heat of bodies crammed inside the sooty walls, she faced their questions with a straight face – How far were the Bolsheviks from recapturing the Kremlin? Was Moscow aware of the Indian situation? Had she already met the city's various revolutionary factions? They chuckled as Ramakrishna recounted how Anna had called the bluff of *Venus's* owner, then ordered another round of the dark and sweet coffee. She had excused herself in a desperate bid to find the loo.

Over the next few months, she saw more of the three unknown men. Ramakrishna accompanied her at times, at others she went alone to their hideouts – to tea shops scattered throughout the city. Later, half awake on her bed, she'd wonder what made her go, search for an answer. It was true that her routine craved diversion. She had spurned her few Western friends out of boredom, and her plans to trade in fake pearls had fallen deaf on Ibrahim's ears. She felt anxious, waiting for Ramakrishna to visit her at *The Terrace*. But neither the city of seventeen ugly sisters nor the centurion *Venus* held clues to her strange behaviour. It was as if the mysterious bells had released a mysterious urge to step out of her costume and step into a dusty old cloak from her past life. In truth, she went not to learn about the revolution, but to be near the revolutionaries. Her secret meetings with her three friends, full of plotting and scheming, were strangely comforting. She sensed, at times even without speaking a word, the bond that had snapped the day she fought with her mother and left for the dancehall. And there was a strange longing for an omnipresent Russia, rather, the Soviet Union. *The Soviet State, the Supreme Soviet*....words that rolled off her tongue as if she had known them all along. Gradually, her Bryansk ceased to be simply the midpoint between Moscow and Kiev, but a 'child of the revolution' teeming with young and unwed 'mothers of the nation.' Locking arms with the three, she imagined marching on a cold Petersburg night to the Red Army Band; or waiting in queue at the Red Square for a glimpse of a dead Lenin. The orchestra at *Venus* reminded her of the full-throated *Moscow by Night*. Her friends told her the fable of the real Anna Pavlova – the queen ballerina of the Bolshoi – and her magic heels. And, when they raised their teacups to toast her arrival, she beamed... 'Tovarisch !'

Despite her caution over the meetings, she received an early warning. In one of his visits to *The Terrace*, Ibrahim sat on her bed turning pages of a magazine, then blurted out.... 'You have betrayed me, Annie.' His outburst, so unlike him, took her by surprise. In an unusually harsh voice he had demanded full knowledge of her 'friends,' then crushed his cigarette violently over her protest. What did she know of politics, he fretted. What did she know of police lock-ups and jails? Why didn't she stay back in Russia if she wanted to be a communist?

She was convinced he was spying on her. Looking down from her balcony she spotted Rahim, the likely culprit, polishing a mango on his dirty sleeves. Regaining composure, Ibrahim had mapped out her boundaries: She, most certainly, could pick and choose her clients; even her contract at *Venus* was negotiable. He didn't mind her occasional tantrums, and had chosen to ignore the business about her return ticket. But to protect her he needed her confidence. All his plans were useless if she herself decided to give him the slip. Holding his white cap in his hand, he had pleaded with his shimmering eyes.... 'Please, Annie, let nothing come between us.'

Ramakrishna had calmed her. Seated cross-legged like a sadhu, he had provided the perfect counter-argument – why should the pious pimp care about her whereabouts as long as he had his monthly commission? In any case, the very meaning of protection was relative. Falling back into Dostoevsky, she asked him if he ever searched his own mind. If he saw his own paradox; the end-result of his life.

'Of course, Annie,' he had quoted from his favourite in a flash, 'I too have kissed the filthy earth with bliss and rapture!'

She slept uneasily.

Once again, Kajal was the messenger, but this time she brought glad tidings. The owner was planning a facelift – fixing up the peeling walls and the leaky urinal as an excuse for hiking up the ticket prices. The troupe was set to open a new play. Bored, Anna heard her drone on. Observing the worry beads on her face, she was tempted to invite Kajal to her secret meetings, but held back recalling one of her comrades, 'We don't want to involve others in our plans.' She felt Kajal needed her advice, if only to survive the owner's advances and Jyoti's prodding to give in. Secretly, she relished her distance from others in both spheres – from the revolutionaries and the 'Misses' – felt like a friendly spirit among them, moving in and out at will, without raising an eyebrow. The rains had weakened her digestion and when she returned to the Coffee House after a week of Doctor

Lama's treatment, her friends seemed tense. They were planning an 'action,' and she sensed an unknown story lurking under the table's familiar smoke.

On the opening night of the new play, she was late. The drumbeat of rain on *The Terrace's* roof reminded her of clip-clopping carriages in Bryansk's town square. Awake the previous night, she had read her mother's letter – the first ever – and heard her shuffling feet on her dark balcony. She wondered why her mother had taken the trouble of breaking free of her black and white TV and the dead Tsar to write to her truant daughter. The thought of an imminent loss set her nerves on edge; the laboured lines on the paper dissolving before her very eyes each time she read them over. Reaching *Venus*, she had dashed into the greenroom and fawned over her new costume.

In her wisdom, she had chosen leather. Holding up the black piece, wet and gleaming, she giggled. The satin top didn't add much to it, and she rued missing out on something tarty. Kajal gasped. Twirling her skirt over his head, Ramakrishna asked to see the 'real costume!' Lilly teased her – 'Now you won't even have to open your mouth!' The spot boy minding the lights promised to match her colours.

Exchanging glances with Ramakrishna, she settled down with a cigarette by the wings and waited for her cue, her stomach knotting as the first of the dancers made her way up the ramps. Casting her shyness aside, Kajal danced with her eye on the owner sitting in the first row, marking her entry and exit with a rare abandon. Biting her nails, Anna waited for her to finish, then took a quick look in the mirror.

Next it was Lilly's turn. Draped in green chiffon, Miss Lilly flowed transparent like the ocean. Parachuting on to centre stage she offered no room for afterthought, and in a quick turn revealed her back – a knotted serpent straining to break free. Anna noticed Ramakrishna nodding in approval, and made a mental note to remind him of his pleasure. The crowd clung dangerously on to each other, waving and cheering. With every thrust Miss Lilly brought them closer to climax, then jumping on to the shoulder of a stagehand rolled her torso at the exact beat of a demented conga. Getting up for her turn, Anna knew it would be a hard act to follow – a Russian whore's word over the swell of local tide.

Yet as she made her relatively simple entry, her thoughts strayed to her dancehall band in Bryansk – the happy faces. And she heard a distant jostle at the entrance. A blue beam cut through the darkness and lit her navel. She started to move. The wrap came off as the base warmed up, baring leather. *This one's for you Mamma!* – she whispered, then barked at a drooling usher… 'Wake up!' Picking up a lash she swirled it in a perfect helix, threw down a pair of iron handcuffs and posed like a rogue. A clear voice rang through the heavy breathing sax… 'Tie me up, baby!' The knot in her stomach uncoiled, and she waited for other voices, sucking in her breath, kneeling on the floor, knees parted, yelping…. *Ummmmmmmm…..* Three hundred pairs of eyes shone through the blue haze, and the spark of a Molotov cocktail.

In fact she never heard the blast, but saw flames – streaking like fireflies. The scream, still full in her throat, lasted a minute longer then merged with those of others. Spreadeagled on the floor, she saw the blur of bodies desperate to escape. A chunk of plaster fell by the wings, and she thought she heard Kajal howl. As she looked up, she saw the spot boy fast asleep with a smile on his face. Then, rising on her broken heels, she stood stationary, a head above the fleeing crowd. At the back of jostling bodies, fresh ink marred the freshly painted walls: *Long Live the Revolution!* She glimpsed her three friends pumping their fists in triumph as they sneaked out through the far exit, then collapsed into Ramakrishna's arms, falling instantly into a deep dreamless sleep.

Along with the three 'Misses,' she was charged with engaging in indecent acts in a public place. A diligent officer suspected that she had overshot her stay in India and demanded to see her sponsor. Reluctantly, she called Ibrahim, still busy with his Hajj pilgrims. He came to the police station, and without fuss stood bail. Then he took her to his office and handed her passport back. He said he was leaving soon for Mecca.

On her way to the airport with Ramakrishna, she passed known landmarks. Stopping briefly at Rahim's fruit stall, she offered him a tip. He refused, and gave her a bag of mangoes instead. The grim bar owner waved at her; familiar faces smiled, and she heard the churchbells. The Coffee House blended into the afternoon's haze, and she observed a row of trucks parked before *Venus* tearing down its walls. Soon they were out in open country, and the stench of the dump woke her with a start. She saw Ramakrishna's eyes on her.

'Do you know why Raskolnikov confessed?'

'Why?' She levelled with him.

He sighed. 'Otherwise *everything* would be permissible on this godless earth…'

A month short of twenty two she left Calcutta for Phuket – to the massage parlour where she was most likely to meet the wealthy Japanese that her agent had once promised. Miraculously, Calcutta had cured her rheumatism.

The Last Dalang

His name was Johann Bosco Novi and he claimed to have descended from the royal house of the Tang. 'Look at me,' he said, and I saw a peasant's face from south of the Yangtze, with steep gorges running down the temples and eyes like turrets that sported a pair of darting pupils. A toothless mouth, flared nostrils and an ugly mole on his cheek gave him the look of a living scarecrow – bald, but for a few strands of white. Bald and fat, with an exhibitionist's belly.

In his sixty years he hadn't learned to walk properly, shuffling in short steps of the flatfooted. Besides a tattoo, his skin bore few blemishes, except burns on his fingers and nails discoloured by the soot of kerosene lamps. When I saw him last he had the same half-smile on his face that had greeted me in his shop, blabbering through his toothless mouth and clearing his voice for frequent bursts of singing. He was getting ready, he had said when we first met, for his 'journey to paradise,' which took less than a year to begin.

It was rain that brought me to Johann's shop in the palace town of Yogyakarta – the afternoon rain, a regular feature of the Indonesian tropics. Like a secret valve that opened at midday, it doused summer's fire with a drenching and drove the sleepy fruit sellers from the central market to the safety of their homes, leaving their wares to sparkle in the rain. To the locals it was a moment of premeditated flight, timed perfectly to coincide with their afternoon's feed of rice and jackfruit.

Johann's store lay within my territory – the jumble of shops that sold bric-a-brac and the occasional treasure that still enticed the serious collector to Java. One needed patience to sift, sometimes for hours, cloistered within the damp walls of badly-lit rooms where a sarong-clad seller kept watch while her elderly kin snored in the backroom. The useful jostled with the useless on the crammed shelves: cheap plastic cups ringed a betelnut box made of old brass; rare

Chinese porcelain reflected on rows of pickle jars; real Asmat beads lay buried under fake ruby; old silver among new, or an enormous padlock bearing the insignia 'V', for the Dutch Vredenburg brothers who had fought and lost the battle for the colony here in Yogya.

I had found the rainy afternoons to be ideal to shop for pottery and silver, old kris and rare ikat, and much more – when sleep held sway over profit and the bored seller found relief in the chatter of a friendly stranger.

Johann's shop was different, and not simply because he was Chinese. It was cast in the same mould as two-storied shophouses found everywhere in Asia, with a spiral staircase connecting the two floors. A removable floor panel allowed the family to keep watch from above on the children playing in the shop. There was a weighing scale on a tidy showcase; door-gods on the altar, a garland of paper money and burning incense; framed photos of ancestors, and Hong Kong posters of kung fu warriors. Giant copper vessels stored old coins bearing the stamp of the Emperor.

As I ambled down Malioboro, the main avenue that ran past the central market, it wasn't the door-gods or the paper money that caught my attention, but a giant sign of a dog kneeling by a gramophone. On a rainy afternoon, laden with useless locks and used silver, I met Johann at his little shop and saw him at his best: selling his puppets – the Wayang Goleks – while pretending to give a 'free' concert of the Ramayana to a throng of gullible tourists.

I had heard him sing in a nasal voice as he held up a puppet and imitated the humble servant, Hanuman, praying to his master, Rama, to invade Lanka and free Queen Sita abducted by the demons. Surrounded by backpacking tourists, Johann was at a dramatic crossroads – the battle between the good and the evil was about to begin and he needed to hold his audience till the rain stopped and took them out of his shop.

It was difficult in the dark to see what lay beyond rows of fake porcelain and cheap carvings, mounds of tourist beads, and bronze temple bells shaped like adolescent breasts. The table that served as the makeshift stage for his puppet show was bare with the exception of a rainbow of visiting cards lined up neatly under the glass top. The pallid green walls flaunted a Columbia Recording Company poster from 1893, and one that read *Höhner's Harmonica* next to the giant sign from *His Master's Voice*. Changing his voice abruptly, Johann sang Sita's lament from her abductor's prison, then switched effortlessly back to Hanuman, the monkey – 'Oh! How beautiful but sad my lady... thin as a bone, her tresses unkempt. Alas! A vicious crab has stroked her lovely cheeks and turned them to stone!'

Turning around to face Johann and his audience, I found nine pairs of eyes staring at me.

'Tell them what happened to Sita. You *are* Indian, yes?' Johann smiled.

By then, the rest of the Ramayana's cast was out on stage: Ravana, the ten-headed king of demons, Indrajit – his brilliant son, the vicious she-demon Surpanakha, and Kumbhakarna – Ravana's brother, the gentle sleeping giant woken by the thunder of battle.

'Have you forgotten?' He stroked the white strand that sprouted from his mole; sleeves rolled up, shirt open at the belly button, glasses foggy from the steam that rose steadily from the quenched soil outside.

Taking my weak smile for defeat, Johann changed tack and started to speak in German to an elderly couple – 'Kennen Sie Professor Max Müller? Die Deutschen wissen alles über Indien, ja?'

The couple smiled nervously. After a few awkward moments, a young and bearded man picked up Ravana and started to mimic his fury. Breaking away from the group, a tall Nordic woman kneeled before a row of gamelan and filled the shop with unmusical notes. Her companion, taking up the cue, sounded the brass gongs; heads peered through the door to check on the status of the rain.

'So what happened to Sita?' A couple of Irish girls pressed on, but by then Johann had fixed his gaze above, at the hidden window that had parted unnoticed to reveal an old Chinese face. She was bald like Johann, with the same mole on her cheek. The gamelan player looked up and exclaimed. Johann seemed a touch irritated and fumbled with something tucked inside his breast pocket.

Then, as well as later, the abruptness seemed typical of *Het Muziek Huis*, his shop named after the Dutch piano company that Johann was connected to by ancestry as I later came to know. Like the Ramayana, the changes fitted his many moods – Johann the shopkeeper, busily converting dollars and deutschmarks to Indonesian rupiya; and Johann the master puppeteer, the dalang, belting out the epic as he marshalled his troops in the battle between good and evil.

Holding my favourite puppet, I inched forward in queue. At the counter, Johann smiled his toothless smile... 'Ah! Kumbhakarna, the one who is always asleep.'

It was easy piecing his life together. After a few more visits to his shop, Johann had introduced me to the other Chinese: a framed great-grandfather on the wall, who had come to Yogya from Canton in 1887, bringing with him a keen head for numbers and two embroidered tapestries. They hung side by side in his house – scenes from Canton and Hangzhou – places he'd never return to. In Yogya he married a Malay – the daughter of a Muslim guard at the sultan's palace – borrowed money from the clan and started a shop for harmonicas. 'Look at me,' said Johann, 'A pure Tang!' Both he and his twin sister, the bald lady at the window, had taken after their Chinese forefather.

The keen head had spawned a solvent enterprise. The elder Tang had boasted a flourishing business with German and Dutch companies, and eventually with Americans. A diversified merchant for muziek and kunsthandel, he had expanded his business to Surabaya, Batavia and Semarang. His house in Yogya's Chinatown was every bit Chinese – the only language he spoke and educated his sons in. His Taoist faith too remained unscathed despite his wife's regular prodding to convert, and despite his closeness to his customers – the Muslim sultan, and the resident Dutch governor of Fort Vredenburg.

As a child, Johann was sent away to study in Jakarta, and he remembered visiting the dock's seedy warehouses full of men who smoked long pipes as their fingers clicked rapidly over the abacus. 'A real Chinese is never far from business!' – but his own father was a sick man who feasted on his daily quota of small white pellets, and dreamt of playing football. Born in a family of businessmen, his father had rebelled, threatened to abandon the shop and start a football club for the local Chinese men.

While in Jakarta, Johann he had met Indians, plenty of them. They worked in the textile business, owned big shops and tiny homes, spoke Malay like sons of the soil. There were some in Yogya too. 'But no one wants to listen to the Ramayana, or buy my puppets!' he had sighed.

What about him? With a Malay great-grandmother, couldn't he claim to be a son of the soil? Johann shook his head, 'Chinese or Indians can't be anything but foreigners.' They were unwelcome in the Malay village by the mosque – with clean-swept frontyards where little children played with marbles and kites, watched over by gurgling doves in exquisite wicker cages, the crescent moon flag flapping from flagstaffs over every home. It was the colony of 'white people' – those who prayed five times every day and wore immaculate white to mark the Hajj.

'Dogs aren't allowed in there,' said Johann. There was, of course, a time when the Chinese held sway over much of Yogya. That was before the big fire, before the tanks rolled into the city, this time not to lay siege on Fort Vredenburg and the Dutch musketeers, but to drive out the Chinese. Suddenly, the central market had become the stage for a battle between Rama and Ravana, and the dalang – the puppeteer – was merciless.

'Where were you in 1967?' I asked him in a guarded way about the purge.

'You know a lot about Indonesia, Herr Professor!'

By his own account, the Tang had fared better than the other Chinese of Yogya. His uncle had managed to board an oil tanker at Surabaya and jumped ship in Hong Kong where he had become a successful moneylender. His half-brother had left for Rotterdam where he studied law and staged vigils outside the Indonesian embassy until he contracted pneumonia and 'left for paradise.' The shop was shut down and the great-uncles and aunts had retreated up the spiral staircase to count rosaries and listen to the mellifluous gamelan in the safety of the family rooms. Johann, a recent graduate from King's University, was sent away to Banka – tin mines in southern Sumatra – as a clerk's assistant. He had learned his German there from German engineers, polished his Dutch, met Scottish missionaries and converted to Christianity.

He had spent his exile in the jungles, entering ledgers and regaling his foreign friends with tales from the Ramayana. The shop resumed business in the '70s, courtesy of the dead great-grandmother. The then head of guards at the sultan's palace had issued a letter in his own hand vouching for the 'native' roots of the Tangs. Gone though were the harmonicas, pianos and accordions. It was next the turn of puppets – made of wood and leather; new, old and faked.

'Why did you return to the shop?' I had asked him.

'Does an apple fall far from its tree, Herr Professor?' He had given me the half-smile.

There was more to his return than simply family ties. Deep inside Sumatra's jungle, he had discovered his true passion – for the puppets and the Ramayana. 'I learned to sing from our servants,' Johann had confided. That was during the family's heyday when the retinue of Malay servants would sing verses from the epic in the kitchen, or as they hauled up cargo from the rail yard through the narrow lanes of Chinatown. In the evenings he'd slip out to listen to dalangs rehearse with their puppets under smoky kerosene lamps. The epic came easier to him than the abacus. His mother, a small and sweet woman who rarely ventured outside their shophouse, was his proud audience. Others – cousins, half-brothers and siblings – were less kind when it came to such a native and lowly pastime. It took him years to learn the seven acts of the Ramayana, master the twists and turns of a rather simple story. His uncle's friend, a Malay, was then the chief dalang at Sonobudoyo – the ancient theatre where sultans came in disguise to share the passion of commoners. The master dalang had taught him everything – how to sing the high-pitched lament following a tragedy, the chatter of monkeys, the bloodcurdling roar of a demon, even taught him to cry the silent tears of Sita in her prison. He had taught him more: to be a real dalang, he'd have to weave his own story into the timeless tale of the Ramayana.

The pastime had worried Johann's father – the money his son wasted on puppets, the way he neglected duties at the shop, and the nightly jaunts that took him out of Chinatown. He had misread his son's adventure, had seen the signs of a secret plot and was convinced that the youngest of the Tangs was slipping into danger – from trade to politics. And so, the same family that forbade his father's football, had banished his puppets.

'It wasn't just my father. The girls too wanted me to be rich, so I went to university!'

'Why don't you do a full performance, not at the shop but....' I regretted asking him, as it seemed to have touched a raw nerve. As he dusted his wares and shuffled from one corner to another, he seemed breathless, beads of sweat on his forehead. He was wheezing, and had a vacant look on his face as if he didn't recognize me any more than other visitors to his shop.

'Because it's useless.' He answered in a deadbeat voice after a long silence.

'Useless?'

'Yes. The Ramayana is dead now…a dead story, useless…' He saw doubt on my face and went on. 'Football is better. Do you know about Man U, Herr Professor?'

Aah! I understood his sadness. Malioboro shops were full of red and white Manchester United shirts, whichever way one looked. Young men with Hajji caps flaunted them on their backs, as did peasants wearing the fakes, even off-duty policemen sported them, stripping off their official tunic as soon as their duty hours were over. It was a contest between football and the Ramayana, and one didn't have to be smart to know which side was winning.

'There are no real dalangs left anymore. Look at the young… they have money but no wealth…no one to tell them what's good, what's bad….' He shooed away his niece who asked him the price of something. Flushed, and in an uneven voice, he rambled on… 'There's nobody who dares to change the story. It's the same Rama, the same Ravana, the same monkey, the same Ramayana…. just a show for tourists.' Walking swiftly over to the back of the store, he wrenched off the Columbia Recording Company poster and held it out towards me, 'Take it, I know you want it.' He said he had been waiting for years for an invitation from Sonobudoyo, but the fools over there took him for just a poor shopkeeper, a Chinese, ignoring the blood of the wise Tang and the noble sultans.

With clouds fast taking up their midday position and the store filling up, Johann became more agitated, his shirt soaked in saliva as he ran to the toilet and came out with his fly open. His niece had disappeared up the stairway, and leaving my finds at the counter, I inched back towards the door. His eyes chanced upon sleeping shopkeepers on the sidewalk, and he barked at them, 'Everybody sleeps! The war will be over before they even know it!' In a sudden turn of his head, he had looked up at the open window where his twin sister had appeared, and screamed at her, 'I don't need the pills, you idiot! The doctor says I need a wife.'

❧ ❧ ❧

I returned to Yogya in time for spring blossoms. As in the rainy season, the streets were deserted in the afternoons, with the locals resting during the month of Ramadan. There was a power cut, and when I reached Johann's shop it was even darker than usual. A young Chinese woman sat at the counter and fanned herself in the stifling heat. Johann, she mentioned, was out to see his doctor. It was one of those rare days when the tourist got the better of the treasure hunter, and I had planned just a quick look in. There was hardly a treasure in sight beside the sign with the dog. Johann had mentioned his grandfather being the first agent of HMV in Indonesia, and how the store sign had come over all the way from England was part of family lore. It had somehow escaped the fury of the riot mob when the shop was ravaged, survived an electrical fire, and blended in naturally with the peeling wall and the wooden door panels. I pointed at the sign and smiled at the young lady. She held up her fingers to name her price. It was a treasure hard to pass up, and I left the shop a happy collector.

Johann treated me as a stranger when we met the next day. He was busy selling his puppets, breaking into songs and translating rapidly for his audience. I took his neglect to be a sign of friendship. Friends don't need to fuss over friends when they are busy, I thought, sooner or later he'd embarrass me with his Ramayana question and put me in a spot before he showed off his mastery. His paunch had grown by a few inches and the limp had worsened since we'd met last. Also, he seemed now to hurry through his acts, when in the past he paused frequently to lace his singing with comic commentary. His audience though, was just as enraptured, and the sales were brisk.

As I faced him at the counter, he pushed aside my knick-knacks and turned his attention to those behind me in the queue, raising a few eyebrows. After the last of the shoppers had left, he scribbled a line on a note pad and held it up to me…. *Trust is a must for business.*

'We must strike a deal, Professor,' he spoke in a gruff voice.

So here was his true ancestry – the trader's blood from Canton still gurgling in his knotty veins. But what deal was he talking about? 'Of course,' I smiled, unsure.

Speaking laboriously and mopping his forehead, he asked for his sign back. It was the only remnant of the family treasure from the times when they were rich and important, when every musician in the archipelago knew who the Tangs were; even the Germans, the Dutch and the Americans knew them, before a few foolish soldiers could drive them out of their own shop, and cause his poor mother to go barking mad in shock.

'It'll come with me on my journey to paradise.' He had promised something in return – that he'd perform his puppet show for me, not at his shop but at the sultan's theatre in Yogya.

I had agreed, and gone a step further – a deal on condition that he performed the story of Kumbhakarna, my favourite Ramayana character.

You have sinned against Sita – Kumbhakarna had rebuked his brother, Ravana, king of the demons. As a demon himself, he saw Sita's abduction by Ravana as a lowly act, bringing on an unnecessary war with the invincible Rama. You should've consulted us before you lost your head and acted like a fool. The giant Kumbhakarna had seen the fear of death in Ravana, and agreed to help him out as a brother. Only a small problem remained – who'd wake Kumbhakarna from his legendary sleep to fight his battle against Rama?

Waiting for Johann, I went over the story of Kumbhakarna: he had asked for a simple boon from the gods – a happy life, as happy as one feels when in deep slumber. The gods had tricked him, blessed him with sleep, six months of uninterrupted sleep, when he'd be all but dead to the world, waking for a single day to eat then fall asleep all over again. Of what use was he on the battlefield? – Ravana had fumed, when the battle for Lanka started. I recalled Johann telling me that Kumbhakarna was the toughest character to portray in all of the Ramayana.... 'How do you play the part of a sleeping man and keep your audience happy?'

When he arrived to take me over to the theatre, I could see that he was calm, like a seasoned performer before a show. His forehead was free of the few unruly strands of hair; he had exchanged cheap plastic slippers for black pumps, and wore horn-rimmed glasses that gave him a sombre look. They belonged to his sister, he explained – they had the 'same eye-trouble'. The pleats of his Malay sarong fanned out every time he took a step; the batik shirt was open to the chest to take in the breeze, and a red carnation stuck out from behind his left ear – Jayakusuma, the Flower of Victory, Johann explained. He'd be allowed to perform a few acts at Sonobudoyo, not the whole Ramayana, of course…. 'That'd cause a revolt!' Just one act was enough, he had boasted – 'You'll see *real* war, Professor!' Why didn't his sister come with him, or his niece? Before I could seize on his lack of a wife or the mystery behind the pills, notes of gamelan ushered us into the sultan's theatre.

Exactly as Johann had described, the setting was perfect for the epic. The audience sat facing the puppets and the performers under a giant wooden canopy along with the musicians – men in sarongs and women in matching dresses wrapped firmly round their breasts – faces gleaming from the kerosene lamps that hung low from high ceilings. Magnificent silk framed the wings through which the puppets made their appearances.

As we made our way through the crowd, Johann caught me drooling over a trunk full of puppets. 'Those aren't for sale, Professor….they belong to the palace!' The show, of course, had started hours ago, and the first four acts of the Ramayana were already over. The crowd was restive as the fifth act started with preparations for the final assault on Lanka. It was a handsome crowd – men and women sat cross-legged on the floor, showing off their finery. The old had captured the front rows, to give their ears a fair chance of catching the commentary; new mothers leaned against floor posts, their babies wrapped securely in sacks behind them. Smoke rose steadily as bark-wrapped cheroots passed from hand to hand. The tamarind juice seller did brisk business, and despite a few look arounds, I failed to spot the sultan in disguise. The master of ceremonies announced each act with the clash of cymbals.

The puppet box was half empty. Barring Kumbhakarna and his followers, all other characters had already made their appearances and lay in a pile on the floor – slain demons with flashing teeth and elephantine ears; and their leaders who had failed to persuade King Ravana to make a bid for peace with the invader Rama. The apes, unquestionably the stars of the show, were waiting for the dalang to bring them back to life so that they could follow the godlike Rama into Lanka and set the demons' capital on fire. It was the turn of Ravana to scheme.

At Johann's turn, he snatched the wooden rattle from the master of ceremonies, took his place on the stage and started to hum along with the gamelan. Then, with a practiced whip of his arm, he brought forward his first puppet, the fearsome Ravana. The clash of cymbals was matched by the crowd's roar as the demon king arched his bow and took aim at his rival Rama. Arrows started to rain down and flames erupted all over the battlefield. The earth rumbled, warriors on both sides let out bloodcurdling screams, yet there were peals of laughter as Hanuman, Rama's most trusted follower, teased his enemy, dancing around them with his tail ablaze. At the end of the first scene, as Rama held Ravana at his mercy, Johann intervened – *Never kill the enemy till he's had time to repent.....* and sent Ravana back to recover and resume fighting the next day. Bringing down the curtain, he had cleared his throat and given me a sly glance.

From a distance, he looked the half-Malay that he was, and the lights made him seem younger. The round glasses had dilated his pupils and his lips were crusted a ghostly white. He seemed to be trembling.

'Wake Kumbhakarna from sleep!' – Johann shouted in the voice of Ravana to his court of demons, and silenced the chattering crowd in the theatre. It was time to bring on his best warrior, the giant who had the measure of gods let alone the mortal Rama. 'Wake him up, by hook or by crook...' Expertly shuffling the cast, Johann sent off the beleaguered demons to Kumbhakarna's palace where he slept on his golden bed snoring like the ocean. Like the ocean breeze, his heavy breathing lifted up his mane in giant surfs. The demons had come with gongs and drums, but his breath threw them out of the palace. The crowd roared with laughter as the ones who had escaped being blown away were sucked in through Kumbhakarna's nostrils, only to emerge dazed on the tongue that flapped out of his gaping mouth.

They stomped on his arms and legs, and poured boiling oil on his torso. Johann's sleeping giant merely turned over on his side. They lit a fire near his mouth, to have him choke on the smoke, rammed him with red hot spikes, tore his hair in vain, and collapsed exhausted. The orchestra was tempestuous as it imitated the din. A herd of donkeys were brought in and made to bray into Kumbhakarna's ears in a chorus, but his snores drowned the braying. Next, it was the turn of seduction.

His chest was anointed with lavender and sandalwood. Women of immense beauty danced all over him, stroked him with their tresses, nuzzled his ears and sang love songs. There were sighs and giggles in the audience, but Kumbhakarna remained unmoved. Johann broke with the dalang's monologue and sang – 'Who do you dream of dear friend, for whom do you sigh so deep…?' Sheep and boar – live bait for his appetite – paraded on stage along with servants carrying bowls of wine.

'Why wake him, if he must die…' a grandmother in the front row muttered. Tempting his audience, Johann brought the torso up, then had the giant fall back with a thud. Why was he taking so long? He wouldn't be able to keep Kumbhakarna asleep for much longer. His audience knew the story of the Ramayana by heart and waited for the real action to begin, for the demon to rise and make his way over to Lanka's battlefield. Looking around, I saw the same question on everyone's face. The comic relief was waning and the chattering had resumed. A fretful air seemed to stifle the laughs as Johann toiled on. The few tourists checked their watches; children eyed the tamarind juice seller and nursing mothers turned in a circle to nurse their infants.

He couldn't keep Kumbhakarna alive for much longer even if he wished to. Sooner than later, the demon would have to face Rama, fight fire with fire and battle the ape army. Badly outnumbered, he'd have to carry on till the flick of the dalang's arm brought him down on the stage and announced his end with a clash of cymbals.

The master of ceremonies had inched closer to Johann and nudged his elbow. The gamelan players had fallen silent. Only Johann's voice, quivering and gravelly, droned on as he brought out one puppet after another from the trunk – more demons, more apes, more dancing girls. More donkeys were brought out to bray, molten wax poured on Kumbhakarna's forehead as he slept on. The cloud of smoke had grown, and I couldn't see his face any more. A child wailed for his mother; shuffling feet and yawns sounded louder than the hiss of kerosene lamps.

Suddenly, Johann stood up. Dropping the giant puppet without a word, he staggered through the crowd towards me.

'Let's go, Professor.'

He was silent as we walked back through the paddy fields. The fireflies were gone and a gentle breeze blew with the smell of rain. I could hear his wheezing and he breathed through his mouth. His eyes, without the glasses, seemed to have taken on a deeper slant – he looked more Chinese, despite the sarong and the Flower of Victory, now limp behind his ear. We walked back to his shop and sat in the dark with a solitary lamp lighting up the puppets. What was he thinking about? Of his childhood… the songs that he used to sing for his mother? Was he still thinking about Kumbhakarna? A faint clash of cymbals sounded in the distance. Johann made a long face, as if he had just heard the swish of Rama's golden arrow strike the giant's heart, and the earth rumble as he fell on his back.

If it wasn't for the rains, I'd have missed the small crowd on Malioboro outside *Het Muziek Huis*. Piles of jackfruit and the slush made it impossible to cross over, as I gazed at a dozen Chinese – men and women in white gowns and caps – waiting on the pavement beside a coffin. A white silk cloth covered Johann up to the neck, the sprout on his mole had been trimmed and two large lotuses flanked his ears. He had died in his sleep, I was told by one of the mourners. Recognizing the twin sister, I waved at her as she was about to retreat into the shop. A van held the funerary offerings – a paper shophouse, chests full of fake porcelain and the sign of a dog kneeling beside a gramophone.

Wet from the drizzle that had just ended, I managed to catch a final glimpse of Johann, scion of the Tang, on his journey to paradise.

The Pearlfisher

*D*uring her birth, Mouttou Lachemy was half inside her mother's womb with only her head sticking out for one and a half days. The doctor had wanted to cut her up and her father had agreed, but God saved her and she came out.

Born on the eighth of September 1957 in Am-Siogo, she was named Mouttou Lachemy Fateme Zara after her paternal aunt and her Arab mother. It was then that her father Mouttou Sittaramane told Bouchara – the newborn's mother – he had another child, a boy from an Indian wife whom he had left behind in India. He was helpless, he told her. As a soldier he didn't think he would ever be able to leave the French Legion and return to his native land. His friends, Diklou and Vaity helped him find a nurse who took care of the baby girl. They cooked with him and prepared a grand feast, dancing for three straight nights – men in flowing djellebas and women in delicate gabak. Afterwards, Mouttou Sittaramane lived with his wife Bouchara and their daughter – my mother – in Kala, till he left Chad after her independence from the French.

This is the man, Monsieur, my grandfather, Mouttou Sittaramane whom we lost before I was born, that I plead you to find. God willing he is still alive, in healthy body and mind, and cared for by his Indian family. He told my grandmother that he was born in Pondicherry – a French colony. Perhaps, after all his travels in Africa, he returned to Pondicherry to live by the river for he loved the river so much. Will you find him for me? For my mother, my brothers and sisters, cousins and aunts? The consul at your country's Embassy in Djamena gave me your address. He said you could write in your paper about my grandfather and maybe one of your readers would know him, know where he lives.

For three years after his marriage my grandfather lived in Chad as a farmer growing paddy rice and brewing mérissée from the millet. But his heart belonged to the river. At dawn he would fish, standing waist deep in the shallow marsh overgrown with weeds holding a line with a small bait *or an osier basket, sometimes with a dam of woven straw placed across the trickling stream. At noon he would return from the fields and join the fishermen on the Chari, sweeping long nets over their heads. In the evenings they would set lanterns on their canoes and beat along the wooden sides attracting the fish, then scoop them up like glistening pearl. Back from the river he would sit inside their thatched home and sing to his little girl....* '*Mouttou Lachemy, sital kileil a djambi....*'

*No one knows exactly when Mouttou Sittaramane left our country except that it was after all his Indian brothers had left. Neighbours remember the day when a messenger came for him from Fort Lamy. Mouttou was in the field, but as soon as the man stepped off the boat, he knew his time had come. Stacking his hoe, he called for Bouchara who was gossiping in the shade of the granary, and went to bathe in the river. Then he had dressed in the style of a soldier, worn the Legion's hat. Holding Mouttou Lachemy in his arms he sat with the villagers. He said he was leaving the girl in the care of Issa Kanembou, Gusmane Doba, Ahmat Marada, Abokar Idriss (one who had solemnized his marriage with Bouchara), Ousman Gadou, Khera (the nurse), Am-brahim, Faigue Adoum (Bouchara's sister), Issa Masry (the Deputy), Souleymane and Ariette. He told these people, '*I am giving my daughter to you to raise as your own. But I am asking you never to marry her off to a soldier like me who will leave her one day. If it comes to that it would be better to let her marry a beggar. At least he will not let my girl suffer.*'*

Please, Monsieur, won't you help me find my grandfather?

In my life there are no surprises. Sitting at my desk among the reporters, I wait for the stack to pile up then go through the motions: tossing, saving, pruning, squashing errors like fruit-flies. I am the Editor's favourite – the old boy minding the Letters page – happy to let young hounds sniff out the hot leads and feast on the carrion. Every day I open envelopes and practice the art of the reader, which will see me through my last years. Before the press-boy comes calling for the day's catch, I'll have put together a bunch of them – a side dish to go with the bloody carrion. Most of the time, I admit, I skim – rarely read the letters in full. People write to complain about people, about telephones and roads, smelly sewers, the state of the economy, Iraq and Iran, and more. They blend with the wheezing fan, taste no worse than the watery tea. Sometimes there is mark of clever composition – a student honing his skills, or a professor showing off. Once in a while one hits on a retiree: the persistence of a bloodhound. Mostly they are angry – sweltering over stubborn typewriters or in long hand ripping the page like a tiger's claw.

Foreign ones are always welcome. I clip out the stamps, relish the burst of politeness....*Dear Sir, I have been charmed by India*.... Occasionally, they are tinged with pathos....*my purse was stolen in Jaipur... passport, money, my mother's photo...everything.* We are the altar for their tears, the bedrock of nostalgia. Once in a while I read 'search and find' requests – from the English looking for elderly souls who have disappeared in the Himalayas. It is easy posting these; one feels one has done one's duty. None, of course, demand that I leave my desk, play the sleuth, or dive into rescue. That would be too much. I shall leave Delhi when I die, I've told myself.

Approaching call time, I finger the letter, unsure. Shorn of the stamps – the lovely butterflies – the envelope looks naked, violated and empty. It's too long, I decide. How would you frame the inquiry? There just aren't enough leads. I'd have to write her letter for her, and that I find uninspiring. We are likely not the venue anyway, not a favourite among farmers from Pondicherry. Besides, I expect this to be her first and the last. Their river won't flow this far.

He came by the Logone on a whale-boat, soldier in the French army, ninth division of the Senegalese Infantry Regiment. In Chad, they wondered where he and his brothers were born. With his chin covered in a lehfa he looked like an Arab merchant from Ouaddai travelling east to Mecca. Up close, they found him black like the Toubous. But he didn't speak any Tourkou – the tongue of the Prophet spoken in the southern deserts. In a bark he could have resembled a Sara, a Sou or a Kotoko, but then he wouldn't be dressed like a white man and resting a gun on his shoulder, would he?

The soldiers disappeared behind the Governor's palace, didn't come out for a whole week. It was time for the February feast known as the Feast of the Snake. By five o'clock everybody had gathered by the river bank, when the tam-tam started. Men moved in a circle behind women. There were those who carried a sheaf of scarlet feathers, and fanned the fires that were set around them. The men brought out whips and attacked each other in mock battles. Then it was the turn of Bangs – sorcerers dressed in frightening masks and covered from head to toe in wood and leather. The audience followed them around the fires but kept their eyes lowered, for it was forbidden to look at the Bang. Everyone was at the feast – Bouchara Adoum, recently divorced from her first husband who was also her cousin, her sister Faigue Adoum, their maternal aunt Nafissa Abdoulaye, their friend Helen born of an Egyptian father and a Chadian Arab mother. The women began to dance in a cloud of brilliant dust. Raising his voice in a weird chant, Ahmat Marada, chief of the town's abattoir, whirled himself like a dervish then collapsed with exhaustion. The millet beer made them adventurous, and many were seen entering the huts at the end of the pier in pairs. Then the Indians appeared. They were dressed no longer in their soldier's beret, chéchias and pantaloon, but were bare chested like the fishermen, wearing a sack-like white cloth from waist downwards. Their foreheads bore white stripes like Fianga warriors and they wore gold earrings gleaming against their dark skin. 'It was dark when he arrived and bathed in mist when he left,' that is how my grandmother would describe him. Every time Bouchara started to talk about Mouttou, her voice would choke, so my mother, Mouttou Lachemy, knew very little about her father. She knew this much that Mouttou had seen Bouchara at the February feast and followed her to her house. Some days later he came to ask for her hand.

You are looking for him, aren't you Monsieur? This time I am sending you two pictures, one of Mouttou and his wife. The other showing my mother with my grandfather.

Seven butterflies float in a bowl on my desk: the *African Euphaedra*, each a different shade of blue. Smart girl! She must know of the collector's pride in owning a full set. I don't mind her letters anymore, getting fatter by the week, don't mind the wandering tales of an Indo-Arab family that lived way back when in the back of beyond. At this rate I'll have to start a new album soon, full of moths, frogs and lizards.

I must tell you about my grandmother too. She was a true Sara Kaba, a desert Arab descended from the stock of the sultans. After her marriage with Mouttou she left her sister and her family behind in Koussouri, but the first years with her husband were unhappy. For a while they didn't

*have a child, and she spent her days making necklaces from beads or visiting
silversmiths. She neglected everything and one day Mouttou told her....
'Listen Bouchara, you are throwing away all our money. The day will
come when you'll regret it, and you'll be searching for it like a chicken
looking for something to eat.' He went away to find medicines that would
get her pregnant, and they say he went where no man goes till he's ready
to die. He took his friend Anourougame Vaity from his native land with
him, rowing their whale-boat up the Logone towards Lake Chad. In
moonlight they entered a swamp smelling of rotting carcasses and overgrown
with amback, papyrus, water-lilies and bindweed. Beasts threw themselves
into the water as they passed by, giving them the glimpse of a disappearing
snout or a tail. They heard the hoarse cry of bats skimming the shores with
their necks outstretched and saw enormous birds – carrion-crows, marabous
and eagles perched on driftwood. Vaity, on his return, had sworn he had
brushed against a hippopotamus. At dawn they were struck by a mass of
yellow water... yellow as the sky, yellow as the sun...*

A storm rushes in from the northern desert. From my window I see
columns of sand swirling like the dervish, hear the rush of deserters
leaving through the corridors. Alone, I return to the lake.

*They passed through the ruins of an ancient city where hyenas, foxes and
aardvarks burrowed, searching for the blue nomads of the desert. Mouttou
had heard about them from men in his Legion. They alone could call for
the Margai. You know about the Margai, don't you? Arabs call them
Genie, the Dougouri believe they live in the souls of fishes. The Margai
could cure disease, fill a womb, send a cloud of locusts even to your field.
Meeting them in the ruins, Mouttou took his blessings from the nomads
and returned to Kala.*

    *Then Bouchara became pregnant with Lachemy, but her love for silver
remained.*

Normally, I am given to stillness: an unwavering mind that reads and
discards; unspeculative, unoccupied. My trap doesn't call for periodic
exits. I'm happy inside. The stream of letters keeps me assured – the
world turns as I warm my lair, nab errors and scathe the graceless

with flair. Without a wife or very many that are near and dear, there is no use keeping up with life's seasonality. Friends too have left me alone. My clean desk sports two full trays: 'In' and 'Out.' The butterflies lie in-between. Soon, I'll need a new tray for river tales, voodoo tales, baby tales.

Loathe as I am to admit it, something turns: I wait for her letters. Perhaps it's the novelty – as clean a break as I can get from nagging pensioners and bovine tourists. Perhaps it's her tongue – the seductive taste of the desert.....*egnéchi, fiassou, borogue, foufi*... Perhaps it's the failed historian still bleeding inside after so many wraps of newsprint. I turn pages in my meagre library; a whole continent flashes by.

Somewhere, she had mentioned 'concessions.' I zero in on A.E.F – *Afrique Équatoriale Française*, read memoirs and maps, linger over black and white nudity. It is a world removed from ours – the French are an unknown quantity here, better known for their wines than their colonies. I catch a young one from Pondicherry, quiz him about ex-Legionnaires, about Tamils returned from Africa. But he's more American than French, hasn't even heard of the Legion. Tempted as much as I am to take up the pen and ask my mademoiselle a few pointed questions, house rules forbid two-way contact: there are a lot of lonely hearts out there, the Editor warns. 'We're the press not the police,' he offers the kind of logic one would to someone senile. What would I ask her anyway? Perhaps she could tell me how they lived without Mouttou – mother and child. Did Bouchara marry, once again? What kept their February feast alive?

I worry less about Mouttou, assume and bequeath him to soldiering. Privately, I chuckle at a Tamil's plight in the French Legion, conjure up his small agonies. Maybe I conjure too much; maybe he was acculturated. A stranger to Pondicherry, I imagine a 'concession' – the white town set amidst the black; the play of sunbeams on mansions and marquees fostering an illusion; the line of blue beyond the lawns bringing back the Mediterranean. I see white women on palanquins, hear splashing and slapping of water on houseboats readied for afternoon tea. I sense the likes of Mouttou lined up for a drill. Maybe he was willing, or gagged.

I can see him at Koussouri too – a dark Tamil and his Arab wife. *Some days later he came to ask for her hand*... What took him so long? Did he think of his Indian wife and his boy? Did he confer with his native brothers in the Legion before coming to a decision? Or wait simply for desire to build up? Like a good soldier of fortune had he resigned himself to many wives in many lands...?

I must tell you a story my mother told me. When Bouchara was pregnant with Lachemy, she wanted silver anklets called 'houdjoule.' But Mouttou asked her to wait till her child was born as it would be unwise to place anything new on her body. She became angry and in the middle of the night in pouring rain ran to her uncle's home. He asked her to return but she didn't for five months till my mother's birth. For full five months Mouttou waited for her. It was the season of rain, the time for mangoes, plums, pomegranates, papaws. And flowers too – the giant hibiscus and the lovely little mauve and white Madagascar Periwinkle. He waited till the day Lachemy arrived. Then Bouchara saw Mouttou coming to her uncle's home, holding something for her in his hand. She greeted him warmly.

.....and mine would be the same sensation......of long-drawn-out hours, of waiting and sinking into a delicious dream.

The business about the child has me foxed. Why take the trouble of a pilgrimage when he already has his boy back in India? Why the urge to recreate a simple life by the river? He would be difficult to trace. Where could they have taken him from Chad? To date-palm oases up country ruled by the méhariste, the camel corps? Perhaps even further north to Tripolitania, escorting prisoners to yet another concession – that of the Italians? Maybe he followed the river down to Mossaka – birdless and songless. If he were lucky, he could've given it all a miss and ridden the ferry back to Bordeaux with his new-found Algerian princess – well-settled by now in Lyon and singing Tamil lullabies to his great-grandchildren. He could simply be dead in Africa – from flies or bullets or both.

But the letters keep him alive. Somewhere, I start believing in her story, try to imagine what he would look like from the faded photos. In one of these, he wears a tie and a shirt with long white cuffs, hair combed back like an obedient clerk. In another he is bare chested, wearing his lungi folded up to his thighs and seated with his baby girl on an indigo-blue roll that gives the impression of waves. Nowhere do I see him attired, I mean dressed as a soldier. Calculating the number of years that have passed, it seems reasonable to expect a seventy-ish man, and wonder whether he is indeed down here, living rather comfortably on his Legionnaire's pension. Getting ahead of myself I plan a stop at the archives – heaven knows they might even keep track of old desert wolves down there.

Her next brings better sight of his character.

He was swimming one day, my grandmother said, when he heard cries for help. The river had overflown in the rainy season and the whole village was a sea of mud. It was difficult to fish because of the floating papyrus, and the overfed crocodiles snapping the fishermen's nets for mischief. My grandfather was a powerful swimmer. The drowning man was one of the Banana – people who live south of the Chari. When Mouttou swam ashore with the man, they surrounded him and demanded an explanation. I must tell you first about these people, about their strange beliefs. My grandfather didn't know that the Banana thought ill of those who try to deny a man his fate. If the drowning man was destined to die, why did he have to go save him? They spoke to him in a tongue he couldn't follow and led him up river to a Saras chief. By then his friends had gathered in Kala and Issa Masry, the deputy, led them searching for Mouttou. When they found him, he was sprawled on the ground, bound by both feet. The Saras priest was chanting a prayer and a large bourma of water was being boiled on a clay oven. They realized what was about to happen. Mouttou would have to experience the Ordeal of Water. He would have to plunge his right hand into the bourma and fish out a chosen piece of metal. If he scalded himself, he would be pronounced guilty and the Margai would be called to punish him for his sin.

One by one, men from Kala begged him not to accept the challenge. His native brothers – Vaity, Salva, Bonami, and Krishna offered to pay in animal heads for his release. Ousman Gadou and Souleymane threatened to take the matter up with the Commandante at Fort Lamy. Bouchara stood before him and pleaded with her eyes. But my grandfather sat with his legs bent and said that he was not afraid of the water for he had committed no sin. And he wetted his hands in the boiling pot without burning them to prove it to everyone.

✤ ✤ ✤

...Maybe he asks Bouchara for her silver anklet and drops it into the boiling water, then fishes it out in one sweep and returns it to her smiling.... I savour the story more for its poetic fantasy than for any truth it might contain.

But Monsieur, it is now almost half a year since I started writing. Do you receive my letters? Do you follow my untidy hand, do you follow my story? It is getting late, Monsieur, I must find my grandfather. I wish I could give you an address. He left behind a few postcards and some letter paper. But my grandmother was illiterate. She tore everything up. She felt since her husband had left her, she had no use for such things.

We know he still thinks of his African family. In 1978 he sent a man – a doctor or somebody from India – to find us. The man came with his address and his message. He had asked his daughter, my mother – Mouttou Lachemy Fateme Zara – to come to India as he wished to see her. But unfortunately, the man had to leave Chad soon as he had a heart attack. Again in 1985 he sent a Frenchman to find my grandmother. He spent a long time looking for her at Kala along the southern shores of the Logone, but by then we had moved to Djamena. We learned all about it after he had left.

It is important, Monsieur, very important, to find him. They call my mother a bastard, for no one knows where my grandfather is. And they think we are children of a bastard. But it is not true as you know. Mouttou Sittaramane and Bouchara were married a few days after the February feast. Abokar Idriss solemnized their marriage. It was attended by many people – my grandfather's native brothers, the Arabs, the Sara, the Sao, the Kotoko.... Most of them are dead now. There are a few still alive, but too old to remember the details. Unless we find him, no one will ever know who our forefathers were, know who we really are....

Something stirs. The ink in my arteries that I have exchanged for blood begins to flow. From my forgotten corner, I think I've read it all. But my instincts surprise me. I didn't think I'd be moved by fishing tales, or the saga of love and desertion in the Dark Continent. The letters hold me in a morbid clutch; I've started leaving early, making calls, lying awake to piece the puzzle together then teasing it apart. In this, I'm alone. I wouldn't trust the hounds to trap the Tamil; I'd like to find a full body, I'd like a happy ending. Meticulous as I am, I have searched the archives, looked up dusty journals no one reads. Perhaps it's the fathering business that has me so obsessed: the girlish voice that I never had missed till the butterflies landed between my trays. I am cut up about the 'bastard' thing as well, feel the need to restore her honour, father and grandfather the lot, once and for all. In any case, I plan my journey – leave Delhi as I die of April's thirst.

Down south, not far from Pondicherry, I search for a river. In my mind's eye I see the Legionnaire standing above the mist, silhouetted by the sun; keep imagining him behind an oar, lugging baskets, shining like the day's catch. Fumbling with names, I recruit a local. We set out on an expedition.

I surprise the natives as much as they surprise me. In my northern skin I could pass for a white man. I feel like a desert Arab crossing the land of Bouchara and Idriss, Gusmane and Ahmat. Passing villages of clay homes, I see sculpted forms, dark like the Sara and Sao – men lying back to back in the shade, women dressing up their hair in a variety of shells; children and herds grazing in the silence of the fields. Without my desk, I feel lost. We cross dust-blown paths, wait for country buses; sometimes we walk all day, enter towns and search for names. My guide grows used to my impatience.

I carry her letters. Searching for clues, I read them over; the experience grows. I feel I've entered her world. Half-asleep on a makeshift bed, I watch a baby running to its mother, from a distance hear cries in a half-familiar tongue.

One day Lachemy was very sick and Bouchara took her to her uncle, a Houssa Arab. The man tattooed a small flower on her neck. Lachemy cried and fell asleep on her way home with her mother. When Mouttou came back from the fields, he saw the tattoo. Horrified, he ran to his neighbour's home, thinking that something terrible had happened to his daughter...

But we don't find the river. At each mile, the smell of dried fish grows; my guide hastens, his appetite doubles. We fight with flies; my city-stomach churns at the sight of coarsely served meals. Luckily, I resist turning back. It is Mouttou who keeps me going – setting aside the bare facts, I begin to examine his vagrant soul. Did he

suffer for his journeys? I mull over him: soldier, fisherman, father....
Nothing convinces me, but I detect a familiar strain – a strong pattern
spread over two continents; I sense I'll soon know.

He was born in Pondicherry, she had written – *a French colony*.
We have gone beyond the 'concession'; we are now in open country.
In every village we repeat the same routine: call on the elderly, show
them photos, recite names – *Mouttou, Vaity, Salva*...as if they were
our very own friends. The men hold the photos in their fleshy palms,
stare hard, then resume their chatter. What are they hiding? I grow
suspicious. Actually, they ask us more questions than we ask them:
where did he live; whose son; whose father; farmer or fisherman or
potter? Women too join the passing circus, comment on his shiny
black hair and grin – add to the confusion. He is a moneylender, we
hear, savage and raunchy, the head of a large family. We discard that
rumour, move on to the next. There's silence when we describe his
soldiering. Nobody has heard of the Legion; even elders frown at
the mention of the French. At best they can remember their own
fighters – young and dreamy – stumping their enemies with bare hands.

He told my grandmother that his son was his carbon copy. The boy was
fourteen at the time of Lachemy's birth. His cousin back in India was
raising his son for him. He always wanted to bring his daughter to India
to meet her brother. If you meet the boy....well, my uncle, give him my
mother's photo.

In my satchel I carry a family tree. Somehow they all seem related
– the men and women of the letters and those that we meet on the
road. Each could pass for an aunt or cousin – drawn from the blood
of Mouttou Sittaramane. I am tempted to invent stories, weave the
characters together, tangle up the two continents. Halfway through
the journey, I realize our mistake. Ignoring grown-ups, we huddle
with the children. They would know perhaps of a disappeared man,
might even have heard the tale of a soldier returned after years spent
in strange lands. They tell us more than we comprehend; one – barely
four – points through a row of palms. We face the sea.

My guide goes off for his dried fish. Restless, I pace the slatey
shore, more grey than even imaginable. In the haze of midday I see
ocean trawlers hanging lifeless from the horizon. A heron or two
venture that far, the rest have chosen the marsh-like beach overgrown
with prickly thorn. Their uncanny flapping quickens my heart; I look
for shade. The wind, unduly violent, shears the palms and like a

mirage on a desert I spot a leafy roof sitting on stilts resembling an abandoned hut.

Inside, it is empty, but for a few goat skins and clay jars for storing water and food. An old blue blanket hangs from a line cutting the room in half. A hole in the earth shows up what might've been a clay oven, ringed by burnt coal. Sitting on the coir bed, I hear the sea and the twittering of sparrows, follow a line of crabs crawling out of the oven.

....if he is alive, tell him we are waiting.

The room appears still yet strangely alive. As if someone had lived here till just a moment ago, but left never to return. As if it was more than a home – a station for gazing at the sea. I have the sense of living the life of the absent owner – a whole life spent spreading the nets and folding them in. How many years did it take him to compose his soul before he could leave it all behind? I doze; an ant climbs my toe; I give it a flick then doze on. How long before desire finally goes...

Then I am awakened by shouts and come out of the hut. My guide clambers up the slippery bank trailed by frolicking urchins. I see him holding something in his hand and waving. Nearer, he keeps pointing behind me. I try to follow his incoherent chatter. He says he's found him; he's sure, he says. Several people in the village have picked out his face in the photo and confirmed our tale. And he keeps pointing at the abandoned hut behind me. That's where he lived when he was alive, he says. Here by the sea?

'Yes!' he pants.

'Our Mouttou?'

'The pearlfisher.'

OTHER TITLES FROM THE AUTHOR...

RACISTS

1855: on a deserted island off the coast of Africa, the most audacious experiment ever envisaged is about to begin. To settle an argument that has raged inconclusively for decades, two scientists decide to raise a pair of infants, one black, one white, on a barren island, exposed to the dangers all around them, tended only by a young nurse whose muteness renders her incapable of influencing them in any way, for good or for bad. They will grow up without speech, without civilization, without punishment or play. In this primitive environment, the children will develop as their primitive natures dictate. The question is: what will be left when the twelve years of the experiment are over? Which child will be master, and which the slave? For surely one will triumph over the other. Or will they all, children and scientists alike, reap the fruits of breaking the taboo, as they discover love and loneliness on the wild but beautiful island of Arlinda.

THE MINIATURIST

In the sumptuous court of the emperor Akbar, in 16th century India, a group of artists begins the painstaking task of chronicling the emperor's life. Bihzad is the son of the chief artist and as such, he is groomed to follow in his father's footsteps. A child prodigy, Bihzad is shielded from life as he grows up in the stunning fortress town of Agra. But as word of his talent spreads, rumours about the wild, passionate nature of his secret drawings bring his enemies out into the open. When the young artist breaches the rules of the court, they will use his art to destroy him.

THE OPIUM CLERK

Hiran is born in 1857: the year of Mutiny and the year his father dies. Brought to Calcutta by his widowed mother he turns out to have few talents, apart from an uncanny ability to read a man's lies in his palm. When luck gets him a job at the auction house, Hiran finds himself embroiled in a mysterious trade, and even more deeply embroiled in the affairs of his nefarious superior, the infamous Mr Jonathan Crabbe and his opium addicted wife. An unlikely hero, Hiran is caught up in rebellion and war, buffeted by storms at sea, by love and intrigue, innocently implicated in fraud and dark dealings.

for more details please visit our website www.harpercollins.co.in

HarperCollins Readers' Club

Become a Member today and get regular updates on new titles, contests, book readings, author meets and book launches.

Join the Readers' Club today!

You can share your reviews and build a literary network of your own.

Register at www.harpercollins.co.in